JUN - - 2016

HOLLOW CRIB

A MAGNOLIA PARISH MYSTERY

HOLLOW CRIB

BJ BOURG

FIVE STAR
A part of Gale, Cengage Learning

GALE
CENGAGE Learning·

Farmington Hills, Mich • San Francisco • New York • Waterville, Maine
Meriden, Conn • Mason, Ohio • Chicago

GALE
CENGAGE Learning

LIBRARY OF CONGRESS CATALOGING-IN-PUBLICATION DATA

Names: Bourg, B. J., author.
Title: Hollow crib / B. J. Bourg.
Description: Waterville, Maine : Five Star Publishing, 2016. |Series: A magnolia parish mystery
Identifiers: LCCN 2015050624 (print) | LCCN 2016010075 (ebook) | ISBN 9781432831424 (hardback) | ISBN 1432831429 (hardcover) | ISBN 9781432831493 (ebook) | ISBN 1432831496 (ebook)
Subjects: LCSH: Detectives—Fiction. | Murder—Investigation—Fiction. | Clergy—Fiction. | Louisiana—Fiction. | BISAC: FICTION / Mystery & Detective / Police Procedural. | FICTION / Thrillers. | GSAFD: Mystery fiction. | Suspense fiction.
Classification: LCC PS3602.O89255 H65 2016 (print) | LCC PS3602.O89255 (ebook) | DDC 813/.6—dc23
LC record available at http://lccn.loc.gov/2015050624

First Edition. First Printing: May 2016
Find us on Facebook– https://www.facebook.com/FiveStarCengage
Visit our website– http://www.gale.cengage.com/fivestar/
Contact Five Star™ Publishing at FiveStar@cengage.com

Printed in the United States of America
1 2 3 4 5 6 7 20 19 18 17 16

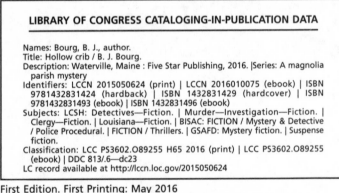

JUN - - 2016

HOLLOW CRIB

CHAPTER ONE

7:00 A.M.
Friday, November 19, 2004
Magnolia Parish, Southeastern Louisiana
"Wake up, Daddy, it's a beautiful day!" I rolled onto my back just in time to see my four-year-old launch herself through the air. She landed with a gleeful screech, knees digging into my gut. The momentum caused her body to lurch forward and her forehead smashed into my nose. My heart sank with the sickening thud of the collision. I quickly sat upright and lifted Samantha. I blinked the tears from my smarting eyes and was relieved to see the deep dimples that Samantha's wide grin drilled into her cheeks. "Pumpkinseed, you need to be careful. You could hurt yourself."

Samantha rubbed her forehead and screamed, "Head-butt!"

I scooped her up and carried her to the kitchen, where the smell of fried dough caused my empty stomach to ache. I kissed the back of my wife's neck and eased Samantha into her booster seat. Debbie turned from the stove and flopped two beignets onto my plate. "You're up early," she said.

"Yeah, and I'm sure you had nothing to do with that." I brushed the large smudge of powdered sugar from the front of Debbie's nightgown. Some of the powder floated onto the red hair that dangled across her shoulder, but she didn't notice.

"I have no idea what you're talking about." Debbie glanced up and feigned a look of surprise. Her tanned face suddenly paled and her mouth dropped. "What happened to your nose?"

"Our human cannonball was at it again."

"My God, it's so swollen." Debbie reached out to touch it, but I turned my head and sat at the table. Debbie sat beside me and gawked. "You need to go to the doctor."

"Don't have time. I have court this morning and then I have an interview after lunch."

Debbie got up and walked to the sink. As she clanked dishes around she said, in a casual tone, "So, what do you have planned for tonight?"

Having been married to Debbie for ten years, I had learned a thing or two about her mannerisms and I knew something was up. I scanned the bytes of memory in my "standing room only" brain and tried desperately to figure my way out of this trap. Thanksgiving was next week, but I knew she wasn't talking about that. Her birthday was in September, so it couldn't be that. Samantha was born in March—

"Hello, are you there?" Debbie sounded a bit impatient.

Samantha leaned over the table, her arm dipping in her syrup bowl, and rapped her knuckles against my forehead. "Knock, knock, Daddy, anybody home?"

"Sam, lights are on in Daddy's head, but nobody's home." Debbie wiped the syrup from Samantha's arm and stared down at me, a look of scorn in her eyes. "You forgot, didn't you?"

It struck me like an uppercut to the liver . . . *our anniversary!* I hung my head. "Baby, I've been so busy at work. I'm sorry."

"I've heard that before." Debbie turned away, but I grabbed her arm.

"Look, I'll make reservations for tonight at Skel's Seafood and Steak House. I know how bad you've been wanting to go there."

Debbie's eyes lit up for a second, but then a wind of doubt blew in and put out the flame. "Do you promise?"

"I promise." I kissed her forehead to seal it.

"I want to come! I want to come!" Samantha exclaimed.

"Sure, baby," Debbie said, patting Samantha's head. "It wouldn't be special without you."

I walked around the metal detectors and grabbed a key from the overweight security guard who stood in wrinkled garb scanning the herd of people trying to get their day in court. I jerked my Beretta 9 mm pistol from its paddle holster and stuffed it in the lockbox. I dropped the key in my inner coat pocket and couldn't help but smile as my hand brushed the three-inch Smith and Wesson revolver that was suspended from my concealed shoulder rig. I might not be the brightest, but I knew better than to leave my safety to a man who cared more about food than he did about shooting a qualifying score once a year during firearms requalification.

I pushed my way through the crowded hallway of the 56th District Courthouse, which was better known as the Hickory Five Six DC. The locals called it that because of the 16-ounce hickory-handled sledgehammer that was mounted above Chief Judge Rick Landry's bench. Rumor was he also had a sawed-off 12-gauge shotgun on a swivel under his bench. Not the kind of judge you wanted to appear before when you were on the wrong side of the law.

I made my way up the flight of stairs and paused outside the courtroom door to hear if court was in session. It was. I cringed when I opened the door to the packed courtroom and the hinges squealed in protest. Every head in the courtroom, from the minute clerk to the prisoners in the jury booth, turned to look at me. I nodded my apologies and stood against the back wall of the courtroom, where a number of patrol deputies had already gathered. They waited impatiently for their names to be called.

I glanced at my watch. Ten-thirty. My interview was scheduled for one o'clock in Seasville, a small town in the southernmost part of the parish. It was an hour drive on a good day. The Hickory Five Six DC was in Chateau, the parish seat for Magnolia Parish, and as far north as one could travel without leaving Magnolia. Things were not looking good.

Judge Landry trudged through the docket like he was appointed to the position for life. I shifted my feet a hundred times within the next hour and my chest ached with every name that was called. It was nearly noon before Assistant District Attorney Nelly Wainwright finally said the magic words: "Your honor, in the matter of State of Louisiana vs. Jarvis Chiasson, the defense has filed a motion to suppress the confession."

"Is counsel for both sides ready to proceed?"

Both sides acknowledged they were ready and Judge Landry told the state to call their first witness.

"State calls Detective Brandon Berger to the stand."

I almost ran to the stand. After getting through my name and occupation, Nelly asked me how I had come into contact with Jarvis Chiasson. "I was investigating the burglary of Jed Smith's black Ford Mustang, from which his cell phone was stolen. I subpoenaed the phone records and found that the burglar had made nearly a hundred calls from it. I began calling the numbers the burglar called and one common denominator kept coming up; Jarvis Chiasson. I then proceeded to Jarvis Chiasson's house and met with him there."

"First of all, is Jarvis Chiasson present in court today?"

"Yes, ma'am. He's sitting to your right, next to Mr. Mac-Quaid."

"Your Honor, please let the record reflect he's properly identified the defendant."

Judge Landry nodded. "So ordered."

Nelly glanced at her yellow notebook. "Okay, what date and

time did you meet with the defendant at his house?"

"It was last month, October 7, at about 3:30 P.M."

"What happened when you met with Mr. Chiasson at his house?"

"I asked him to accompany me to the station and he agreed to do so. When he got in the car with me, I read him his rights."

"Did you question him in the car?"

"No, ma'am. I just talked with him about fishing, hunting . . . small talk. I was trying to establish a rapport with him."

"At what point did you question him about the burglary?"

"When we arrived at the office."

"How did that take place?"

"I met with him in an interview room. After a short conversation, he admitted to smashing the window on the black Mustang and stealing the cell phone from inside."

"Did you promise him anything or threaten him in any way to get him to talk to you?"

"No, ma'am."

"Did you pressure him or coerce him in any way?"

"No, ma'am."

"Was the statement he gave free and voluntary?"

"Yes, ma'am."

"Did he appear to be under the influence of any type of drugs or alcohol?"

"No, ma'am."

"Was he responsive to the questions?"

"Yes, ma'am."

Nelly paused for a moment to look over her notes. She took off her glasses and said, "Answer any questions Mr. MacQuaid might have for you."

Red MacQuaid stood and walked to the front of the lawyers' table and leaned against it. He crossed his thick, stubby arms and tucked his hands under his sweaty armpits. "Detective, isn't it true that Mr. Chiasson told you he wanted a lawyer?"

"No, sir."

"Well, if Mr. Chiasson were to testify here today and say that he told you he wanted a lawyer, what would you say to that?"

"I'd say he was committing perjury."

Red MacQuaid's neck started to burn. "Isn't it true, Detective," he asked, "that you told my client you would beat him with your stick if he didn't say he did the burglary?"

"No, sir. I don't even carry a stick."

Red's face was ruby. "You testified that you read my client his rights. Do you have a card that you read from?"

"No, sir. I did it from memory."

Red's eyes lit up. "From memory? Well, can you recite the same rights you read to my client for the Court?"

"Yes, sir. I told him, *You have the right to remain silent. Anything you say can and will be used against you in court. You have the right not to incriminate yourself. You cannot be required to be a witness against yourself in court. You have the right to the assistance of a lawyer. If you cannot afford one, a lawyer will be appointed by the court to advise and represent you, without cost to you. If you choose to answer questions or give a statement, either with or without the advice of a lawyer, you have the right to stop at any time.*"

Red nodded his resignation. The color slowly drained from his face. "No further questions, Your Honor."

I took my place at the back wall and Red MacQuaid called Jarvis Chiasson to the witness stand. On the day I arrested him he wore faded, muddy jeans and a stained T-shirt. Today he was dressed in his Sunday best. I was betting that the same person who posted his ten-thousand-dollar bond paid for the clothes.

"I told Detective Brandon that I wanted my lawyer and he told me I didn't need no lawyer," Jarvis said. "And then he threatened to beat me up if I didn't tell him I did it, so I was scared. That's why I said I did it. I was scared of him."

Jarvis talked for twenty minutes about how I'd mistreated him. At the conclusion of the hearing, Judge Landry said, "This is an easy decision for the Court. I can believe that the defendant is telling the truth or I can believe that the detective is telling the truth. Now, let's put aside the fact that Detective Berger is a seasoned and decorated officer whose credibility is impeccable, and focus solely on the defendant's testimony." He removed his glasses and glared down at Jarvis Chiasson. "Son, I don't believe a single word that came out of your mouth. Motion denied." He turned to the clerk. "Give the defendant notice of the pretrial date. Next!"

I descended the steps two at a time on my way out the courthouse. I was almost to the street when a voice behind me called my name. I turned. Ray, the overweight security guard, approached at a stumbling jog. Annoyed, I said, "Look, I'm in a hurry—"

When he reached me, Ray bent over to catch his breath and it was then that I realized he was holding my pistol. "Sorry, sir," he said, panting. "You forgot your gun."

Shamefaced, I took my pistol and gave Ray a grateful pat on the back. "I appreciate it, Ray. You're a lifesaver." Ray seemed to stand a little taller as he waddled back to his post. As I watched Ray, I saw Jarvis staring at me from the front steps of the courthouse. I waved, but he turned away and strode down the sidewalk. I shook my head. I would definitely be seeing him again. I glanced at my watch. 12:30 P.M. I'd have to fly to make the interview in time. I jerked my cell phone from my shirt pocket and called dispatch.

"Hey Julie, it's Brandon. Can you look up Skel's Seafood in the book and patch me through?"

"I'm not Bell South."

"I know, I know. Please, I need this. I'll owe you big time."

"But isn't that in New Orleans? I don't have a New Orleans

phonebook."

"We have a New Orleans phonebook in the library." I tried to remain patient.

With a grunt, Julie put me on hold. She returned a minute later. "Hold on, I'll patch you to the number."

The phone rang several times and then the automated answering machine picked up telling me that all their circuits were busy and to please hold. I held on for twenty minutes, as I raced through traffic, but finally gave up. I called Julie back and explained my troubles. "Could you call them and make reservations for three at eight tonight?"

"Bran, I'm not your personal secretary," Julie said.

"Right. I know this. But I'm in a bad situation. If I break my word to my wife, there'll be hell to pay."

"Then don't."

"Julie, can you do this one thing for me? I'll be forever in your debt."

"Will you come out with me if I do this?" There was no mistaking the flirtatiousness in her voice. "Bourbon is awesome this time of year! I can get some of my girlfriends together—"

"Jules, you know I can't."

"Then I guess it's not that important to you."

"Look, it's very—"

A car abruptly pulled onto the street in front of me and stopped to make a left turn. I smashed the brakes and swerved to the shoulder of the road. I whizzed past the car at nearly seventy miles per hour and narrowly missed taking the side mirror off. Rattled, I said, "Julie, will you do this or not?"

"Hey, first of all, I didn't ask you to make a promise to your wife that you couldn't keep. Secondly, I don't get paid to make personal phone calls for you."

Chapter Two

3:00 P.M.
Friday, November 19, 2004
Skybald National Forest, North Louisiana

Loose gravel rolled beneath the tires of the green Thunderbird. An occasional rock popped against the undercarriage. The pitted road snaked through the steep hills of the Skybald National Forest like a python slithering after its prey. Wondering when the next rough bend in the road would be the last, William Chandler kept the Thunderbird to a modest speed. One wrong move could send his family plunging over the embankment and down to the rocky rapids of the upper Skybald River.

Miles later, the road veered away from the river and a gradual descent brought them to a spacious, paved parking lot at the end of the forest road. William eased his car to a stop in front of a large timber fence. The fence stretched in either direction and disappeared into the dense forest. A break in the fence marked the beginning of a trail that led to the campsites along the banks of the Skybald River. He glanced at his sleeping wife and child and shook his head. *Those two can sleep through anything.*

William opened his door and stepped out. The thick aroma of pine that clung to the cool afternoon breeze and the sound of the rushing rapids greeted William like an old friend. He looked around. Nothing had changed in the twenty-two years since he'd been there last. He had only been a boy back then, but everything was still familiar. Well, almost everything. He didn't remember the aged and worn soldier crouched beside the beat-up station wagon. The soldier wore faded BDUs and spoke in a rough voice to a black pit bull. He didn't seem to notice that a car had driven up. William watched with a curious eye as the soldier drew circles in the red dirt with a twig.

"The sun rises over there in the east," the soldier said intently to the dog. "We're gonna wait until it gets to right about—" He slapped the ground with the twig and the pit bull's ears came alert. "Pay attention when I'm talkin' to you, Satan, boy!" Shaking his head, the soldier continued, "Now, where was I? Oh, yeah, we're gonna wait for that sun to get right about here before we start blowin' things up. We're gonna send a slew of them commies to the other side . . ."

William shuddered and wondered if bringing his new baby to this place was a mistake. There were several other cars in the parking area. A white Honda minivan was parked on the same side of the lot. He glanced at his wife. Still sleeping. So was Gracie. Two hours ago Claire had coaxed Gracie to sleep with a bottle and then stuck a pillow against the window and drifted off herself. It made the remainder of the trip boring and William had stopped twice to help stay awake; once for beef jerky and a drink and once to use the bathroom.

A tan Lincoln Continental and a silver Mitsubishi Galant sat at the far end of the parking lot. William could see the bright orange of two tents in the woods just beyond the vehicles. Voices echoed through the trees. He remembered seeing several camping areas within a hundred yards of the parking lot when he was a kid. His dad had wanted to camp there because it wasn't far to walk, but at little William's insistence, they trudged off deep into the forest and "roughed it."

Not liking the looks of the soldier, William started to get back in the car when movement up the trail caught his eye. He strained to see through the dark shadows. Could that be? He shook his head and looked away. When he looked back, she was still there. She wore a long, pink dress that seemed blood red against her snowy complexion. Her black mane floated in her wake. Had to be early twenties. She flashed a smile at William when she got closer, revealing a row of bright teeth.

William waved. "How're you?"

The woman sighed and leaned against the fencepost. "I'll be doing better when my husband decides it's time to get out of this Godforsaken wilderness."

"Godforsaken?" William threw his hands up and waved them around. "This is real unadulterated beauty."

"It's nice for a few days, but it gets old. I want my bathroom back."

Right then Gracie let the world know she was awake and hungry. The woman walked past William and looked into the Thunderbird. "Oh, you have a baby. What's her name?"

"Gracie. Well, Grace, but I call her Gracie. I think Grace sounds old for a baby."

"I love that name. She must be, what, about six months?"

William nodded. "Exactly."

"She's adorable." The lady leaned into the back seat and tickled Gracie's cheek. "Hey there, how are you?"

William stared uneasily at Claire, who stirred at the sound of the woman's voice. As the woman continued to talk, Claire sat upright and rubbed her freckled nose with the palm of her hand, a habit she had acquired long before William knew her. Her eyes turned curious. She looked past the woman at William. "What's going on here? Are we there?"

The woman offered Claire her hand. "I'm Gaby Arthur," she said. "I couldn't resist. She's so adorable."

Claire shook Gaby's hand and turned back to William. "Is this the place?"

"Yeah, but I think we'll go back a ways. I saw a place up the road that looked quiet."

"This place is quiet," Gaby offered.

William glanced back at the soldier, who was still talking to the dog. The guy could be completely harmless, but he didn't want to chance it, not with his wife and child along. "There's another campsite about ten miles up the Scenic Trail."

Claire pouted. "I don't think I could take another minute in this car. Let's just stay here."

William hesitated. "I guess we could."

Gaby's blue eyes brightened. "Please do. I don't want to be the only lady in this part of the jungle. And besides," she tilted her head toward the soldier and lowered her voice. "That weirdo and his dog give me the creeps."

As though he'd heard, the soldier lifted his head and glared at the trio. William looked away. "Come on, Claire, let's unpack before it gets dark."

"When you guys are finished, holler at us," Gaby said. "Jake will be thrilled to see other humans. He loves to talk and I'm not much for conversation. We're only about a half mile down the trail." Gaby retrieved a bag from her van and flashed a parting smile before she disappeared down the trail.

William didn't realize he was staring until Claire cleared her throat. He abruptly looked away and opened the trunk. With a grunt, he heaved his father's worn five-man tent to his shoulders. He watched as Claire sifted through the trunk.

"Just get Gracie for now," he said. "I'll come back for the rest of the stuff after I get the tent up."

Claire nodded. She eased Gracie's wriggling frame out of the car seat and followed William down the steep, bumpy trail. He cast an occasional glance back at Claire, who walked in circles, trying to see everything through wide eyes. As she turned, the sun glistened off her shoulder-length golden hair. "Will, you were right, this is beautiful!"

"Would I lie to you?"

"This isn't at all what I imagined. The forest looks wild, menacing even, but at the same time so peaceful and safe. It's like a giant oil painting."

"Wait 'til you see the creek."

Five hundred yards along the trail, William changed direction and trudged off into the forest. The vegetation was thicker here, walking a little more difficult, but the descent was more gradual. "Watch your step," he cautioned, looking back to see how Claire was making out. She picked her way like a soldier walking through a minefield and she clutched Gracie tightly to her chest.

"Where're you taking us?" she asked.

"Same place my dad took me—*if* it's still there." William stopped and balanced the tent with one hand while he pointed with the other. "See that bright spot up ahead?"

Claire nodded.

"That's where the river cuts through the forest."

Claire cocked her head. "What's that roaring sound?"

"The rapids of the Mighty Skybald River." William smiled. "Music to my ears!"

"Is it safe?"

"As long as you don't fall in." William pushed on and excitement surged through him when they reached the clearing where the ancient pines stood guard along the high bluffs. He let the tent fall from his thirty-three-year-old shoulder and walked to the edge of the bluffs. The dropoff was about eight feet. It had seemed like more when he was eleven. When the initial excitement wore off, he felt the aching in his shoulder and performed shoulder rolls to loosen it up. "Sucks to get old."

Claire didn't seem to hear him. She kicked off her sandals, shuffled her feet in the pine needles that blanketed the earth, and danced around with Gracie. "This is better than a carpet massage!"

William smiled and plopped on top of the tent. "All these years and nothing's changed. It's just like my dad and I left it."

"You think the old rope's still there?"

"I don't know." William stared dreamily at a large limb that was being tossed about by the rough currents of the raging river. He had told Claire all the stories about him and his dad swinging from that old rope and dropping into the deep swimming hole that was located just north of their campsite. It was a place where the river took a sharp bend to the north and the deep water was not as rough. He remembered how raw his palms would get from the rough nylon. When his grip had weakened so that he could no longer hold on, he and his dad would swim across the river and search for buried treasure along the beach. He still had a collection of fossilized wood he had found in the woods surrounding that area. "That'll be Gracie's now."

Claire stopped twirling Gracie and looked down at him. "What?"

"Nothing," he said. "I was just thinking out loud." He pulled himself up and started back up the trail to unload their gear. He lost count of the trips. Each time he made it to the top of the trail he had to pause to catch his breath—and each time he did, the soldier stopped talking and glared at him. On the last trip William said "Hi," but the soldier didn't even acknowledge William's existence.

William hurried back to the campsite. "Something's up with that soldier," he told Claire as he set up the tent. "I knew I should've brought my pistol." It was an old single-action semi-automatic his father had left to him.

"There's no place for guns on a family vacation," Claire said.

"Tell me that when a bear's knocking on the door to our tent." William pounded the last of the stakes into the soft ground and Claire ducked into the tent with Gracie. William gathered twigs and had a modest fire going just as the sun started to slip behind the line of trees across the river. He crawled into the tent and dropped to the hard floor. Claire shoveled spoonful after tiny spoonful of vegetable beef dinner into Gracie's mouth. Most of it dripped down her chin.

William closed his eyes and the sounds of the rapids began to slowly fade . . .

William's dad called him in from the water. He ran, high-stepping through the water, his mouth watering from the smell of barbecue that clung to the warm breeze. As he reached the beach, he heard a loud crack that was barely audible over the roaring of the rapids. He watched, frozen in horror, as a large branch broke free from an ancient pine tree and descended in slow motion toward the ground— toward his father, who smiled from the barbecue pit, unaware of the danger. With a thunderous boom, the tree crashed on top of his father, burying him beneath an onslaught of rough timber and needles. Flames and coals from the pit shot skyward—

William jerked awake and stared wildly about. Gracie was on her belly at the center of the tent and Claire lay watching her. He let out a long sigh.

"Are you okay?" The concern in Claire's voice was obvious.

"Just a bad dream." He stared at his little girl, who made her best attempt at crawling. She buried her face in the blanket, hiked her knees up and shoved off with her feet. For her efforts she succeeded in doing nothing more than plopping onto her side. Her arms and legs flailed and she uttered frustrated baby talk. Doggedly, she tried again.

Claire sat motionless on a balled-up sleeping bag. Her eyes were moist. "Thank you, Will."

William rolled to Claire. "Isn't she the greatest? She's beautiful like you. I just hope she doesn't have your temper."

Claire's mouth dropped and she elbowed William in the ribs. He doubled over and feigned injury. When Claire bent over to check on him, he snatched her off the sleeping bag and tickled her. Her screams caused Gracie's head to snap around and it teetered on her fragile neck. She smiled and the pacifier spat from her mouth, leaving in its wake a line of drool. William could see a glint of humor in Gracie's eyes as she watched them tumbling on the ground beside her.

Suddenly, something crunched outside the tent. William froze in place. He strained to hear. Claire stared wide-eyed at him. A twig snapped. A boot crunched. The sound got closer. Claire scooped Gracie in her arms and moved behind William. The crunching drew closer. William's heart beat against his sternum. A shadow suddenly fell on the wall of the tent and Claire buried her nails into William's forearm.

CHAPTER THREE

1:30 P.M.
Friday, November 19, 2004
Magnolia Parish Sheriff's Office Substation
I pulled into the rear parking lot of the Magnolia Parish Substation in Seasville. I jogged through the back door and made my way quickly up the long hallway. "Hey, Becky," I whispered to the front secretary, "is Bernadette Mayeaux here?"

"Yeah, she's been here since twelve-thirty."

"Oops!"

Becky shook her head and leaned close to me. "It's not a problem. I told her you're the best detective we have and that you're in big demand. She didn't mind waiting."

"Thanks, Beck, you're the best. Of course, you give me way too much credit." I turned to go to the waiting room and then stopped. "Hey, do you mind calling Skel's Seafood and Steak House and making reservations for three at eight? I wouldn't ask, but I'm in a fix."

Becky smiled. "Of course I will."

Becky had been the front secretary at the substation for the past eleven years. She was by far the nicest employee in the entire sheriff's office.

I walked into the waiting room and found Bernadette Mayeaux patiently reading the newspaper. She was a robust woman, dressed in an oversized plaid flannel shirt and brown polyester pants. Her hair was thick and curly, held together by too much hairspray.

"Hello, ma'am, I'm Brandon Berger."

Bernadette looked up and smiled.

I extended my hand. "I'm so sorry to keep you waiting."

She took my hand in both of hers and gently squeezed. "Thank you so much for agreeing to see me." She had a heavy Cajun accent.

When we were seated in my office, I asked her what I could do for her.

"It's my daughter, Meagan. I haven't seen her or my grand-child in almost three weeks."

"Did you file a missing-person report?"

"No, sir. I don't guess I can say they're missing. You see, Meagan called me last week from her cell phone to let me know they're okay, but she won't tell me where they are."

"How old is she?"

"Twenty-three."

"And the baby?"

"A little over six months."

"Is she married?"

Mrs. Mayeaux grunted. "Yeah, and I think her husband's the problem. Since they've been married, she hasn't been able to go out with any of her friends unless he's with her. My God, she can't even go shopping without him. The only place he lets her go by herself is my house. I thought he would like to stop that, too. I guess he finally done it."

"What's his name?"

"Tom Banks."

"Does he work?"

"He's an assistant preacher at the Magnolia Faith Church."

I booted my computer and ran a name inquiry for both, Tom Banks and Meagan Mayeaux Banks. They were both clean. Not even a traffic ticket. "When was the last time you saw them?"

"Two Sundays ago. No, well, three Sundays ago. Two Sundays ago she called early in the morning and said she was coming to my house for dinner. She called back later to say she couldn't make it. When I asked her why, she couldn't give me an answer." Mrs. Mayeaux shook her head. "It's not like Meagan to go that long without seeing us. She visits me nearly every day. I think Tom is holding her and Nikki against their will."

"Is Nikki the baby?"

Mrs. Mayeaux nodded and bent her head to wipe a tear. "I'm just so scared that we won't get to spend time with Nikki on her first Christmas."

I leaned across the desk and squeezed Mrs. Mayeaux's shoulder. "Ma'am, if Meagan's taking good care of Nikki and she's where she is of her own free will, then legally there's nothing I can do."

Mrs. Mayeaux nodded her understanding.

"But," I said, "I'm going to look into this. I am a little concerned, since you say this is out of Meagan's normal pattern of behavior. I'll need all her identifiable information—cell phone number, names of friends, names of Tom's family, stuff like that. A picture would also be helpful."

Mrs. Mayeaux's eyes lit up and she dug through her oversized purse. "I have most of that already written down." She handed me a piece of stationary and pointed to a number at the top of the page. "This is Meagan's cell number, but she's been keeping her phone off." She removed a family picture from her wallet and handed it to me.

"How about friends?"

"She hasn't had any since joining that crazy church."

I rubbed the stubble that had started to sprout on my chin. "I'm really going to need to talk to her."

"Well, she told me she would call me tonight. She usually calls between seven and seven-thirty. If you'd like me to meet

BJ Bourg

you here, I can."

"I could go to your house. That would save you from having to be out on the road at night."

"Oh, you're so kind." Mrs. Mayeaux's eyes were shiny wet. "Thank you so much for agreeing to look into this. I understand this is not an important case, like the others you work . . ."

"Ma'am, if it's important enough for you to drive out here to meet with me, then it's important enough for me to look into."

"You're a kind man." Mrs. Mayeaux gathered her purse and stood. I walked her to the door and then joined Becky in the front office. She was on the phone giving directions to some poor soul who had forgotten to pay a speeding ticket and now had to visit with Judge Landry. I picked up Becky's newspaper and sat at the spare desk.

When Becky hung up the phone, she handed me a pink sticky note. "Your reservation has been made, sir. At first they told me they couldn't—"

"Shit!" I slapped my forehead and my eyes smarted when my palm brushed against my bruised nose. "Double shit!"

"What's wrong?" There was genuine concern in Becky's voice.

"I just set up a meeting with this Bernadette Mayeaux woman for tonight."

Becky covered her mouth with her hand. "Do I need to cancel the reservation? Because I had to do some smooth talking to get you the table and they're not going to be happy with me if I cancel."

"No, uh, maybe . . . hell, I don't know what to do." I leaned back in the chair and threw my legs up on the desk. "Today's my anniversary. It just crept up on me this year." I said that more to myself. I stared at a spot on the ceiling. If Tom didn't let Meagan have friends, then who would know where Meagan was? I shook my head. It seemed she was closer to her mom than anyone else . . . if her mom didn't know, no one would.

26

And what if Meagan didn't call tonight? That would mean I let my wife down for nothing. I stood and paced the hallway. What to do? I could feel Becky's eyes on me, but she didn't say a word. Like a good friend, she knew when to remain silent. I pulled the stationary from my pocket and stared at it. There had to be a way I could locate Meagan before tonight. It suddenly struck me—the Magnolia Faith Church! If Tom Banks was an assistant preacher, they would have to know where he was.

The Magnolia Faith Church parking lot was empty except for two cars parked near the front door to the office. I had driven past the church many times, but never realized just how big it really was. The steps leading up to the front office were made of marble, the hand railings solid brass. I opened the door and found myself in a plush waiting room. Paintings of Jesus, rich in detail, lined every wall. Above the reception glass, beside one of the pictures of Jesus, was a portrait of a man. There was a golden placard on the bottom framework that read, "Father Isaac Stewart."

I scanned the rest of the room. A red leather sofa set, solid oak coffee table, and two matching end tables made up the furniture arrangement. I grunted. *I can't afford this stuff for my living room and they've got it in the waiting room.* I took a deep breath. Even the air was rich. I smashed the brass bell and waited. A minute later the secretary slid the frosted window open.

"May I help you, sir?"

"Yes, ma'am. I'd like to speak to the preacher."

"Father Isaac is out of town at the moment."

"What about Tom Banks?"

"He's with Father Isaac."

"When will they be back?"

"I'm not sure. They're doing the Lord's will."

I puckered my brow and started to ask what was supposed to be the Lord's will, but just shook my head instead. "What about a cell number?"

"Father Isaac has a cellular phone, but he doesn't allow us to call him unless it's an emergency."

"Well, this is an emergency." I showed her my badge. "I'm Detective Brandon Berger. I need to speak with him immediately."

The girl hesitated.

"I can get a search warrant and tear this place apart until I find his cell number, or you can get him on the phone."

"Please, I'll be a minute." The girl shut the window. I heard her muffled voice from somewhere deep within the room, but was unable to make out what she said. I leaned closer to the window. Footsteps clanked against the marble floor and the door to the left burst open. It was the secretary. "Come with me."

I followed her down a long corridor. She stopped near a large solid door and opened it. I stepped inside. An enormous Judge's bench served as the desk. It was made of quarter-sawn oak and the writing surface was lacquered sailcloth material. A leather wingback chair with ball and claw feet stood guard behind the desk. One entire wall served as a solid oak bookshelf. There were books from floor to ceiling and wall to wall. I whistled. This place made a rich man's office look like a washroom. *I'm definitely in the wrong profession.*

The secretary smashed the button on the phone that indicated line one. She handed me the receiver. "It's Father Isaac."

I shoved the phone against my ear. "Isaac? Howdy, I'm Detective Brandon Berger."

"What can I do for you, Detective?"

"I'm actually looking for Tom Banks. Is he with you?"

"Brother Banks? What business do you have with him?"

"I need to ask him some questions."

"Questions? About what?"

"His mother-in-law reported them missing."

"Missing?" Isaac bellowed on the other end. "They're not missing. Brother Banks has been with me for a couple of weeks now."

"What about his wife and—"

"They're all fine."

"Well, I still need to speak with them. So, if you have a number . . ."

There was a long pause. "I'll have Brother Banks call you this evening."

"Great. I appreciate it." I gave Isaac my cell phone number and handed the receiver back to the secretary.

I called the flower shop on my way back to the office. "I need to get two dozen white roses delivered."

"When and where?" The girl on the other end asked.

"This afternoon to—"

"Oh, I'm sorry, sir, we close in half an hour. There's no way we can get the order out in that time. If you like, you can stop by and pick out an arrangement."

When I got back to the office Becky stopped me. "Bernadette Mayeaux called for you."

I glanced at my watch. It was five o'clock. "Did she say what she wanted?" Even as I asked the question, I was dialing the number on the spare desk phone.

When Mrs. Mayeaux heard my voice she grew excited. "Detective, Meagan just called me. She said something about the police going to the church to look for Tom and she said that they're coming home tomorrow. Thank you so much! You're every bit as good as the secretary said!"

I couldn't help but smile. "I didn't do anything, ma'am."

"Yes, you did! You went over there and put the heat on them and now my daughter's coming home."

As soon as I hung up with Mrs. Mayeaux, I quickly dialed my home number. Debbie must have looked at the caller ID box because she answered the phone singing, "I called up to say I'm sorry, I just can't have lunch today, because the boss just called—"

"Be ready for seven o'clock," I said victoriously.

Debbie screamed. "Oh my God! Really?"

"Yes, indeed. I have a few things to tie up here and then I'll be home."

"Thank you, Brandon." I could sense the tears of joy in Debbie's eyes. "This is really important to me."

"Me, too. See you in a few."

Becky was beaming. "Is she happy?"

"Oh yeah!"

"It's important that you put your family before your work," Becky lectured. "You can get another job, but you can't replace your family."

"I know, I know. Things just kinda crept up on me."

I thanked Becky as she left for the day and sat at my computer to catch up on reports. The light started to fade outside and I soon found myself typing in the dark. My desk phone rang. "Hello?"

"Where are you?" Debbie's voice was anxious.

The clock at the bottom right corner of my computer told me it was six-fifteen. "I'm wrapping up this report and I'll be home in a minute."

"Okay, I was just getting—"

The scream of my pager interrupted her. I pulled it off my belt and glanced at the display screen. It was the radio room

. . . and there was "911" behind the number. That was never good.

"Is that your pager?" Debbie wanted to know. "Are you getting called out?"

"No, I just have to call the radio room."

"They're calling you out, aren't they?"

I tried to be optimistic. "There's a two-for-one sale on doughnuts down at the bakery . . . they're paging all the cops."

"Damn it, Brandon, that's not funny. What's going on? Why are they paging you?"

"They probably just have a message for me. I'll make this call and I'll be right home."

"Are you sure?"

"Baby, I'm not going back on my word this time. Nothing can stop me from taking you out tonight."

Debbie reluctantly let me go and I called the radio room. A young dispatcher, whose voice I'd never heard, answered in a panic. She told me there had been a death at 1701 East Jillian Street. "You're needed right away," she said.

My heart sank to my toenails. "Tell me you're kidding."

"No, sir. The Sheriff wants you over there ASAP."

I gently placed the phone receiver back in the cradle and slowly stood to go. I exhaled deeply and stared at my reflection in the window. "Can you spell *divorce*?"

CHAPTER FOUR

5:00 P.M.
Friday, November 19, 2004
Skybald National Forest, North Louisiana

"Is that the soldier?" Claire's breath was hot against William's ear and he could smell the spearmint on her breath from the gum she always chewed. The shadow moved closer. Claire's fingernails dug deeper and broke the skin on William's arm . . . he knew it by the burning sensation he felt. He pulled her hand away and reached for the black twelve-inch Cold Steel Recon Tanto knife that protruded from the side pouch of his duffel bag. He lifted the Tanto and sidled toward the zippered door. His heart pounded in his ears. He took the zipper gently in his fingertips and started to ease it upward. The tent suddenly jerked in front of him. He jumped back, dropping the Tanto. Claire yelped when a deep voice called out, "Hello the camp!"

William froze in place. Claire held Gracie close and tried to keep her quiet.

"Are you guys there?" a lady's voice called.

William sighed audibly when he heard the familiar voice of Gaby Arthur. "Yeah, coming right out." He unzipped the tent door and held it open for Claire and Gracie. He followed them out and when he straightened, he had to look twice at Gaby's husband, who was not at all what he had expected. The man was short, somewhat plump, and even paler than Gaby. His thick-rimmed glasses made him appear much older than Gaby.

"Name's Jake, Jake Arthur."

William shook Jake's outstretched hand. It was a weak handshake, sticky and wet. William subtly wiped his hand on the back of his jeans and said, "We were about ready to put some burgers on the pit. Care to join us?"

Gaby scrunched her nose. "We don't want to be a burden. We were actually just heading back to the car to get some things before it gets dark."

Jake nodded. "We don't go around the parking area after dark."

"The soldier?" William asked.

"Yeah. He gets really weird when the sun goes down."

"How 'bout Gaby stay here with Claire," William suggested. "I can give you a hand with the stuff."

Jake cast an inquiring glance in Gaby's direction. She nodded her approval and Jake said, "Okay, let's do it."

William slipped his leather sheath onto his belt and shoved the Tanto into it. "Protection," he offered when Claire scolded. He joined Jake and they trudged along the rough and gradually ascending trail. William made a conscious effort to walk slowly enough so the shorter man could keep up with him. They dipped and dodged to avoid the outstretched arms of shrubbery that lined the narrow trail. An occasional wind peeled the pungent odor of stale sweat from Jake Arthur's body and smeared it into William's nostrils. William grimaced and prayed for the wind to shift. After several minutes of silence, he said, "How long have y'all been here?"

"Two weeks."

William whistled. "Must be nice. I don't think my wife would be able to handle being here that long." *And if we smell like you do now,* William thought, *I don't know if I'd want to stay here that long.*

"Gaby doesn't particularly like camping, but sometimes you

just do what you got to. Anyway, it's a good family outing."

"How many children do you—"

Jake stopped abruptly and pointed to the clearing where the vehicles were parked. "What's he doing?"

William looked in the direction Jake pointed. The soldier was crouched beside William's Thunderbird examining the wheel-well above the front driver's-side tire. William stepped out into the clearing and took a cautious look around. The pit bull was nowhere in sight. He dragged his Tanto from the leather sheath.

Jake stepped back. "What are you doing with that?" he asked in a hushed voice.

"That guy looks dangerous."

"So, what? You're gonna stab him?"

William shook his head and waved the knife in a dismissive manner. "This is just for protection. In case he attacks us." William moved forward one slow step after another. He scanned the area for the pit bull. When he was fifty feet from the soldier, he stopped. He kept the knife concealed behind his back and took a deep breath. In as demanding a voice as he could muster, he shouted, "What the hell are you doing?"

The soldier didn't even flinch. He continued to examine the wheel-well. When he was satisfied, he moved to the passenger-side tire. William took a bold step forward. He opened his mouth to speak again, but movement caught the corner of his eye. He froze. The pit bull had stepped out from behind the Thunderbird and fixed its eyes on William. Their gazes locked. The pit bull's lip curled into a growl. William's fingers tightened around the Tanto's handle and he pointed the blade in the direction of the dog. They stood poised for what seemed like hours. The soldier finally straightened and turned to the pit bull. "Come on, Satan, all's clear." His olive drab BDU blouse hung loose on his thin frame and he sauntered by William and Jake as though they weren't even there. His leathered face bore no expression. Satan followed the soldier, but kept a wary eye on William. The soldier returned to his post near the station wagon and slid to the ground. "Something stinks, Satan, and we're gonna find out what."

Neither man uttered a word while Jake grabbed a bundle of clothes from the back of the van. William cast an occasional nervous glance in the direction of the soldier. He wished the man would just leave. Why have a pit bull out here, anyway? The people who camped in this primitive area were exposed to enough danger without having a mad dog running around. At least the black bears, coyotes, and wolves were afraid of humans . . . that pit bull was not.

When they were a safe distance up the trail, Jake said, "What do you think he was doing?"

"Planting a bomb?"

Jake chuckled. "Did you see the name on his uniform?"

"Too faded."

"You think he was really in the military?"

William shrugged. "You can never tell." He thought of his old neighbor and smiled. "When I was a kid my neighbor's dad used to tell us stories about how he killed a bunch of Viet Cong in the Vietnam War. He always wore those battle dress uniforms, jump boots, dog tags . . . the whole nine. When I got older I found out he'd never even read a military book, much less been in a war."

"In any event, I'll be happy when he's gone."

"How long has he been here?"

"He showed up about three days ago. I tried to talk to him when he first showed up, but he acted like I wasn't even there. He gives Gaby the creeps."

"He's definitely a strange one." William looked up. Daylight was fading fast and the tall dense treetops cast dark shadows along the forest floor, making it hard for them to follow the faint trail that led to the campsite. Leaves rustled behind them. William touched the handle of his Tanto and looked over his shoulder. It was too dark to penetrate the shadows. *Why didn't I bring that pistol?* He knew the dangers and he had argued the point with Claire, but she wouldn't relent. He had told her about the bears he saw there when he was a kid. She'd laughed at him and said, "Well, it didn't get you, did it?"

William shook his head. What did Claire know about the dangers of the wilderness, anyway? The closest she'd ever come to camping out was in her dad's tent in the backyard of her childhood home. It had been her double-digit birthday party, or something. The only animals they'd seen were the neighborhood cats and a few mosquitoes.

William didn't relax until he saw the orange glow from their campfire. He smiled to himself. What was it about campfires that gave such a feeling of comfort and security? Through the gaps in the trees he could see Claire bent over the butane stove. The alluring smell of barbecue beef reached out and invited him closer.

Jake stopped him. "I'll run this over to our tent."

"Need a flashlight?"

"Naw, it's just down the trail."

Claire looked up when William approached the campsite. "Where's Jake?"

"The soldier got him."

Claire glowered at William.

He threw up his hands. "Just kidding. He ran to his campsite."

Claire rolled her eyes and turned back to her cooking. "I just flipped the burgers. They'll be ready in five minutes."

William glanced at Gaby. She hadn't looked up. She sat in a lounge chair by the fire and bounced Gracie on her lap. Gracie's dark eyes sparkled and she laughed hard. Gaby's face beamed and she seemed completely captivated. William understood the feeling. The day they took Gracie home from the hospital he and Claire just stared at her for hours. It was the happiest they had ever been.

William removed the knife and holster from his belt and placed it on the picnic table beside the stove. He then sat beside Gaby. "Having fun?" His voice apparently startled her and she blushed.

"Sorry," she said meekly. "I didn't realize you guys were back. Your daughter is just too precious!" Gracie slapped two wet fists together at the sight of her dad.

William smiled. "Yes, indeed. I couldn't ask for more. Of course, with a mom like Claire, what would you expect?"

"Oh, stop it," Claire called from the picnic table, trying to sound indifferent.

William winked at Gaby. Claire wasn't fooling him. She had always responded well to flattery. "I have to keep a good supply of brownie points on hand. Lord knows I need them."

"Wow," Gaby said, "you two seem to be so much in love."

"We're good actors," William explained.

Gaby laughed and wiggled her pointy nose against Gracie's plump smeller. "What do you think, Precious?" Gracie giggled and grabbed Gaby's face in her arms. She bit down on Gaby's forehead with wet gums. A long line of dribble fell across Gaby's eye, but she didn't seem to mind.

"You're so good with her," William said. "Do y'all have children?"

Gaby frowned and put her head down. "No, but I want one really bad."

When she looked up, William noticed Gaby's eyes were moist and red. He felt a twinge of sorrow for this young woman. *Was it that she couldn't have children?* William felt compelled to say something, but he didn't know what. To say the wrong thing might make things worse for Gaby, so he sat silently and stared into the fire. He was actually relieved to hear Jake's goofy cry of, "Hello the camp!"

It made Gaby smile. She cleared her throat and subtly wiped a tear that had escaped her eye. "He always says that when he approaches the campsite," she explained. "He read it in a Western novel."

"That's right" Jake dropped a six-pack of sodas on the table where Claire had spread out four plates. "It's the polite thing to do. You don't want to walk up on a camp and surprise a man and a woman." He smiled big, exposing a row of yellow teeth. "Know what I mean, Will?"

Gaby blushed. "Jake, there's a baby here!"

William helped Claire dress the hamburgers. When they were done, the two couples sat around the fire and ate. As they talked, William noticed that Jake dominated most of the conversation. For a short plump man he displayed a healthy dose of confidence. He was also funny and William couldn't help but like him.

They talked late into the night, with William excusing himself several times to feed the fire. Finally, Gaby, who had rocked Gracie to sleep hours before, stifled a yawn and turned to her husband. "Jake, I think it's time we let them get to sleep." She rose gently to her feet, tiptoed to Claire and eased Gracie into Claire's waiting arms.

"It was so nice to meet y'all," Claire said. "I've had a great time."

"So did I." William stood to his feet and nodded in Jake's direction. "How long are y'all staying?"

Jake looked at Gaby, who cocked her head to the side and shrugged.

"It's up to you," Gaby said.

Jake scratched his head in thought. "I'd love to stay longer now that you guys are here, but," he wrapped his arm around

Gaby's neck, "my wife is getting a bit tired of this place." He looked up at Gaby, who was an inch or more taller than him. "What do you say we leave tomorrow evening?"

Gaby smiled. Her eyes lit up. "That would be great." She looked at Claire. "The first thing I'm going to do when I get home is take an hour-long bath!"

William and Claire watched as Jake and Gaby disappeared into the night. "They're nice people," Claire said.

William nodded and he and Claire squeezed through the opening in the tent. He zipped it shut behind them. He hung the flashlight from the ceiling of the tent and watched as Claire positioned Gracie on a flat, narrow mattress. Gracie didn't even stir. "She sleeps like you," William said. He unrolled a large sleeping bag and spread it on the opposite side of the tent. He reached for his knife, but remembered placing it on the table. He started for the zipper.

"Where are you going?"

"Get my knife."

"Leave it."

"But, what if—?"

"For me . . . you know I don't like those dreadful things."

William sighed. He stripped down to his boxers and turned the flashlight off. The only light was the flickering glow from the campfire outside and he and Claire fumbled for several minutes with the sleeping bag before finding the opening.

"Can we really fit in there together?" Claire wanted to know.

"Yep. And you won't have to worry about being cold . . . I promise."

Claire slid into the sleeping bag and William followed, their bodies pressed together. Claire snuggled closer to him and let out a long sigh. "This is the life," she said in a dreamy voice.

William nodded and closed his eyes. His tired muscles started to slowly unwind. He sank into the ground. The night sounds had a hypnotic effect on him and he slipped into a dreamlike state. *This ain't so bad,* he thought. A lazy smile tugged at his mouth. *I can beat this monster.*

William was almost asleep when a loud crack from off in the distance brought him instantly alert. It had been twenty-two years since he'd heard that sound, but he immediately recognized it for what it was—a tired tree limb losing its grip on the mother trunk. Moments later came the loud boom as it crashed to the ground. William shuddered. He was much older now, but that sound still sent a chill through him that made icicles form around his heart. Sweat pooled on his forehead. His heart pounded like a bass drum in his chest. Frozen in place, he stared wide-eyed into the darkness above. *Was this a mistake?*

CHAPTER FIVE

7:00 P.M.
Friday, November 19, 2004
Magnolia Parish, Southeastern Louisiana

It was almost seven o'clock when I turned down East Jillian Street. Patrol cruisers lined one side of the narrow street. Their strobe lights flashed blindly against the blackness of the night. I drove around the cruisers until I found the address. The yard was wrapped in yellow crime-scene tape. It was a small lot with an old gray trailer situated near the center. A seventies model Chevy station wagon, up on cinder blocks and minus four tires, was parked on the cement drive and a push-lawnmower was shoved under the trailer. Other than those two items, the yard was bare.

I parked in front of the driveway and picked up my cell phone to dial home. I paused, thumb suspended over the "send" button. What was I going to tell Debbie? What wouldn't sound like all the other times I called to say I couldn't make it? Missed birthday parties, late Christmases, too many all-nighters. Debbie had said many times that life with me was a highway filled with potholes of broken promises. I couldn't argue with her. Hell, I was working the night Samantha was born. I punched the steering wheel. *Why was this shit always happening to me?*

I flipped my phone shut and dropped it in my shirt pocket. Several deputies huddled near the station wagon and they looked up when I ducked under the yellow tape. Dawn Luke,

41

who was the department's crime-scene investigator and photographer, walked out the front door. She ejected a roll of film from her camera, scribbled something on the outside, and shoved it in the side pocket of the camera bag that was draped over her shoulder.

"Hey, Dawn," I said in as cheery a voice as I could. "What's the prognosis?"

Dawn was just over five feet tall and had a body that was proportionate to her height. This was a fact that she was well aware of and she took every opportunity to flaunt it. On this day, she was squeezed into a pair of faded jeans with a tight red sweater that accentuated her firm breasts. Her short brown hair, which capped off her tanning-bed complexion, was tucked under a baseball cap. She shoved an ink pen up under the right side of her cap, aimed her flashlight at my face, and looked directly into my eyes. "You don't look happy," she said.

I grunted. "Is it that obvious?"

"It is." She pouted and slid closer to me. Her eyes softened. She allowed her fingers to dance gingerly across my chest. "I can help make it all better."

"Yes, you can." I walked past her. "You can wrap this up so I can get home to my wife."

Dawn sighed. "You're such a killjoy."

I picked my way through the front yard, searching for evidence as I walked, and finally made it to the front steps. I carefully ascended the splintered boards. They were unsteady and shook under my weight. I stopped at the doorway to pull on a pair of latex gloves and carefully pushed open the door. The doorjamb was splintered.

The smell of Dawn's sweet perfume warned me that she had followed me up the steps. "The body's in the back bedroom," she said.

"What's with the doorjamb?"

"The deputies had to kick the door in to gain entry."

"What brought them here?"

"A call that someone was murdered. They found the body in the master bedroom."

I turned and looked around the yard and the street in front of the trailer. There were only law enforcement officers present. "Who called it in?"

Dawn shrugged. "He didn't leave a name. Dispatcher said it was a guy, sounded young."

The doorway led into the living room. The furniture setup was modest, the room immaculate. Other than a few dirty dishes in the sink, the kitchen was as clean as the living room. Even the garbage can was empty. Dawn pointed down a dark hallway. "The body's down there."

I followed her to the master bedroom at the end of the hallway. The door was open and the ceiling fan and lights were on. To the right was a window. It was broken. Shards of glass peppered the carpet and the curtain danced wildly in the cool breeze that blew through the gaping hole.

"What do you know about that?" I asked.

"The deputies say it was broken when they arrived."

I turned my attention to the interior of the room. A full-size bed took up most of the space. Atop the bed was a woman. Her body was covered to the neck with a multicolored quilt. She was mid-thirties, but looked older. Her face was pale and ghostly . . . cheeks hollow . . . eyes closed and sunken. I tested her jaw—it didn't move. Dawn stared down at the woman, her playful eyes somber.

"You shot enough photos?" I asked.

"Yeah, I'm done."

I eased the quilt down to expose a bony frame clad in a faded blue nightgown. I grabbed her bare foot and gently lifted—it was stiff and cold. I pulled her nightgown up and saw that her blood had settled to the back of her legs and torso. When I pushed my index finger against the rosy skin, it didn't blanch. "Hmm, she's been dead a while. What time did the call come in?"

Dawn pulled her notebook from the waistline in front of her jeans. She thumbed through the pages before answering. "6:02 P.M."

A visual examination of the body revealed that there were no bullet holes, knife wounds, or ligature marks on her neck. I opened her eyes. "No petechiae."

Dawn's face scrunched. "A what?"

"Pinpoint hemorrhaging." I glanced around. "Anything missing?"

"I can't be sure. I wasn't able to find a purse, wallet, or any form of identification for the victim. No bank records, checkbooks, nothing." She pointed to the closet and a dresser across from the doorway. "That's been rummaged through."

"Any fingerprints?"

"Not so much as a smudge. I think somebody wiped this place clean. I should've found the victim's prints at the very least."

"Okay, here's what we know: We have a broken window, a dead woman with no obvious cause of death, possibly some things missing from the trailer, and a mystery man called it in." I rubbed my chin. "We need to find that caller—"

My cell phone rang and I suddenly remembered Debbie. I snatched it open. "Hey, Deb, what's up?"

"Brandon, where are you? It's ten after seven!"

"I know, I know, I got this call. You see, a woman's dead—"

"No, tell me you're not . . ."

"Deb, it's an emergency, this lady's dead and it looks like—"

"I don't give a shit if the President's dead! You promised me you'd be here!"

"I know, and I'm sorry, but it's my job."

"And what are we?" Debbie cried. I could hear Samantha fussing in the background. "Here, talk to your father," Debbie said.

"When are you coming home, Daddy?"

"Hey, Sam, put mom back on the phone."

"Daddy, Mommy said you love work more than me."

"No, Baby, that's not true. Look, give your mom the phone."

"Mommy told me to tell you bye." The phone went dead.

I hit the redial button on my phone. It rang several times with no answer. I hung up and tried again. Still no answer. Dawn tapped my shoulder. "You can go if you like," she said. "I can finish up here."

"I appreciate the offer, but you know I don't shirk my responsibilities." I called home again and still no answer. I tried Debbie's cell phone. An automated message told me the phone was turned off. I cursed myself.

Dawn put a warm hand on my cheek. "Go home, Brandon. I'll finish up here. There's nothing more we can do tonight anyway."

"But—"

"Go! We'll get back on this tomorrow."

I pulled Dawn's hand from my face and gave it a squeeze. "Thanks, you're a good friend."

My heart stopped beating when I pulled into my empty driveway. Debbie's new Mercury Mountaineer was gone. I rushed into the house and called out for her and Samantha. Nothing. Every room in the house was empty. I jerked my phone from my pocket and dialed Debbie's parents' number. Her mother answered.

"Hey, this is Brandon." I tried to sound casual. "Is Debbie there?"

"Is she supposed to be here?"

"I'm not sure. I just got home from work and she's not home."

"Try her cell."

"I did."

"Oh dear, I hope nothing's wrong."

"I'm sure everything's fine." I pulled the phone from my ear and rubbed my forehead. Debbie's mom's muffled voice called from my palm.

"Brandon? Are you there?"

"Yeah, I'm here."

"Is everything okay?"

"Everything's great. Just have her call my cell if you hear from her."

"Sure."

I called Dawn to find out how things were going.

"Fine, fine. Don't worry about a thing."

"Okay, well . . . I'd better let you go."

"You don't sound good."

"Debbie took Samantha and left."

"She's probably at her mom's house."

"No. I called."

"She probably drove around to cool off. I do that sometimes when I'm mad."

I paced up and down the living room. "I don't know. She's never done anything like this."

"I could drive around, see if I spot her."

"No, I don't want to inconvenience you."

"It's no bother."

"I know, but I'll go ahead and do it." I walked briskly to my unmarked cruiser and made the round of our small town. Her Mountaineer was nowhere to be found. I tried to imagine where Debbie could have gone. The grocery stores turned up nothing. A dozen tries to her cell phone met with the same results—

turned off. I called the two area hospitals . . . nothing. I'd been monitoring my police radio and hadn't heard any reports of accidents. I called the radio room to be sure.

"No, sir," the dispatcher said. "Knock on wood, we've had no wrecks tonight."

The later it got, the more worried I became. I drove aimlessly around town, as I watched the minutes tick by on the dash clock. Nine-thirty found me parked in front of the Seasville Substation. As I mulled over what had become of Debbie and Samantha, a thought struck me like a javelin to the throat—kidnap! Panic gripped me.

There'd been a report of a home invasion in the news the previous month. Just sixty miles to the east, a woman had been forced from her home at gunpoint. When her husband returned home from work, he hadn't even suspected anything. It wasn't until her nude body was discovered two hours later in a field that her husband knew something was wrong.

I spun my unmarked in the street and mashed the gas pedal, trying desperately to remember if the door to my house had been locked when I first arrived home from work. *What if someone did kidnap them?* The names of every person I'd ever arrested flashed through my mind. It was a long list of bad people, the worst of whom were either dead or doing life without parole. *Did they have contacts on the outside who could get this done for them?*

When I arrived home, I raced through my house and searched for signs of forced entry. Nothing. Every window was locked, every door secured. Confused, I leaned against the kitchen counter. Debbie had never done anything like this. *What if she met someone?* "Get a grip," I said out loud. I shook my head to clear it. *Not Debbie. She's a classy woman.* I checked the caller ID box—I was the only one who had called all day. I pressed the redial button on the house phone and a moment later my cell phone rang.

I snatched a longneck from the refrigerator and walked aimlessly into the living room. My recliner groaned when I dropped into it. I wolfed down the beer and yearned for another, but dared not. Dejected, I closed my eyes and leaned back. *Why are you doing this to me, Debbie?*

CHAPTER SIX

3:00 A.M.
Saturday, November 20, 2004
Skybald National Forest, North Louisiana

William tossed and turned. He tried to shake the fear that gripped him like a vice. He flinched with every branch that snapped and shuddered every time a pinecone dropped on the roof of the tent. Leaves crunched nearby and he remembered the soldier. His heart raced. He pulled the sleeping bag over his head, but then stopped himself. *Come on, fool,* he thought, *you're a grown man!*

Sometime later, the glow from the campfire faded. William opened his mouth and listened closely to Claire's breathing—sound asleep. He eased out of the sleeping bag, crawled quietly across the plastic floor, and unzipped the door. After scanning the area for danger, William scurried the short distance to the fire and threw on more wood. An uneasy feeling enveloped him. He glanced often over his shoulder while he waited for the logs to catch. When the fire blazed again, he darted back into the tent and slid beside Claire.

The fire crackled a welcome tune and cast dancing shadows against the tent. William closed his eyes and tried to sleep, but it was no use. He got up twice more during the night to feed the fire. Each time he returned to the sleeping bag he prayed for sleep, but it was a prayer that fell on deaf ears. He feared his tossing and turning would awaken Claire, so he stretched out on the floor. He wasn't aware of when it happened, but sometime late in the night he managed to drift off to a restless slumber.

William opened his eyes. The sun shone through the thin walls of the tent. He heard voices outside . . . Claire was talking to Gracie. He sat up and rubbed his eyes. A pain shot down his back when he bent to pull on his jeans. After he was dressed he crawled slowly out of the tent and stood cautiously to his feet.

"Good morning," Claire called cheerfully from the picnic table. There was a stack of pancakes on a paper plate and two plastic cups filled with milk near the butane stove. Gracie lay on a blanket beside the table. William smiled when he realized Gracie was wearing the all-in-one he had bought for the camping trip. It was a yellow striped outfit with a girl teddy bear on the front and a sign that read, "Daddy's Pumpkin." A matching knit cap was pulled down to her eyebrows to keep her head warm. Her brown mitts matched the brown shoes on her tiny feet.

William bent to play with Gracie and yelped as a sharp pain coursed down his back. "I don't remember the ground beating me up like this when I was a kid."

"Why didn't you stay in the sleeping bag? It was much softer than the bare ground."

"I couldn't sleep and I was worried I'd keep you up."

Claire laughed as she served the pancakes. "You know I can sleep through a war zone."

"You're right about that."

"Oh, before I forget, a Forest Ranger person came by here about an hour ago. He said we forgot to fill out the day pass."

"Day pass?"

"It's two dollars a day to camp here. We have to fill out a card and hang it from the car mirror."

"Hmm, I don't remember doing that when I was a kid. Did he give you a card?"

"He said there's a metal box in the parking lot with envelopes. He said to put the money in the envelope and drop it in the slot."

William pulled two dollars from his wallet. "I'll be back in a second."

"Hurry, I don't want the pancakes to get cold."

William set out at a jog, but gave up after a hundred yards. He proceeded at a brisk walk and didn't slow until he neared the fence that marked the parking area. He could see the soldier's station wagon through the trees. He instinctively reached for his Tanto and cursed when he realized he'd forgotten it. He stepped out into the open and scanned the area. The soldier was nowhere in sight and neither was the pit bull. The metal box Claire described was on the other side of the station wagon, hence the reason he hadn't noticed it earlier.

William retrieved a pen from the Thunderbird and walked cautiously to the box. A pink envelope protruded from a slot at the bottom of the gray metal box. A narrow rectangular opening at the top of the box marked the pay slot. As he reached for the envelope, he glanced around. All seemed quiet.

William walked back to the Thunderbird and wrote his name, license plate number, city, and state on the appropriate lines on the envelope. He slipped the two dollars inside and hung the day pass on his mirror. A roar from a large engine drew his attention to the rock road. He was relieved to see a green Ranger truck drive into view. The truck drove past him and parked near the station wagon. An elderly man stepped out. He wore a green faded coverall and a jacket that read, "Forest Maintenance." He limped to the bank of garbage bins that was located near the pay box.

The soldier was still nowhere to be seen. William walked to

the pay box and nodded at the man as he passed. "How's it going, sir?"

The elderly man looked up. His wrinkled face was strangely familiar to William. He returned the nod. "Not too bad, if I must say so myself." The man removed the garbage bags from the bins and tossed them into the back of his truck. He relined the bins with fresh bags.

William paused by the pay box. "My wife tells me we have to fill out one of these passes each day. Is that right, or can I fill out the three of them now?"

The elderly man paused over the bin. "It's one per day. Safety reasons. We make a pass each day and check the cars in the lot. If there's not a current day pass on the car, we go looking for the campers. Most times, the campers simply forgot to fill out the pass, but sometimes we find that the campers ran into trouble."

"Wow." William was impressed. "That sounds like a good system."

"Yeah, we started that a good many years back, right after a man was killed by a falling tree. His young son was out here alone for three days before anyone found them."

William swallowed hard. "Okay, well, thank you, sir." He turned away, but the elderly man's voice stopped him.

"Be certain you don't leave food around your tent."

"Is there a problem?"

The elderly man shrugged. "Not a real threat, but one of the black bears been getting too close to the campers lately. I suspect someone's been feeding her."

"You don't think—"

"No, there's nothing to worry about. Just keep an eye out and secure your food."

William waved his thanks and walked briskly down the trail. Claire looked up when he reached the campsite.

"Where've you been?" she asked. "The pancakes are cold."

"Sorry," William mumbled and took his place at the table. He didn't say much during breakfast. He knew Claire would question his silence, but he couldn't force himself to make conversation. When he'd finished, he spun around on the bench and leaned against the table. Claire scooted next to him and put her arm around him.

"Missing your dad?" she asked softly.

William swallowed the lump that had formed in his throat. "I thought coming here would help put it behind me. Maybe I was wrong."

"Give yourself a break." Claire climbed onto the tabletop behind William, with her legs straddling him. She rubbed his shoulders. "You said it would be hard to come back after so long and you were right. You also said this trip would help put it to rest. I believe you were right about that, as well. Just give yourself a little time."

"I was okay when we drove up and I was fine last night while Jake and Gaby were here. It's just . . ."

"What? You had a nightmare?"

"No. I heard a branch break in the forest, a big one. I've heard that sound millions of times in my dreams, but to hear it again for real . . ." He shook his head. "It just killed me."

"You need to stop blaming yourself."

"There's no one else to blame. It was just the two of us. I did nothing. I just stood there . . . and did nothing."

"You were eleven. There's nothing you could've done to save him. You were too far away. Had you been closer, who knows? The tree might've killed you both."

"I could've warned him, yelled out, or something. Instead, I just stood there. Frozen. Hell, I wanted to warn him. I tried to scream, but nothing came out. Like the coward that I am . . . I was too scared to act." William buried his face in his hands and tried to squeeze back the tears.

Claire wrapped her arms around him and held him tight. "Baby," she whispered, "your dad is looking down on you right now and as sure as I'm sitting here, he forgives you. It's time you forgave yourself."

William finally gave up and just let the tears flow free. He didn't know how long he cried, but Claire held him the entire while. When the tears would no longer flow, he looked up. His eyes squinted at the bright sunshine that slipped through the opening in the trees. "You know," he said after a long silence, "you're the best thing that's ever happened to me."

"No, no, no!" Claire corrected. "The best thing that's ever happened to you was Gracie. I'm just a close second."

William smiled and wiped his face with his shirtsleeve. "Without you, there would be no Gracie." He glanced over at Gracie and his mouth dropped open. She was up on all fours with her head held high like a prized poodle. He tapped Claire and pointed. They both watched in silence as Gracie eased one hand forward. Her knee followed. She repeated the shuffle with the other side.

"Oh my God!" Claire clasped her hand over her mouth. "She's crawling."

William slid off the bench and dove through the tent door. He fumbled in his duffel bag for the camera, but heard Claire's groan of disappointment before he could find it. He turned to find Gracie sprawled out on the blanket. She kicked her legs and chewed on her fists, unaware of the significance of what had just happened.

Claire tried to coax Gracie into crawling again. Instead, Gracie scrunched her body and rolled onto her back. She celebrated by wriggling her arms and legs in the air and shrieking in delight. "Come on, Sweetie," Claire said in baby-talk, "crawl for mommy."

William and Claire were so engrossed in Gracie's stunts that they both jumped when they heard Jake bellow, "Hello the camp!"

William turned to see Jake and Gaby approaching. He greeted them, but kept his face turned away for fear his eyes were still red.

"Y'all want breakfast?" Claire offered.

"No, but thank you. We're just packing up to leave," Jake said.

William pointed to a box of food on the picnic table. "How 'bout some chips and drinks for the road?"

Jake hesitated, but relented when William insisted. "Thanks. We do have a long drive ahead of us." Jake picked out a bag of chips and handed it to Gaby. "What do you guys have planned for today?"

William shrugged. "Hang around here, mostly. We'll go down to the swimming hole later, so I can show Claire where we used to swing from the rope. We'll probably hang out on the beach for most of the day."

"Would y'all like to come to the beach with us?" Claire asked.

Jake frowned. "We'd love to, but we want to try to get a head start on the drive."

Gaby grimaced. "Yeah, it's 251 miles from here to my driveway, and I get car sick easy."

"Wow!" Claire exclaimed. "That's a long drive."

"It's not so bad," Gaby admitted. "We travel the interstate the entire—"

"No need to complain, Dear," Jake said. "Besides, it was well worth the drive."

Gaby grunted. "If you say so."

"Well, good luck with everything and enjoy your stay here." Jake stepped forward and shook William's hand. His grip was stronger than William had remembered.

Jake then leaned to give Claire a hug and Gaby moved toward William. She wrapped her arms around his neck and whispered in his ear, "Be careful." When she pulled back, William noticed that her eyes glistened just a little.

"I hate goodbyes," she explained quickly.

CHAPTER SEVEN

7:43 A.M.
Saturday, November 20, 2004
Magnolia Parish, Southeastern Louisiana

I opened my eyes. The sun shone brightly through a window above me. It took several blinks for me to comprehend what was going on. I covered my eyes with my arm to block out the sun. Debbie had really left. It hadn't been a nightmare. I exhaled deeply and felt on the floor for my phone. After flipping it open, my thumb slid over the rubber pad on its way to dialing Debbie's number. Still turned off.

I smelled it for a full minute before realization struck me. I lunged off the sofa and ran to the kitchen.

Debbie was scraping the last of the scrambled eggs from the frying pan. I rushed to her and wrapped my arms around her. She gently pushed me away. "Brandon, I really need to finish breakfast."

She bustled about the kitchen, making wide circles around me and avoiding eye contact. "Deb, where the hell were you last night? You worried me half to death."

She didn't look up from her work. "I had plans."

"With who?"

Debbie glared at me. "What are you implying?"

"I'm not implying anything. I simply asked a question."

"Well, if you must know, I *had* plans with you."

"I got called out to a death case, possibly a murder."

Debbie rolled her eyes. "It's always a murder . . . or a rape
. . . or an escaped convict terrorizing a neighborhood. Always
something, but never us. Sam and I are an afterthought."

"That's not true. I love y'all more—"

"I'm not playing second fiddle to your job anymore." There
was a sound of finality in Debbie's words that worried me.

"What are you saying?"

"I've already said it."

"Well, what do you plan to do?"

Debbie set a plate of eggs on the table. "Your breakfast. Eat
it before it gets cold."

I'd never seen Debbie like this. I moved next to her. "You
still haven't told me where you went last night."

Debbie stared into my eyes with a coldness that would have
given Cedric Dempster a run for his money. I'd arrested Cedric
the previous year for the rape and murder of two Jasper
teenagers. He'd laughed throughout most of his confession. "If
you care about where I went," Debbie said in a slow, deliberate
voice, "you should've been here at seven o'clock yesterday—like
you promised."

My blood pressure started to rise. I opened my mouth to
speak, but thought better of it. I just shook my head and walked
out the kitchen.

"You're not going to eat?" Debbie called after me.

"I'm not hungry," I lied. I walked down the hall and stopped
outside Samantha's room. I glanced inside. She lay on her back
in the bed and clutched a stuffed baby lion to her chest. Despite
the anger I felt, I couldn't help but smile. When I had first given
her the lion, she thought it was a puppy and had named it
Honey Bear—after her grandmother's yellow lab.

My cell phone rang and interrupted my moment. I pulled it
from my wrinkled shirt and flipped it open. Dawn's cheery

voice scratched in my ear. "Hey, the autopsy is in an hour. Coming?"

"They're not going to wait until Monday?"

"They were, but when Dr. Wainwright found out I was attending, he changed his mind."

"But, I cut my grass on Saturdays."

"Grass don't grow in November."

"It does in my yard." I sighed. "Let me get showered and dressed."

"Pick me up at the substation in thirty?"

"Sure." I wasted no time showering. After I toweled off, I pulled on a pair of jeans and a burgundy sweatshirt. I shoved my Beretta nine-millimeter pistol in my belt, grabbed my wallet and keys, and walked through the kitchen. Debbie was making an exaggerated effort to clean up. I paused by the door before leaving. "Even though you won't tell me where you went, I'm glad you and Samantha are okay. I was worried about y'all."

"Oh, Brandon!" Debbie rushed to me and wrapped her arms around my neck. "I can't stay mad at you."

I hugged her back. "I didn't mean to break my promise to y'all, I just feel obligated to the people of this parish."

"I understand and respect that, but I wish you'd reserve the special days for us."

"I have no control over when people commit crimes." I leaned back and shook my head. "Although, it does seem like there's a conspiracy against me, because shit's always happening at the most inopportune times."

"Well, you don't have to go every time they call you. You can tell them no, you know?"

"A lot of people are depending on me."

"So are we."

I nodded and kissed Debbie on the forehead. "I'll make a concerted effort to do better."

I turned to walk out the door, but Debbie grabbed my arm and stopped me. "We went to Skel's."

"Skel's Seafood and Steak House?"

"Yeah, Samantha and I kept your reservation. I know I should've called you, I knew you'd be worried." She pursed her lips. "I was just angry."

I smiled. "I would say I forgive you, but that would be letting you off too easy. I just hope you never do that to me again."

"I hope you never break a promise to me again."

I bowed. "Touché."

Dawn was waiting outside the substation, black leather satchel in hand. She got in and tossed me a computer printout. I looked it over. It was from the local telephone company.

"What's this got to do with anything?"

"While you were sleeping, I was on the horn with the phone company. The anonymous call came from a pay phone outside Nadene's Groceries."

"We need to get out there before too many people touch that phone."

Dawn stretched back in the seat and smiled triumphantly. "Say I'm good."

I raised my eyebrows at her.

"Come on, say it," she coaxed.

"Okay, you're good."

"I already dusted the phone. Got a set of latent prints just waiting to be fed into AFIS."

I nodded my approval. "Did we ever get an ID on the dead girl?"

Dawn pulled her yellow legal-size notebook from her bag. "A lady by the name of Rosie McKenzie pays the electric bill."

"You run her?"

"Yeah. Nothing."

"Canvass turn up anything?"

"Her immediate neighbors say over the last couple of weeks there's been a lot of traffic to and from her trailer at all hours."

"Drugs?"

"Hard to say. Usually addicts will drive up, get what they want, and leave. In this case, they'd hear a car drive up. A few hours later another car would drive up and the first car—or so they assume—would leave. One of the neighbors said it sounded like they were working shift-work over at that trailer."

"Any descriptions on the cars or people in them?"

Dawn shook her head. "They were too lazy to get up to look. Hell, they didn't even get up when I knocked on their doors." She pulled a small envelope from her satchel and removed a cassette tape. "This is a copy of the 911 call."

I pushed it in the cassette player and turned up the volume. The dispatcher answered and asked what the emergency was. A muffled voice said, "I need to report a murder."

The dispatcher said, "Excuse me, did you say murder?"

"Yes," responded Muffled Voice. "A girl has been murdered at 1701 East Jillian Street. Y'all need to hurry." The line went dead.

When we reached the coroner's office, I stopped in the parking lot and turned to Dawn. "I appreciate you covering for me last night."

She smiled and leaned toward me, brushing my still-swollen nose lightly with her index finger. "My pleasure. You've always been good to me."

We entered the coroner's office and found Dr. Wainwright bent over the nude body of the female. She lay in a supine position on the stainless steel table. Dr. Wainwright's eyes angled upward and fixed on Dawn for a long minute. "Good to see you again, Detective."

Dawn smiled. She was accustomed to the constant attention she received from men. She took it in stride.

"I'm here, too, Doc," I said.

Wainwright's jaw dropped. "Oh, hell, Brandon, I didn't notice you standing there. Sorry about that."

"Yeah, yeah." I walked over to the table. "Who killed her?"

"Not *who,* but *what.* This girl died from dehydration. Case history says she lived alone and had no family or friends in the area, is that right?"

I looked at Dawn. She nodded.

"Well, I'm no detective, but I'd say this poor girl got sick and just lay there thinking it would pass. Before *it* could, she did."

"You're ruling this a natural-cause death?"

"Yep, unless you give me something that says different."

"We have a 911 call saying it's a homicide."

Wainwright cracked a cocky smile. "What doctor called and said that?"

Dawn and I left the coroner's office and drove to the detective bureau. I followed her into the lab. It was a spacious room at the end of the complex. She pulled an envelope from her desk drawer and removed a fingerprint card from inside. The prints were some of the best I'd ever seen recovered. "Great work!"

"Why, thank you, but I already knew that." Dawn's eyes twinkled as she set about scanning the prints into the AFIS machine. I wandered around her office until she gave me the news. "Nope," she said. "If our caller has ever been arrested, his prints were never entered into the AFIS system."

"What about surveillance tapes? Did you check those?"

"The manager said the pay phones are out of view."

"Won't it pick up people walking to and from the pay-phone area?"

"I thought of that, but do you know how many people shop

at Nadene's on any given day?"

"Forget about any given day, just focus on 6:02 P.M."

Dawn smiled. "Why didn't I think of that?"

It was an hour past dark when we returned to our conference room to view the surveillance tapes. "That loss prevention guy was a bit of a prick," Dawn complained.

"He was just trying to impress you." I shuffled through the tapes we'd recovered from Nadene's Groceries. There were six possible angles. The tapes were all labeled and we began with the one from the front door. We watched from 5:30 P.M. to 6:30 P.M. We were on the third tape when I saw someone in the tape walking toward the front door of the store. The cocky walk was familiar. I stood and moved close to the screen.

"You see something?"

I looked at the time on the tape. It was 6:00 P.M. The person disappeared through the front automatic doors. Before the doors shut, I could see that he ambled in the direction of the pay phones. At 6:03 P.M., the same person exited the store. He looked to the left and right, as though he thought he was being followed. I hit the pause button. "Jarvis Chiasson!"

"That kid you just popped for that burglary?"

I nodded and scribbled his clothing description on my note pad. The faded blue jeans with holes in the knees and the black and gold sweatshirt. "I bet he paid an extra thirty dollars for the holes in the jeans."

"Hell, I bet those are stolen. You know he doesn't buy anything."

I packed up the tapes and held up my car keys. "It looks like it's time for a stakeout."

CHAPTER EIGHT

Saturday, November 20, 2004

Skybald National Forest, North Louisiana

William stuffed sandwiches and drinks into his backpack. He zipped it shut and glanced around. "Where's my Tanto?"

"You don't need that dreadful knife."

"I might. That crazy army dude might be dangerous."

"Don't say that!"

"Well, you never know. Where is it?"

"I don't have it."

"Where'd you put it?"

Claire hoisted Gracie into the kangaroo pouch that hung from her shoulders. "I didn't touch it."

"Are you sure?"

"Positive."

William sighed and adjusted the knit cap that dangled from Gracie's head. "Does she really need this?"

"It's too cute to take off."

"But she'll get hot."

"Better than being cold." Claire poked at Gracie's stomach. "Besides, it matches her outfit."

William turned and led the way to a faint trail that squeezed its way through the dense forest. If everything were as he remembered, the hike to the beach was half a mile along the narrow trail. The landscape varied from sandy paths to rocky slopes. As they walked, he kept a close eye on Claire and spent some tense moments holding onto her as they sidestepped an area of the trail that veered dangerously close to the edge of a high bluff. He chanced a peek over the edge and quickly pulled back. The dropoff was close to thirty feet and if the fall onto the jutting rocks didn't kill you, the wicked rapids certainly would.

The trail turned sharply away from the banks of the Skybald River and led them deeper into the woods. After a two-hundred-yard zigzag through the thicket, the trail descended into a bed of brown leaves. William turned to Claire. "Let me take Gracie. This'll be slippery."

Claire eased Gracie out of the baby pouch and handed her to William. "How much further is it?"

William pointed to the bottom of the slope where the trees thinned. A sea of white sand peeked through the leafy wall. "That's the beach."

Claire's face lit up and she broke into a stumbling jog down the slope. William picked his way carefully behind her. He was about to caution her to slow down, but was too late. A surprised screech ripped from her throat as she lost her footing and ended the last few feet of the trail on her back.

William Chandler stifled a laugh. "You okay?"

His wife stood and brushed leaves off her shirt. "Good thing you took Gracie."

"Yeah, I'm good."

A sheepish smile played at Claire's lips. "I'm glad no one saw that."

William's mouth gaped. "Gracie and I are no one?"

"You two don't count . . . y'all love me." Claire clutched the crook of William's arm. "Now take me to my paradise."

William led the way out onto the open beach. The sand stretched from the edge of the forest to the lapping water of Skybald River. The river took a sharp turn away from the beach at this point. The current at the beach side of the river wasn't as powerful as the opposite side, which was lined with a stretch of high rocky bluffs covered with sparse vegetation that overlooked the beach below.

William instinctively glanced up at the trees along the edge of the beach. He took a deep quivering breath as the horrors of his last visit rushed to the surface.

Claire moved close, slid her arm around his waist, and looked up into his eyes. "You okay?"

"This is it. This is where it happened." He walked to a spot on the beach and checked his surroundings for verification. He indicated with his foot. "This is the spot." He jutted his chin toward the water. "I was about two hundred feet out into the water when I heard the branch snap."

"Will, at that distance there's nothing you could've done."

William nodded somberly. "I guess you're right. Even if I would've yelled, there's no way he could've moved in time to save himself."

"You hadn't realized that?"

"It never occurred to me. I just remembered being frozen in fear." He took a deep breath and walked to a stump that protruded from the soft sand. The area around it was shielded from the sun by a large oak tree whose limbs extended far out from the trunk. Switching Gracie from one arm to the other, he shrugged the backpack off his shoulders and propped it against the stump. He lifted Gracie high into the air and spun her around. She giggled and drool rained from her mouth and fell in William's eye. He squinted and rubbed the drool with the sleeve of his shirt. "I guess I deserved that."

Claire kicked off her boots and ran to the water's edge. She tested the water with her toe. "It's cold!"

"It's November—what do you expect?"

William and Claire spent a joyous morning running around

the beach and building sand castles with Gracie. They engaged in sand fights, buried each other, and created sand figurines until noon. Exhausted and hungry, they gathered around the stump. William pulled a blanket from the backpack and spread it out on the sand. While he threw together some ham sandwiches, Claire spoon-fed Gracie from a jar of baby food and then gave her a bottle to go with her nap. By the time they had finished eating, Gracie was sound asleep. The bottle had drifted from her mouth, but her lips were frozen in a pucker.

William stretched out on the blanket next to Gracie. A deep groan of satisfaction escaped his lips.

Claire jumped to her feet and, with a devilish grin on her face, backed away from William with feline grace. "The baby's asleep and it's just you and me," Claire said. "We're all alone in the wilderness."

William smiled. It had been a year since he'd seen Claire this playful. She stopped at the water's edge, took a cautious look around, and peeled off her jeans. She tossed them onto the sand. She made a show of unbuttoning her shirt and let it follow her jeans. Clad in nothing but bra and panties, which were a matching set of crimson that accentuated her flawless, porcelain complexion, Claire waded out into the water. "Ooh, it's so cold!"

William nodded his understanding, as the cold was evidenced by the duck bumps on Claire's body and her protruding nipples. "You're crazy," he said.

Claire waded out until the water reached her waist. "Wow! The current is strong even in the shallow water."

"I know." William stood and walked to the water's edge, a sense of foreboding coming over him. "Don't go out too far. If the current catches you it'll wash you out to those rocks."

Claire splashed water up into the air and squealed when it rained down on her. "You coming in?"

William looked over at Gracie. She slept soundly on the blanket. He plopped onto the sand and pulled off his boots. He had just lain on his back in the sand to shake his jeans off when he heard Claire scream. He looked up in time to see her drop down to her neck in the water. She stared up at the bluff across the river, eyes wide and flashing and her mouth open.

William followed Claire's gaze and sprung to his feet. A shadowy figure stood beside a tree at the edge of the bluff. William shielded his eyes from the sun and the figure came into full view . . . the soldier! The pit bull stood beside him, tongue hanging. "What the hell are you looking at?" William screamed, rushing into the water. Eyes glued on the soldier and oblivious to the water's temperature, he broke into a stumbling run to where Claire was crouched. He shook his fist at the man and his dog. "Get the hell out of here!"

William ripped off his shirt and wrapped it around his wife, who was shaking. As he guided his wife toward the shore, anger burned deep inside of him like nothing he'd ever felt. When Claire was safely on the shore and wrapped in a blanket, he returned to the water's edge and glared up at the soldier. "What the hell are you doing? Huh? What the hell do you want?" The veins bulged on William's temples; he could feel them throbbing. "Get the hell out of here before I kill you, you sick bastard!"

The soldier slowly turned away and disappeared over the top of the bluff. The pit bull followed.

William walked back to Claire, seething and breathing hard. Claire squeezed his neck. Her eyes were moist. "Oh my God," she wailed, "I'm so sorry!"

William returned the squeeze. "You did nothing wrong. There's no reason to be sorry."

"I should've kept my clothes on. I forgot that freak was even out here."

"So did I." William cupped Claire's face in his hands and kissed her forehead. "I don't think we need to worry about him bothering us again."

Claire nodded vigorously. "I think you scared him away!"

"Yeah, he's lucky I didn't climb that bluff and kick his ass."

"I've never heard you talk like this before." Claire rubbed William's chest seductively. "I like it when you talk tough."

William blushed. "It just made me mad that he would stand there staring at you. I knew he was creepy, but I didn't think he was a Peeping Tom."

Claire glanced over at Gracie and smiled. "I can't believe she slept through all that hollering you did."

The couple spent the remainder of the afternoon playing with Gracie on the beach and taking turns posing for photographs. William explored the area and located the tree from which he used to swing as a kid. The thick nylon rope had been replaced by a slender rope with a stick tied to the end of it. "If the water wasn't so cold and rough, we'd go swinging."

Claire frowned. "Why is it so rough?"

"All the rain we've been having. Most of the times when I came here as a kid the rapids were just a trickle and we'd walk clear across the river."

They sat on the beach and watched a large stump glide past them in the churning water. Gracie clapped as the stump crashed into the distant rocks and tumbled through the rapids. "So violent," Claire whispered.

As daylight started to fade, William found himself looking over his shoulder. Sure, earlier he had talked tough in his moment of anger, but the fact was he didn't know what the soldier was capable of doing. He wondered if it would've been better to keep his mouth shut. *What if the soldier is waiting for us at the campsite? Or waiting along the trail to ambush us?*

"Will, is everything okay?" Claire's voice was edged with tension.

"Oh yeah, everything's fine." A branch snapped in the forest and William's head jerked around. His eyes strained to penetrate the deepening shadows. Leaves rustled. A lone coyote cried out in the distance. A chill reverberated up and down William's spine.

Claire clutched Gracie and moved closer to William. "I want to leave . . . now."

William nodded. Without saying a word, he stuffed their belongings into the backpack and Claire quickly changed Gracie's diaper. When they were set, William shouldered the pack and searched the tree line along the beach until he found a stout walking stick. He struck it against a tree to test its rigidity. Solid. He turned to Claire. "Stay close to me and walk quietly." He led the way cautiously along the trail, stick poised and eyes alert. The painstaking pace put them back at the campsite just as nightfall cloaked the forest in total darkness.

William quickly lit the Coleman lanterns and placed them on either end of the campsite. He then set out to restart the campfire. Claire remained beside him, holding Gracie in her arms. Once the fire raged, William began to relax. He plopped into his chair and took Gracie from Claire. "I'll rock her to sleep if you cook supper. Deal?"

Claire gawked. "Deal for who?"

"Baby, you know it's against the law to eat what I cook."

Claire laughed. "Yeah, you can't even toast bread without burning it."

When the beans and chicken were cooked and the places set, Claire unzipped the tent door so William could put Gracie down for the night. William eased Gracie onto her sleeping area and smiled as the "Daddy's Pumpkin" emblem rose and fell with each tiny breath she took.

William didn't speak much during supper. He knew he had to display an air of confidence in order to ease his wife's fears, but the continual rustling of leaves and snapping of branches in the deep darkness was more than unnerving. He tried to cast a casual glance about the area, but with each turn of his head he could feel Claire's penetrating stare upon him.

"Can we leave first thing tomorrow morning?" Claire asked.

William nodded. "It's been a great trip, a healing experience, but two nights are plenty enough."

She looked deep into his eyes. "I want you to know I've had a great time with you and I'm glad we made the trip."

William scowled. "It wasn't as perfect as I wanted it to be. I definitely didn't count on that soldier being such a problem."

"It's okay." Claire leaned and kissed William full on the lips. "Meet me back in the tent after I scrape these plates?"

"Just leave them 'til tomorrow."

"Are you crazy?"

"What do you mean?"

"After what the Ranger man said about that bear . . ."

"I think he was telling stories, because we would have seen one by now."

"Well, I'm cleaning them anyway. I don't want to wake up with a bear licking my toes." Claire grabbed the pot of dirty dishes and slid down the embankment to her wilderness kitchen—a narrow, sandy spot along the edge of the raging river. She had cleaned there for the past two days and had become familiar with the area.

"Want one of the lanterns?" William offered.

"I can see good enough," Claire called from the darkness.

"Be careful."

"Relax, I'm just scraping these plates."

William dug through his bags in search of his Tanto. He sifted among the supplies on the table, rummaged through the garbage bag, searched through the bag of dirty clothes—nothing. He scratched his head and tried to remember the last time he'd seen it. A twig snapped behind him. He glanced over his shoulder. "Baby, are you—?"

A piercing scream shattered the tranquility of the night like a bomb exploding in a church during a funeral service. William's heart stopped beating. The scream was followed by a deep splash and more shrieks. William lunged ahead and slid down the embankment. The reflection from the moon was bright on the water and there was no mistaking what he saw—Claire's body tumbling and sinking into the dark, jostling rapids of Sky-bald River.

CHAPTER NINE

8:30 *P.M.*

Saturday, November 20, 2004

Magnolia Parish, Southeastern Louisiana

I killed the headlights long before we turned onto Jarvis Chiasson's block. I eased up on the accelerator and shut off the ignition. My unmarked cruiser coasted to a stop beside the curb. I pointed to a little shotgun shack four houses down and on the opposite side of the street. "That's it."

Dawn leaned closer. "Does he have a car?" The fresh smell of spearmint blew gently from her soft breath.

"Why are you whispering? We're in a closed car, four houses down. He can't hear us . . . I promise."

Dawn cracked a sheepish grin. "I don't know. It just seemed like the right thing to do."

I pulled a set of binoculars from under my seat and trained them on the front of Jarvis's house.

"See anything?"

"Everything's dark."

"I guess we're in for a long night."

Dawn was right. The seconds ground into minutes and the minutes stood still. When my dash clock told me several hours had dragged by, I checked all my mirrors for the thousandth time. Nothing in sight. Everything was quiet. "Wait here. I'm going to take a closer look."

"Not without me."

I knew it would be futile to argue, so I eased out of the car and held the door for Dawn to slide out. The night air was cool and Dawn wrapped her arm around mine and leaned close. "Just staying in character," she said.

I tried not to laugh as we strolled casually down the street past Jarvis's house. The thick oaks that lined the street blocked out the dim lampposts and painted the sidewalk in black. I cast a casual glance toward Jarvis's house as we walked by. No movement, no light—nothing.

"Do you think he's inside?" Dawn's voice was barely a whisper.

"There's only one way to find out." I tugged on Dawn's arm and walked to the house. We climbed shaky cement steps to an equally unsteady porch. The wooden boards were soft and creaked under my weight. I stepped to one side of the door and waited for Dawn to step to the other side. I banged on the screen door that hung partially open and leaned back. I listened intently. No movement or sound from inside. I banged several more times and then motioned to Dawn. "Wait here."

I stepped off the porch and walked through the cluttered yard to the back. I tripped on a pile of bicycle parts and other garbage and nearly fell. I paused to listen. Still nothing. I felt my way through the dark to the back door of the house and rapped loudly on it. After several minutes of waiting, I returned to the front.

"You think he's hiding inside?" Dawn wanted to know.

"His mom lives two streets down. Let's go talk to her."

"But it's almost midnight."

"We can't help that."

Jarvis Chiasson's mother answered the door wearing a night robe. Her wrinkled face was curious. I recognized her from the court hearing of Friday morning. "Hello, ma'am, I'm Detective—"

"I know who you are, young man. Don't you get tired of harassing my son?"

"Ma'am, I'm sorry for bothering you this late at night, but we need to talk to Jarvis. We think he might've stumbled onto something."

"Do you have an arrest warrant?"

"No, ma'am. We just need to talk to him."

"Well, if you don't have an arrest warrant, you can just leave." Mrs. Chiasson slammed the door shut.

"I could kick the door down," Dawn offered.

"Sure." I walked back down the long sidewalk toward the car and Dawn followed. "We need to set up surveillance on his house and apply for a search warrant."

"I'll call the patrol lieutenant and get him to put a couple of cars on the house."

"Good idea. Meanwhile—"

A door slammed behind me and I spun around. Jarvis jogged toward me and stopped a few feet away. He was still wearing the clothes from the video. "Detective, look, I'm sorry about lying in court." Jarvis was out of breath. I couldn't tell if it was from his short run or his nerves.

"I'm not worried about that, Jarvis. Almost everybody lies when they're facing jail time."

Jarvis looked around. "Okay, well, I just wanted to say that and, uh, I hope there's no hard feelings."

"Look, Jarvis, you were wrong."

"What are you talking about?" He tried to look uninterested.

"You were wrong about the girl." Jarvis's eyes widened a little. I let that thought sink in and then said, "She wasn't murdered. She died of natural causes."

His eyes seemed to sparkle just a little and relief pushed the color back into his face. "I don't know what you're talking about."

"Really? Do you mind giving us consent to search your house?"

"Sure, I don't have nothing to hide."

Although I had never known of Jarvis to carry weapons, I frisked him and opened the front passenger-side door of my unmarked cruiser. "You can sit up here with me."

Dawn slid behind me, where she could keep an eye on Jarvis. I drove to his house and we all exited the car. After I filled out a consent form, Jarvis signed it. "What are y'all looking for, anyway?"

"We're investigating a burglary."

Jarvis's face twitched. "You're crazy if you think I'm about to get in trouble while I'm out on bail."

Dawn and I followed Jarvis inside. The house was stuffy and smelled of urine. The kitchen was cramped. A flimsy card table was shoved against one wall and dirty dishes were piled precariously high atop it. A box of fried chicken was on the counter. Dawn walked over to the box and looked inside. She shook her head. "You fired the maid?"

"Why don't y'all just get this over with?"

I kept a wary eye on Jarvis as we combed every inch of his cluttered house. There was nothing in the house that we didn't touch. When we were done, I sidled up to Dawn. "Anything?" I whispered.

"Not a thing."

"He must've ditched the stuff." I rubbed my rough face.

"What now?"

I turned to Jarvis, who leaned against the grease-stained wall, trying to look casual. "I'll need you to come down to the office with us."

"But, why? I thought you said she died of natural causes?"

Jarvis sucked in air when he realized what he had said.

"You know why." I nodded for Jarvis to lead the way out of the house. His chin rode against his chest as he walked past me and out the doorway. Dawn mashed the lock on the doorknob and pulled it shut.

CHAPTER TEN

Sometime after dark
Saturday, November 20, 2004
Skybald National Forest, North Louisiana

"Claire!" A low-lying branch jutted out over the water for about twenty feet. William clutched the branch and plunged feet-first into the water. He high-stepped through the rushing water, moving hand-over-hand along the length of the branch, wild eyes glued to the spot where he'd last seen his wife.

"Claire! Claire!" Just as the words left his mouth, William's foot slipped on a rock and his legs shot out from under him. The branch dipped under his weight. His fingers locked around the branch in a grip of death as he struggled to hold on. With a mighty heave and a grunt, he pulled his body upright. *This isn't working,* he thought. Panic propelled him forward. He dragged himself out of the water and broke into a blind sprint along the sandy shore in the direction that the rushing rapids had taken Claire. Branches and vines tore at his body. His breath came in labored gasps. Pain, like a branding iron, pierced his lungs. He didn't feel any of it. He just ran . . . and ran . . . and called out to Claire.

"Claire! Oh, my God! Claire!" After running for what seemed like miles, William collapsed against a bed of rocks and sobbed out loud. His mind flashed back to the day he and Claire met. It had been his twentieth birthday and he'd gone bowling with a couple of his buddies. Bowling next to them was an angel. His

78

buddies told him she had some friends with her, but he hadn't noticed. It took a few beers for him to muster up the courage to walk over and introduce himself. Two years later they were married. It was the happiest he'd been since losing his dad.

William pounded his head against the rocks . . . once, then twice, and again, oblivious to the pain. "Claire! No! Not you, too! Oh, my God! What have I—"

The sound was barely more than a raspy whisper and could not be heard over the roaring rapids that taunted William. He paused and listened. *Could that be?* He cocked his head and opened his mouth. There it was again! He sprang from the ground and ran down the trail like a wild man possessed with a new demon. A renewed sense of hope pushed him forward. The further he ran, the louder the sound became. He turned a bend in the trail and the sound was to his immediate left, almost at his feet. He dove into the wall of briars that separated him from the familiar voice that had been a pivotal part of his life for the past twelve years. Prickly vines encircled him. Tiny green daggers sliced through his jeans. His hands and arms burned as he pushed and pulled on the strips of briars that stood between him and his wife.

After struggling for what seemed like days, William broke through to the other side and tumbled head over heels down the sandy embankment. When he righted himself, he saw her.

Claire was nearly twenty feet away. She clung to a cluster of cypress knees. The moonlight reflected off her pale face, which was accentuated by the utter blackness of the murky water. The angry current jostled her about and threatened to break her grip from the life-saving anchor.

"Claire . . . hold on . . . I'm coming!"

"Hurry! I'm slipping!"

William took a cautious step into the river. Cold water rushed into his wet shoe and the current pushed against his leg like a bulldozer ripping through a field of toothpicks. He clutched a nearby sapling and slid his other leg into the river. He reached out a trembling hand. Just a few more inches . . .

"Please catch me," Claire said in a tired voice. "I can't hold—"

Claire's hands slipped and she disappeared into the murky water. Without thought, William threw himself into the strong arms of the Skybald River. The shock he experienced when his body hit the cold water caused him to take an involuntary breath and he sucked in a lungful of water. He surfaced choking. Before he could catch a good breath, the current rolled him and smashed him into a rock that jutted from the river's floor. *Don't panic,* he told himself, *your life and Claire's depend on you staying calm.*

Fear warmed him. His love for Claire fueled him. William free-styled with the current. Between strokes, he caught glimpses of Claire being tossed around like a pirogue in the middle of the Gulf of Mexico during a hurricane. She flailed and screamed, going under and popping back to the surface, each time staying a little longer underwater.

William grabbed a slimy log that whizzed by and, using it as a flotation device, kicked with tired legs. Each kick got him a little closer to Claire's desperate fight to stay above water. When he was within lunging distance of Claire, the log snagged on something in the water and Claire darted away.

William abandoned the log and swam forward with the last of his waning strength. He reached Claire just as she disappeared beneath the roaring current. Taking a deep, painful breath, William dove into the wet mob of blackness. Water shot into his mouth, got sucked up into his sinuses, burned his nose. He refused to come up for air, despite the fire in his lungs. His efforts were rewarded when his hand brushed against a soft leg at the rocky bottom of Skybald River.

William latched onto the flesh with one hand and sprung off

the bottom with both legs. He pulled with his free hand, fighting for the surface. After what seemed like two lifetimes in Hell, he fought his way to the surface. Still clutching the leg, he struggled toward the shore. A bend in the river brought him nearer the shore and he clawed his way through waist-deep water along a bed of slippery rocks, jerking the limp body along with him.

When he stumbled to the shore, William dragged the body out of the water and dropped to the sandy shore beside it. Horror filled his every fiber as he stared down at Claire's ghostly face. He fumbled at her neck with wrinkled fingers, desperately feeling for a pulse that wasn't there. *This can't be happening!*

"Claire! Open your eyes!" William blew a lungful of air into Claire's mouth and began chest compressions. "Damn it, how many chest compressions am I supposed to do?" he wailed aloud. He worked feverishly, pausing after every set of chest compressions to feel for a heartbeat. After the fourth set, he felt a faint pulse. His heart raced. He delivered another breath of air into Claire's mouth and she coughed water up into his face. He turned her onto her side and she spat up more water, coughing and choking until she finally settled down to heavy breathing.

William's dam of emotion broke. He lifted Claire to his chest and cradled her. His tears fell like rain onto her face. "I thought I lost you," he cried. "God, I couldn't live without you!"

"You came for me," Claire said in a weak voice. "You saved me."

"Just lie still."

Claire nodded.

William cradled Claire for several minutes. His heart rate slowed to a normal pace and his breathing became easier. His eyes began to slide shut when Claire suddenly jerked up. She collapsed back to the ground and grabbed her head.

William gasped. "Please, just lie still for a while. You need—"

"Gracie! What about Gracie?"

"She's okay. I left her sleeping in the tent."

"Go check on her."

William turned in the direction he thought the tent to be and stared into the blackness. Utter nothingness. Not even a hint of the campfire. "I can't leave you here."

"I'll be okay. You've gotta go check on Gracie. She's all alone."

Claire shivered in William's arms. He wiped his dripping nose and realized that he, too, shook. "I have to get you into dry clothes and take you to a hospital."

"I'm okay, just go."

"I won't lose you again. When you're feeling well enough, we'll go back to camp . . . together."

"But—"

"But nothing. Gracie is safe in the tent." William wiped his face and glanced over his shoulder. "What happened back there, anyway?"

"I don't know. One minute I was cleaning the pot, the next minute I was being pushed into the water."

"You must've slipped."

"I was pushed!"

The darkness closed in, smothered William. "Are . . . are you sure?"

"Positive."

"But who?"

"It had to be that soldier. Remember the way he was looking at me?" Claire shuddered.

"That mother—"

"It's okay now." Claire grabbed William's shoulder and pulled herself to a sitting position. "Let's just go get Gracie."

William stood firm as Claire leaned against him. He gripped her shoulders and they set out through the forest. The roaring river was their guide.

"Are you sure this is the right way?" There was worry in Claire's tired voice.

"All we have to do is follow the river. It'll get us back to camp."

They crunched through ankle-deep leaves and twigs that littered the forest floor. They remained silent, both lost in their own thoughts. William said many prayers of thanks to God as he stumbled along, straining to keep Claire vertical. The relief he felt at having rescued Claire sapped the little strength that remained in his overused muscles. *What if I hadn't gotten to her in time?* He tried to imagine life without his wife and shuddered. *There is no life without Claire.*

"William," Claire hissed. "What was that?"

"What was what?"

Claire buried broken nails in his forearm. "I heard something in the bushes."

"Probably a raccoon. Keep walking."

"What if it's a bear?"

"It's not. Just keep walking."

They pressed on. Twenty minutes later, Claire stopped.

"What is it?"

"My head. I feel like I'm going to pass out."

William helped her to the ground. He looked around. The moonlight strained through the dense treetops and enabled him to see several yards ahead through the trees. He stared directly at it and then lost it in the night. He stared at a dark shadow that was ten degrees to the left and was able to see it clearly in his peripheral vision—a faint trail. It seemed to glow on the forest floor, snaking along to where William knew would be their campsite.

"This is the trail!" William felt a surge of energy course through his body. "We're only a few hundred yards from the camp site."

"Run ahead and check on Gracie. I'll wait right here."

"I'm not leaving you behind."

"Go check on my baby!"

"Gracie is fine. She's safe, locked up in the tent with a healthy campfire watching over her."

"It can't be too healthy," Claire muttered and dragged herself to her feet, "we still can't see the damn thing."

"It won't be long." William lifted Claire's left arm and draped it over his shoulder. He set an easy pace, resisting the urge to sprint ahead to check on Gracie. *She's fine,* he told himself. The beaten path made walking easier and they covered more ground. Claire stopped every hundred yards or so to rest, but she seemed to be regaining her strength. She didn't stumble as often.

They walked in silence for several minutes. Their labored breathing drowned out the sound of the Skybald rapids, which was muffled by the thick underbrush that stood between the trail and the precarious overhang that overlooked the fierce river. William shook his head and wondered why one couldn't just enjoy the beauty of this place without having to flirt with death.

"There it is!" Claire exclaimed.

William looked in the direction Claire pointed. A faint glow marked the remnants of the campfire. He steadied Claire. "Will you be okay?"

"Yes, just go!"

William broke into a run. His feet pounded the packed sand and matched that of his heart beating against his chest. It had probably been an hour since Claire first fell into the water, but it felt like days. All he wanted now was to hold his daughter, to make her safe.

The trail ambled closer to the river, then veered to the left and descended sharply toward the campsite. William hit the descent at a full sprint. The fading embers cast an eerie dim

84

glow around the clearing, barely silhouetting the tent and—

"Holy *shit!*" William tried to stop abruptly. He lost his balance. His momentum carried him forward and dumped him flat on his face. Sand shot into his eyes and mouth, feet went airborne. He flipped over and landed in a violent skid on his back, shooting through the bushes. The branches and thorns reached out at his clothes and skin and clawed him to a stop. He scrambled to his feet and spun to face the shadowy campsite. He spat sand from his mouth and rubbed his eyes. Disbelief and horror stabbed a hole in his heart. When his eyes focused, his fears were reaffirmed . . . even in the darkness, there was no mistaking the shoulders and back of a large bear protruding from the open tent flap.

William stood petrified. He stared wide-eyed as the bear calmly pawed at something inside the tent. He didn't know how long he stared, but a piercing scream caused him and the bear to jump. The bear spun and the tent flap snagged on his nose. He gave it a violent shake and a corner of the tent toppled to the ground. He rose to his hind legs and growled his displeasure at having been interrupted.

William couldn't see Claire clearly in the darkness, but he knew she was afraid. "Stay calm," he said in a soothing voice, "and back up real slow."

Claire took a slow step back, and then another, and another. The bear began to move toward her, shaking his head and roaring in anger. William could hear Claire sobbing quietly in the night, but she continued to slowly move backward. The bear was getting closer to her.

"William," Claire said, barely above a whisper, "this isn't working."

"Just stay calm."

"Fuck calm! Do something!" Claire hissed.

"Just back slowly away, he'll leave you alone."

"He's following me, do something!"

William scanned the ground. There were black blotches mixed into the already darkened ground . . . rocks! William jerked two of them out of the ground and threw the first one as hard as he could, taking a lunging step into it. It struck the bear on its back. The bear jerked around and William began to scream and wave his arms like a mad man. The bear hesitated and William threw the second rock. It smacked the bear beside the head, causing it to scramble sideways. William snatched another rock from the ground and launched it through the air. It landed at the bear's feet. William continued to scream and wave his arms as he felt for more rocks. He heard something *swoosh* through the air and strike the bear across the neck. With a frustrated grumble, the bear turned and jogged off. The thunderous sound of snapping branches and crunching leaves signaled the direction of his retreat.

Claire bolted toward the tent.

William jogged after the bear. He screamed and flailed, throwing whatever he could grab. Behind him, Claire clawed at the collapsed walls. She called desperately for Gracie. Dread filled his heart when he realized there was one sound missing among all the commotion—a baby crying.

Suddenly, Claire's screams filled the night air and turned William instantly around. He broke into a full sprint and slid to a stop near the tent. Claire lay on the ground in the darkness. She clutched a tiny bundle tightly to her chest and rocked wildly. *Gracie!*

"What's wrong?" William's voice was laced with panic, as his eyes tried to penetrate the darkness.

Claire continued to rock. She cried uncontrollably.

With hands that trembled, William pulled gently on her arms. They opened and the fading light from the campfire splashed against Gracie's body. Sucking air, he squeezed his eyes shut and turned away. Bile filled his mouth.

CHAPTER ELEVEN

1:26 A.M.
Sunday, November 21, 2004
Magnolia Parish Sheriff's Office Substation
When we arrived at our office I sat Jarvis in an interview room and read him his rights. "Okay, Jarvis, just go ahead and tell me what you did yesterday. Well . . ." I glanced at the wall clock. It was 1:30 A.M. "That would be the day before yesterday—Friday. Tell me what you did Friday, beginning with when you woke up."

Jarvis chewed on a dirty fingernail. "I got up and my mom took me to court. After court we ate lunch and she brought me back home."

"What time did you get back home?"

"About three in the afternoon, I think."

"What did you do when you got home?"

"Just hung around my house."

"Did you leave your house at any time?"

"Nope."

"What did you wear that day?"

"You know what I wore—you saw me."

"Yeah, but you didn't keep those clothes on all day."

"I don't remember."

Dawn placed the surveillance tape from Nadene's Groceries on the desk. "Jarvis," she said in a soft voice, "you expect us to believe you never left your house?"

Jarvis's eyes darted from the surveillance tape to Dawn. "Uh, yeah, I mean, I don't remember leaving my house."

"Why did you wait so long to call the murder in?"

"I didn't—"

"Look, before you answer that . . ." Dawn moved closer. "What would you say if I told you we found your fingerprints in the dead girl's trailer?"

Jarvis shook his head. "You don't have my fingerprints!"

Dawn nodded in agreement. "Right, right, you wore gloves. But, can you account for every hair on your head?"

"What?"

"Your hair—can you account for every one of them?"

A blank look spread across Jarvis's face.

Dawn glanced down at her shoulder and removed a short brown hair from her collar. "You see this?"

Jarvis nodded.

"Our hair is constantly falling. I'm sure you've noticed hair on your pillow in the morning, hair on your brush, and even hair in the shower drain. Haven't you?"

"Yeah, I guess."

"Right, because your hair is constantly falling . . . even when you're committing a burglary. It tumbles to the floor and stays there until I come along and process the crime scene."

The front of Jarvis's shirt seemed to jump with each beat of his heart. "But . . . but, I didn't steal nothing."

"Well, then, why don't you just tell us exactly what happened?"

Jarvis cleared his throat and shot an uncertain glance my way.

"It's okay, Jarvis," I coaxed. "We already know."

"Alright . . . look . . . wait. What'll happen to me if I tell y'all what happened?"

"That all depends on what you say," Dawn said. "Obviously,

if you confess to committing a crime, there'll be consequences."

Jarvis was quiet for a long minute. "Okay, I did it . . . I broke into that trailer, but I didn't steal nothing."

"When did you do it?" Dawn asked.

"Thursday night. My mom didn't have no money and she was worried that if the judge put me back in jail she wouldn't be able to bail me out."

"Didn't you think about getting caught?"

"I was wearing gloves so y'all wouldn't get my fingerprints. I didn't think about the hair, though." Jarvis hung his head. "I guess I wasn't thinking at all. I just wanted money to get out of jail."

"But you've already bailed out," I said. "You get to remain free until the trial date, unless you screw up again—like now."

"I didn't know that. My mom thought I would be going back and she got me worried. I don't like being in that jail. They do crazy stuff in there."

"Let's get back to Thursday night," Dawn said. "How'd you get to the trailer?"

"I walked. It had just got dark and I decided to look for a place to steal. I saw that trailer and the woods were real close to the back of it, so I thought it would be easy to get in and out. A light was on inside and I waited in the woods for about an hour. Finally, two men walked out the trailer and—"

I held up my hand. "Whoa, what do you mean, *two men*?"

"Two men walked out the trailer. They were carrying plastic bags full of stuff."

"Can you describe them?"

Jarvis shook his head. "All I could see was their legs and them bags because they were on the other side of the trailer. I couldn't see too good because it was dark. When they left, they turned all the lights off in the trailer. I waited about an hour after they left and I figured they weren't coming back, so I broke in."

I leaned back and let Dawn resume control of the interview. "How'd you get into the trailer?" she asked.

"I broke a window and climbed through."

"The window is a bit above the ground."

"There was a green garbage can in the neighbor's yard. I dumped it and turned it over to stand on."

"What did you do when you got inside?"

"I . . . I walked down the hall. Felt my way to the bedroom and that . . . that's when I saw her."

"Well, how'd you see her if it was dark?"

"I got a small flashlight I carry with me." Jarvis leaned over and shoved a hand deep in his pocket. He squirmed around and then pulled his hand out. He tossed a key-chain light on the desk. "It's really bright for a little light."

"Describe what you saw."

Jarvis stared at his hands. "I've never seen a dead person before. She looked like a ghost. She was skinny and her eyes were deep inside her sockets."

Dawn put a hand on his shoulder. "What did you do next?"

Jarvis grunted. "I screamed and ran. I'm no hero. I jumped straight out that window. I'm surprised I didn't cut myself on the glass."

"Jarvis," I said, "is there anything you can offer to help us identify those two men?"

Jarvis pursed his lips and leaned back in his chair. He stared at the ceiling as though he were watching a replay of that night's events. I was about to interrupt when he sprang forward. "They were religious!"

"How do you know that?" I asked.

"I heard one of them say something about the Lord's will, or something."

"Can you remember exactly what they said?"

"It was something like, *I guess it wasn't the Lord's will*—whatever that means."

"Did they call each other by name?"

"One of them called the other one Ray."

"Anything else?"

"Just one more thing. The other one said something about calling her dad."

"What do you mean?"

"He said he'd have to call her dad and let him know what happened. Said if her dad would've been there things would've been different."

"Did this dad have a name?"

"Ike, or Isaac, I think."

"What exactly did the guy say?"

"He said something like, *I'm gonna have to call her father, Isaac.*"

I stared through Jarvis with narrowed eyes. There was something familiar with that statement. Something I'd heard before, but couldn't quite—

"Hey!" I suddenly had it. "Could it have been *Father Isaac*, instead of *Her father, Isaac*?"

Jarvis's eyes lit up. "Yeah! That's it. How'd you know?"

"Lucky guess. Tell me about the phone call you made."

"I couldn't sleep after seeing that dead girl. I didn't know what to do. I wanted to tell you when I saw you outside the courthouse, but I thought you'd arrest me."

"Is that when you called?"

Jarvis nodded. "Yeah, after that day."

Dawn leaned forward. "I'm just curious. What made you call? I mean, why not just go about your business?"

"I might be a thief, but I ain't no killer. Hell, that could've been me they killed."

Dawn stood. "Okay, that'll do it for now."

"Am I going to jail again?" Jarvis's face was twisted into a plea.

"No victim, no crime," I said. "Consider this your last lease on a free life."

CHAPTER TWELVE

Late night
Saturday, November 20, 2004
Skybald National Forest, North Louisiana

The embers from the campfire cast a dim orange glow on Claire's pale face. Her eyes were sunken holes of blackness and her cheeks hollowed. Her soul seemed detached from her body, the flame in her eyes extinguished by grief. "Is . . . she . . . going to be okay?"

William swallowed a flood of vomit. It was hard to be certain in the dark, but it looked as though Gracie's face and neck had been mauled. Visions of his father's mangled body flashed in his mind. Without warning, his stomach convulsed. Spray shot from his mouth as he wretched violently.

"Oh, God, Will, do something!"

William wiped his mouth with the back of a hand. The "Daddy's Pumpkin" emblem at the front of Gracie's outfit reflected off the glowing embers. He tried to focus on the emblem and not on the shadowy gashes and broken flesh that had rendered his little baby unrecognizable. Tears streaked down his face, as he tried to remember Gracie as he'd last seen her.

"We have to get to a hospital!" Clair's scream broke through William's nightmare. Determination surged through him. He hadn't been able to save his father all those years ago, but he would not fail his daughter. Scrambling into the collapsed tent, he felt around frantically for the car keys. When he found them, he clawed his way outside and hurried to the picnic table to retrieve the flashlight. Claire was already stumbling down the trail, Gracie clutched to her chest. He caught up to her and aimed the flashlight ahead of them. They struggled forward, making their way through the dark forest at breakneck speed.

William strained through blurred vision to see the trail ahead of them. A branch snapped in the thick foliage behind them and he jerked around. He cast the flashlight from side to side. Nothing. A chill reverberated up and down his aching spine and a terrified scream brought him back to Claire . . . she was sprawled on the ground. Gracie lay several feet away. Claire pulled her knees up under her body and plucked Gracie from the ground. With a lunge, she tackled the trail once more.

The utter blackness of the forest reluctantly began to give in to the first hint of dawn. William's eyes scanned the area ahead of them, trying to see everything at once, and trying not to look directly at the flashlight for fear he would lose his night vision. He stole an occasional glance at Gracie's limp frame as she bounced in Claire's arms. He longed to hear her laugh, cry. He prayed for a whimper. Anything to indicate that she was still with them. He thought back to the hours he spent rocking her to sleep back home, as he'd take in the new-baby smell and dream of her future. *Please, God, let this be a dream!*

The morning brightened ever so slightly and the surrounding trees that had been ominous shadows just moments earlier slowly came into focus. Also coming into focus was the familiar fence that marked the end of their long trek.

Claire sighed and her pace quickened. "I can see the car."

When they cleared the opening in the fence, Claire sprinted to the Thunderbird. William mashed the *unlock* button on the keyless remote.

Claire slipped into the front passenger seat. "Come on, *drive!*"

William shoved the key in the ignition and revved the engine.

The tires screeched when he smashed the gas pedal and shot out of the parking lot.

The Thunderbird slid sideways when William left the blacktop surface and turned onto the bumpy gravel road that sliced through the hilly forest. He sped along and fishtailed slightly as he took some of the precarious turns at over fifty miles per hour—twice the posted speed limit. The Thunderbird's engine strained up the steeper hills and seemed to sigh on the descent.

"Please be careful," Claire cautioned, her eyes wide. "There's no shoulder on this road."

"I know what I'm doing."

About four miles further, William reached a section in the road where the gravel had been worn down. A minefield of potholes stretched for a quarter of a mile. He zipped in and out like he was dodging cones on a driving course. He hit one of the potholes and the force of the bump gave them a rough jolt. The rear end of the Thunderbird shifted violently to the left and then the right, as William fought to maintain control.

"Jesus, Will, slow down! You're going to kill us."

William sensed the sheer terror in Claire's voice. He tapped the brake. Nothing happened. A sharp curve in the roadway loomed ahead. To the right of the curve were trees. To the left, a sharp descent into a conclave of officious-looking rocks. He smashed the brake pedal. Still nothing.

"What's wrong?" Claire asked.

"I don't know. The brakes, there's something wrong with the brakes." William rotated the steering wheel to the right, taking the curve on the inside. He caught a glimpse of Claire in the glow from the dash lights as he fumbled for the emergency brake—she held the dashboard with one hand and clutched Gracie in the other. Her eyes were squeezed shut. The tires of the Thunderbird bumped roughly as the car left the roadway to the right. The large pine trees that stood like hulking sentinels along the roadway flashed toward them and he jerked the steering wheel to the left. The car veered sharply and William felt the seatbelt tearing at his shoulder as his body wrenched in the opposite direction. Panic-stricken, he rotated the steering wheel back to the right, but it was no use. The Thunderbird began to careen out of control even as his fingers caught—then lost—the brake lever.

Green foliage zipped by. Branches pelted the Thunderbird. Suddenly, where there was once trees and underbrush, there was now dark and empty space. The car took a violent dip as the front tires left the edge of the roadway. William's neck was thrust violently back. They plunged violently forward. Claire's scream pierced the air and intensified as the Thunderbird plunged to the earth.

William tried to lean forward, but the force of the fall pinned his back to the seat. He closed his eyes and began to murmur a prayer. His prayer and Claire's screams were abruptly cut short when the front of the car smashed into a bed of rocks. Airbags punched out and caught the couple square in the face as their bodies wrenched forward against the impact. The Thunderbird flipped end over end and skid on its roof. There was no sound but that of metal scraping rock until the car lurched to a crashing stop.

CHAPTER THIRTEEN

7:00 A.M.

Sunday, November 21, 2004

Magnolia Parish, Southeastern Louisiana

Seven o'clock came early. Debbie groaned when I rolled to the side of the bed and dropped my heavy legs to the floor. "Where are you going?" she asked, eyes half closed.

I leaned over and kissed her forehead. "I have to go to church."

"Church?" Debbie sat up and rubbed her eyes. "Did you say you were going to *church*?"

I nodded and grabbed a towel for my shower.

"You don't go to church."

I laughed and kept Debbie guessing while I showered and shaved. When I was dressed for work I stepped out of the bathroom to find our bedroom empty. I walked to the kitchen. The table was set and Debbie and Samantha were waiting for me. Samantha spun out her chair and made a dash for me. I bent and caught her in mid flight. "Daddy! Are you staying home?"

"No, Baby, I have to go to work."

Samantha scrunched her face into a pout. "How many hours?"

"Not too many." I set Samantha down on a chair and took my seat beside her.

Debbie reached out and touched my hand. "What did you

mean by going to church?"

"I have to talk to this preacher about a case."

"Maybe he can get you on the right track."

"Maybe he can loan me some of the money he's stealing from his parishioners."

8:15 A.M.

I picked Dawn up from the office and we drove to the Magnolia Faith Church. "You're gonna love the great Father Isaac," I told her while we waited in the lobby.

"Judging by the size of that picture, he loves himself enough for everybody. Hell, it's bigger than the picture of Jesus."

The secretary abruptly opened the door. "Father Isaac will see you now."

I nodded my thanks and the secretary led us to Isaac Stewart's office. He sat behind his desk and didn't even look up when we walked in. He was reading a file of some sort. I stood over him and knocked on his desk. "Howdy, Father Isaac. I need to talk to you about Rosie McKenzie."

Isaac's eyes paused ever so slightly. He recovered quickly and leaned back. "I was just beginning to prepare my sermon for Wednesday night. Would you like to hear it?"

"No. I want to hear about Rosie McKenzie."

Isaac shook his head. "I don't know a Rosie McKenzie."

"You should. She comes to this church."

Isaac smiled. "Detective, have you any idea how many members attend my fellowship?"

"I can imagine it's difficult to know each of your parishioners by name, but this girl you should remember."

"Is that so?"

"Yeah, that's so. Ray called you Thursday night to talk about her and what happened with her."

The wrinkles disappeared from Isaac's face as his skin

stretched taut. "Ray who?"

"Did more than one Ray call you Thursday night to talk about a dead girl?"

"Detective, I'm afraid I know nothing of which you speak. So, if you'll excuse me, I have to get back to my Wednesday night sermon and I have another to deliver within the next hour."

"Can I have a list of your parishioners?"

"For what reason?"

"I'd like to see if any of them knew Rosie McKenzie."

"I'd love to help you, but I can't in good conscience divulge that which I consider to be confidential information."

"I understand." I stood and Dawn did the same. "Mind if we have a look around?"

"Do you have a warrant?"

"I thought God's house was open to the public."

"Only the assembly room, during worship and prayer. So please, unless you have a warrant, I have to get back to my sermon."

"Thanks for the time." I held the door for Dawn and then walked out without closing it. When we were in the parking lot, I turned to Dawn. "We need to get a list of those church members."

"How?"

"I can apply for a search warrant."

"Do you think we have probable cause?"

"I don't honestly know. I mean, what crime has been committed?"

Dawn shook her head. "None. Rosie died of natural causes."

"Unless we can show that someone knew of her condition and failed to get her medical attention."

"How do we do that?"

I rubbed my smooth chin and stared down at my fingers. "I

can't think without my stubble."

Dawn laughed. "Then I guess we're out of luck for a few days—wait a minute! Why don't we subpoena the preacher's phone records? We don't need probable cause for a subpoena and that'll lead us to the person who called him Thursday night."

"I guess I don't need my stubble after all."

Dawn sidled closer. "Nope, all you need is me."

I turned away and walked to my unmarked cruiser. "When we get back to the office, call the district attorney's office and get started on that subpoena."

"And what'll you do?"

"Call every bank in the parish and find out where Rosie did her business."

"Why?"

"I want to be sure that Rosie is a member here."

"How will her bank account do that?"

"She might've paid her dues with a check."

CHAPTER FOURTEEN

Early morning
Sunday, November 21, 2004
Skybald National Forest, North Louisiana

William pried his eyelids open. His head felt heavy. He tried several times to blink away the blurriness, but it was no use. Something pulled down hard on his left shoulder and waist. His hands were elevated above his body. He shook his head to clear his vision, but winced as a million branding irons pierced the inner walls of his skull. He tried desperately to recall what had happened. He remembered leaving home to drive to the Skybald National Forest for vacation. He remembered—

Hell, that's all I remember! William turned his neck, first to the left and then to the right. It hurt both ways. He tried to shift his body and it felt as though he set himself on fire. He blinked several more times. Things finally began to materialize out of the fog. He saw the base of a tree directly in front of him, but it was growing upside down. He moved a hand to rub his eyes and it flopped back above his head. *Wait a minute.* Realization hit him with the unforgiving ferociousness of a killer tornado— the brakes!

"Claire! Gracie!" William looked to his right. Claire dangled by her seatbelt in a lifeless heap. Her golden hair covered her face. William reached out with a bloody hand, afraid of what he would find beyond that wall of silk. He gently brushed the hair away. Her eyes were closed. There was a nasty airbag rash on her face. Her right arm was twisted at an odd angle. Blood dripped from a cut on her forehead. Gracie was no longer in her arms.

William broke into a panic. He couldn't do anything for Claire or Gracie while strapped upside down in his seatbelt. Ignoring the pain, he reached to his waist and pressed hard against the seatbelt button. It didn't give. He sucked in and pushed against the roof of the car with one hand and manipulated the button with the other. With a clank, it snapped free and he collapsed onto his shoulder blades. He screamed out loud as his left leg remained attached to the floorboard above him. His head whirled in pain. He peeked through narrow eyelids and saw that the dashboard had a firm hold on his leg. His jeans were saturated in blood.

William groaned and gritted his teeth as he squirmed along the ceiling. He stopped when he was directly under Claire. He reached up and felt her neck. He breathed a deep sigh of relief when he felt a heartbeat. His relief turned to concern when he realized her breathing was shallow. Her position was an awkward one and it was difficult for her stomach to rise and fall. He tried to stabilize her neck with one arm and reached up with the other to press the release button on her seatbelt. The belt broke free and Claire dumped directly on top of William, putting extreme pressure on his leg.

He screamed and writhed in pain. Sweat slid down his face like sheets of rain. When he felt he could no longer take the pain, his eyelids slid slowly shut and everything went black.

Sometime after dark

When William opened his eyes, panic filled his heart. Everything was black. He blinked several times and looked around. Still black. He waved his hand in front of his face. Nothing. *Jesus,* he thought, *I'm blind*! He knew Claire was still on him because it was hard for him to breath. He shifted and felt a wrenching tension on his leg. He groped around in the dark until his fingers found Claire's neck. Her heart still beat strong and her breathing was steady. Leaves rustled just outside the overturned car. William jerked his head around in that direction. Such utter blackness. He strained to hear the sound again. All was quiet, except for the normal night sounds of the forest. He heard the lonesome wail of a wolf in the distance. Crickets chirped a noisy chorus. An owl called out in search of other owls. Mosquitoes buzzed around his head. Tree frogs screamed their prayer for rain.

William sighed and relief extinguished the panic in his heart as he realized it was nighttime. "What night is this?" he wondered out loud. Had they been there for longer than a day? Why hadn't someone rescued them? Were they so far off the road that no one could see? What about Gracie? Tears streamed down his face.

William decided to try and work his leg free. He crunched upward and slid his hands along his leg to where it was trapped. Just the slightest touch to his leg broke sweat on his forehead. He felt around in the dark and gripped the twisted metal that clutched his leg. He pulled with all of his limited strength. His fingers slipped from the fabric and bumped his leg. Tears of pain squirted from his eyes. He decided it was a bad idea and tried to think of another way out of his predicament.

With nothing to do and nowhere to go, William lay panting. He began speaking softly to Claire. He wondered about her condition and worried that it might worsen if they weren't rescued in short order. As he spoke, his eyes drifted shut.

Monday, November 22, 2004
When William opened his eyes again it was daylight. The first thing he noticed was a rancid odor that polluted the air like

stale roadkill on a hot August day. He scrunched his nose and tried to locate the source of the smell. He peered outside the front windshield, but didn't see anything. He checked the side windows. Nothing. He squirmed gently to see out the back windshield. It was then that he caught sight of Gracie's seemingly lifeless body. She was lying in a bundle on the pine needles twenty feet from the car, her mangled face pressed to the ground.

William squeezed his eyes shut. His jaw burned. Tears seeped through and spilled onto the overturned roof of the Thunderbird. The ache in his heart masked the pain in his leg. He glanced at Claire. She hadn't so much as fluttered an eyelid since the accident—that couldn't be good.

"I've got to get help." William took several deep breaths and exhaled forcefully. On the last exhale he gave his left leg a jerk. The pain ripped a scream from his lips and he lay panting. He felt drained. He fought back tears as realization settled heavy. This was it. There was no way out. There would be no rescue. The Thunderbird had traveled too far from the road for anyone to see it.

William lay back in despair. He couldn't just lie there and let his wife fade to a slow death. He closed his eyes and then opened them several times. He drifted off—

Suddenly, a rumble under the ground roused him. He considered the sound and realized it was a vehicle traveling overhead along the gravel road. It sounded like a pickup. It was headed in the direction of the campsite. William began to scream, but the vehicle's engine gradually faded off into the forest, taking with it his dream of a rescue.

He began to count in second intervals, trying to keep track of time. When he'd reach the minute mark, he'd remove a piece of broken glass and place it in a stack. In this way, he knew it was about thirty minutes later that the vehicle made the return trip past the wreckage. He began screaming again and desperately kicked at the dashboard area with his right leg, knowing this might be his only chance to catch the attention of a human. As he kicked, his foot brushed against the horn and it gave a bellowing honk. *The horn!* William abandoned his cries and mashed the horn with his foot. The sound was deafening. His ears rang. He held it until he heard someone hollering from the roadway above.

"Hello? Anyone hurt down there?"

Hope awakened every muscle in William's being. "Help! My little girl . . . a bear . . . I need an ambulance! Get an ambulance! Quick!"

"Hang on," the voice returned, "I'm going to get help!"

It must have been an hour before the vehicle returned, but it seemed like days to William. He heard several vehicles pull up. Before long, sirens echoed in the distance and reverberated through the trees. Firemen and Rangers soon made their way to the vehicle and began to assess the situation.

A young Ranger with a pointed nose and round face leaned over. "How bad are you hurt?"

"I'm okay. It's my wife and my baby. My baby's . . . my little girl's—"

William choked on the tears.

"There's a baby in there?" The Ranger dropped to his belly and scooted through the passenger-side window to have a look. He glanced around.

William shook his head. Before he could speak, someone hollered from behind the Thunderbird. "We've got a baby here . . . oh my *God!*"

The Ranger cast an inquiring glance in William's direction. "How long have y'all been here?"

"Since yesterday morning."

The Ranger nodded at Claire. "The lady?"

"She's my wife—Claire." William's voice cracked. "She hasn't opened her eyes since the wreck. I don't know what's wrong with her . . ."

"Well, we'll get her out in a jiffy." The Ranger's voice was soothing. "You're in good hands here. Tell me about you. Are you experiencing any pain?"

"Yes, sir."

"Where?"

William forced a smile. "The short list would be where I *don't* hurt."

"I see you've kept your sense of humor. That's a good thing." The Ranger looked up at William's leg. "Trapped?"

William nodded.

"Okay, just sit tight. We'll have you out in no time."

The Ranger disappeared and returned later with several firemen. They dragged large pieces of equipment into view and plugged them into a generator. While some of them worked to free Claire, one bent and recovered Gracie's body. He wrapped her in a thick blanket and cradled her in his arms. The tears tumbled like a mudslide down William's face.

A fireman muscled a large hydraulic machine into place on Claire's side of the car. After several minutes, he called out in triumph. "She's clear!" Several other firemen moved in and helped him ease her out of the car and onto the soft ground. Ambulance personnel worked on her while she lay unconscious. William strained to see what was happening.

The firemen brought the machine to his side of the car and went to work. They also used a power saw to cut back some of the metal. Before long, they were poised to pull William from the clutches of the Thunderbird. Several firemen supported his leg.

"Take a deep breath," one of them said. "This might hurt a little."

The hydraulic machine strained. Metal squealed. William grimaced when his leg shifted. He prepared himself for the pain that would follow. The dashboard popped. His leg fell free and into the arms of the firemen. He let out a bloodcurdling scream that sounded like a schoolgirl with her hair on fire. Everything swirled. He felt hands grab hold of him, lift him from the wreckage. His eyelids became heavy . . .

Noon
Tuesday, November 23, 2004
Cote Blanche General Hospital
William awakened to a loud beep. He slowly opened his eyes. There was a plump lady bent over him. She wore pink scrubs. A stethoscope dangled from her neck. She attached something to his finger and straightened. "This thing always comes loose," she explained when she realized he was awake.

"Where am I?"

"Cote Blanche General. You've been in a terrible accident."

William looked down. His leg was encased in a large cast and elevated by a cable attached to a contraption on the ceiling. "Where's my wife? Is she okay?"

The nurse frowned. "She suffered some serious injuries."

"Is she okay?"

"Why don't you just try to get some rest now."

"I want to know how my wife is doing and I want to know *now!*"

"I'll tell you, but you have to remain calm."

William blinked and braced himself for the worst.

"Your wife is in a coma."

"Coma?" William breathed a shallow sigh of relief. "She's going to be okay?"

"Her condition is stable."

"When will she come out of the coma?"

"It's hard to say. Only time will tell."

"Where is she?"

"Second floor."

"I want to see her." William tried to sit up. Chains rattled when he moved and he was yanked back to the bed. He looked down at his arms—handcuffs. He was chained to both sides of the bed.

"Is there a problem with the prisoner, ma'am?"

William looked to where he heard the voice. A uniformed cop was just inside the doorway of the hospital room.

The nurse waved her hand. "Everything's fine, James."

"Hey, man, there *is* a problem," William said. "Why the hell am I cuffed to this bed? And who're you calling a prisoner?"

The cop sauntered over to where William lay. William guessed the cop was about four inches taller than him. His uniform was solid green with gold patches on the shoulders. He had a thick black leather belt strapped to his waist. The only thing attached to the belt was a black pistol. Danny Jerkins, William's cop buddy from back home, always told him not to mess with cops who only carried a gun. He said they were more prone to shoot if things got out of control, whereas the cops who carried mace and sticks had other options.

"Sir, I need to report a crime. We were—"

"You'd better just sit quiet until the detectives come down here to question you. Understand?" There was finality in the cop's tone as he stared icicles into William.

William gulped and only nodded. He turned his head and didn't look back until the clicking of the cop's boots faded into the hallway. The nurse finished up her duties and turned to leave.

"If you need anything, just ring the bell."

"But I'm cuffed," William said halfheartedly.

The nurse pointed to a red button on the rail just inches from William's fingers. "It's right here."

When he was alone, William lay in fear and mused over the possible reasons for his detention. *This has to be a huge mistake,* he thought. *I've done nothing wrong.* His mind raced. *Could they be charging me for the accident? But surely, when they learn of the circumstances surrounding the wreck, they'll understand.* He thought back to everything he'd ever done wrong. Nothing warranted this. He'd never broken any laws.

William spent a restless day in the hospital. The nurse came in every hour to check on him and brought him a lunch tray that he didn't touch. When the light outside his hospital window began to fade, a slender nurse brought him another tray of food.

"Hi," she said in a cheerful voice. "I'll be spending the night with you."

William couldn't help but smile.

"You need to eat something," the nurse insisted when William pushed the tray aside.

"How's my wife?"

"She's doing good."

"Is she awake?"

The nurse shook her head. "But the doctors are hopeful."

When the nurse left him alone, he nibbled on mashed potatoes and meatloaf. Everything felt dry going down. He had to swallow several times and take a gulp of soda before the food would make its way down his throat. When he'd had enough he pushed the tray away and tried to get some sleep. Nothing doing. He shifted restlessly on his back, longing to be with Claire, to hold Gracie one more time. He cried softly and somewhere in the night he drifted off into troubled slumber.

8:00 A.M.

Wednesday, November 24, 2004

William was already awake when the hospital door burst open at eight the next morning. The plump nurse was back. She bustled in and hurried through her duties. She seemed tense and didn't respond when William greeted her. When she was done filling in her chart, she promptly left. Before the door could shut behind her, a large hairy hand stopped it.

William stared anxiously as the door glided open, slowly exposing a looming dark figure—one slice at a time. He wore a black trench coat and black slacks. When he stepped forward the ground seemed to shake beneath his two-hundred-plus pounds. Light splashed off his face. His facial features were tight, with lines of hate etched across it. His brows were thick, his expression stuck in a permanent scowl. He slid a chair next to the bed and carefully removed his trench coat, exposing the silver pistol that dangled from a brown leather shoulder holster. His shirt was white and cardboard stiff. A crisp tie displaying a wilderness scene hung from his neck.

"I'm Detective Oscar London," the man said in an uncharacteristically calm and calculating voice. "How are you feeling today?"

"Okay." William coughed to remove the crack from his voice. "I'm okay."

"Before we get started, I have to read you your rights."

"My rights? Why?"

"Because you're under arrest. Don't you watch TV?"

"Arrest? For what?"

"Murder."

CHAPTER FIFTEEN

7:25 A.M.

Wednesday, November 24, 2004

Magnolia Parish Sheriff's Office Substation

When I walked into the office on Wednesday morning, Becky lifted a yellow envelope from the black tray at the corner of her desk. "A lady from Seasville Bank and Trust dropped this off yesterday afternoon."

I tore open the envelope and dumped the contents into my hand. I walked down the hallway and into the office I shared with Dawn.

"What you got there?" Dawn sat behind the desk looking warm and cozy. She wore a red form-fitted turtleneck sweater. Her nails and lips matched the sweater.

"What're you doing here so early?"

"I can be on time when I need to be." She slid a copy of a subpoena across the desk. "Laci at the DA's office faxed this out today. She said the phone company should have the information within a couple of weeks."

I sat across from Dawn and thumbed through Rosalie McKenzie's bank records from the current year. Her last recorded transaction was on November 5, 2004—two weeks before her death. It was a check written to Mack's Exxon, the only remaining full-service gas station in Seasville. "I like this girl already."

"What is that?"

I handed Dawn the sheet that contained a copy of the cancelled check to Mack's. "She supports the small business people." I continued scanning the records until I struck investigative gold. "Gotcha!"

Dawn's eyes were curious. "What?"

"She gives regularly to the church." I pulled out a highlighter and colored in all the checks that were made out to Magnolia Faith Church. I whistled. "This girl gave over twelve hundred dollars to that church since April."

Dawn leaned across the desk. "Forty dollars a week? Who gives that much money to a church?"

"Now I know how Isaac can afford to pay for the junk in his office." I counted the number of checks to the Magnolia Faith Church. "This girl wrote thirty-one checks to Isaac in seven months. How in the hell can he say he doesn't know her?"

"Did he endorse the back of the checks?"

I flipped the pages over. "I don't have copies of the backs of the checks."

"The bank should be able to get them for you."

I pondered what we had. It wasn't much. "Say we prove he was aware that McKenzie attended his church. What then? What's that got to do with her death?"

"We need to talk to this Ray fellow."

"You're right. We need to know what they were doing there that night." I returned the bank records to the envelope. "Laci said it'll take a couple of weeks?"

"At least. It could be longer."

"Why so long?"

"In case you haven't realized, Thanksgiving's tomorrow. Most people take off this time of year and spend it with family."

I snatched up the phone and called Debbie. She answered and, in my sweetest voice, I said, "Hey, do you have anything planned for tonight?"

"What do you need to do?"

"I have to be somewhere tonight for work, but I shouldn't be too late. I'll definitely be home for Thanksgiving dinner tomorrow."

Debbie gasped. "You remembered!"

"Well, not exactly. Dawn reminded me."

"Here I am, thinking you've changed and you have to go and say that?"

"Would you rather me lie?"

Debbie was silent for a moment. "No, it's okay. Tell Dawn I said thanks. Don't be too late. I might need help getting the turkey out of the oven."

"I'll be there." I hung up the phone and looked over at Dawn. Her eyes were narrow and suspicious.

"You just lied to your wife!"

"No, I didn't."

"You told her you had to work tonight, but you don't."

"Actually, I do—and so do you."

"Where are we going?"

"Where everyone should go on the eve of Thanksgiving—church."

A knowing smile spread across Dawn's face. "I like the way you think."

"Make sure you wear a dress . . . and it better not be revealing. We're going to church, not a nightclub."

"I do have Sunday clothes, Mr. Atheist." Dawn turned and drummed away at her keyboard.

I leaned back in my chair and watched Dawn work. She wasn't paying any attention to me as she ruffled through her notes and typed on a report. *Probably the Rosie McKenzie case.* While most detectives, myself included, liked to wait until the investigation was completed to type the report, Dawn liked to keep her report current. She looked up at me and smiled, then returned to her work. Her eyes held a loneliness that I'd never seen before. Maybe I just hadn't noticed. "What are you doing tomorrow?"

Dawn shrugged. "I'll probably pick up a pizza and a movie."

"What happened to driving up to Arkansas to be with your family?"

"Not this year. Too much going on around here."

I tapped the envelope on the desk and tried to be casual. "Would you like to join us for Thanksgiving dinner?"

"I couldn't impose."

"It wouldn't be an imposition. Besides, you know how much Samantha loves you."

"I don't know."

"Come on, say yes. It'll be great, and you'll be doing me a favor."

"How's that?"

"Every year my in-laws come over. We don't have much in common and all they want to do is bitch anyway. At least if you come, I'll have someone to talk to."

"But what about Debbie? Don't you think you should ask her first?"

"She won't mind."

"I guess I'll think about it."

"It'll beat spending it alone."

"Okay, okay, you—"

The phone beeped loud and Becky's voice came across the speaker. "Brandon, there's a man on line three and he sounds mad."

I picked up the phone and smashed the blinking button. "This is Brandon."

"Detective Berger, this is Red MacQuaid. I received a call from Jarvis Chiasson's mother this morning. She told me you pulled Jarvis in for questioning last night."

"That's correct."

"I represent Jarvis and if you want to talk with him, you have to go through me first. You have violated—"

"Red, let me interrupt you. The judge appointed you to represent Jarvis Chiasson on the matter of the car burglary. We pulled him in on a separate and unrelated matter."

"You still have to notify me!"

"Actually, all I have to do is advise him of his rights. Once he waives them and agrees to talk to me, there's really nothing you can do about that." I could feel Red's face turning to blood through the phone.

"I demand to know what he said."

"Red, this is an ongoing investigation and I'm not at liberty to discuss the case with you. But, since I'm such a nice guy, I'll tell you this: You don't have to worry about any new charges being filed against Jarvis."

"Really?"

"Really."

"Oh, well okay. I just wish you'd keep me in mind if you have to talk to him again."

"Later, Red." I dropped the phone in the cradle and stood. "Let's grab some lunch before it gets too late."

CHAPTER SIXTEEN

8:30 A.M.
Wednesday, November 24, 2004
Cote Blanche General Hospital
William swallowed the sand in his throat. "I didn't murder anyone."

"What do you call what happened to your daughter?"

"A bear killed Gracie."

"Oh, really? And where were you?"

"I left her for just a second. I had to. Claire was drowning and I ran to save her."

"Why was your little baby out there in the first place? Don't you think she's kind of young to be out in the forest?"

"My dad started taking me when I was a baby. I practically grew up out there. Lots of people—"

"Okay, Mr. Chandler, I'm very interested in what you have to say, but before you continue, I have to read you your rights."

The detective pulled a card from his wallet and read it. William didn't hear a word he said. *How can this be happening?*

"Sir, are you listening to me?"

William nodded.

"Then could you kindly answer my question. Do you understand your rights?"

"Yeah."

"Very good. Now I want you to start from the beginning and tell me exactly what happened."

William rushed through the story. He told the detective about when they first arrived at the forest, how they saw the soldier and he was acting suspicious. He told about Jake and Gaby Arthur and how they could confirm the suspicious activities of the soldier. He told of how the soldier had stalked them through the woods and how he had pushed Claire into the water and that while he was rescuing Claire the bear killed Gracie. He told how they had chased the bear away, took Gracie's body, and then crashed the Thunderbird—because the soldier cut the brake lines.

When William was done, Detective London stared down at his notes. "Wow, that's quite a fascinating story. This soldier, does he have a name?"

"I don't know. I . . . I'm sure he does, but I don't know it."

"And your brake lines; how do you know he's the person responsible for cutting them?"

"We were walking to the cars—"

"Who is *we*?"

"Me and Jake Arthur. We were walking to the cars and we saw him crouched down by my front tires cutting the brake lines."

"So, you caught him cutting your brake lines. Did this anger you?"

"Not at the time. I mean, I didn't know he was cutting my brake lines—"

"But you just said, and I quote, *We saw him crouched down by my front tires cutting the brake lines.* End quote."

"I mean, I know *now* what he was doing, but at the time I didn't. I just thought he was snooping around."

"What did you do when you thought he was snooping around your car?"

"Nothing, really. I just yelled at him to get away from my car."

"So it *did* anger you."

"No, I wasn't mad."

"But you yelled and that indicates an angry state of mind. Do you get angry often?"

"What are you saying?" William didn't like the direction the interrogation was heading and his voice revealed that fact.

"I'm simply asking a question." Detective London's voice remained calm. "Do you get angry often?"

"I don't have a temper, if that's what you want to know. I've never laid a finger on Claire and I would never hurt Gracie—"

"I'll get to them in a minute. First, I want you to tell me again how you know this soldier is the person who cut your brake lines?"

"It *has* to be him."

"When you realized he was the one who cut your brake lines, did this anger you?"

"No, I mean—"

"A strange man cuts your brake lines, he places your family in danger, and you're not angry?"

"I'm angry now."

"And you were angry when you thought he pushed your wife into the raging rapids. Isn't that right?"

William stared down at his handcuffs and didn't say a word.

Detective London leaned forward. "I have a wife. If someone ever did anything to her . . ." He shook his head slowly from side to side. "I don't know what I'd do. Being angry, that's a natural response. Now, if you got angry and things got out of hand—"

"What the hell are you talking about?"

"You know what I'm talking about."

"Why are you hassling me?"

"Do you love your wife?"

"What's that got to do—"

"Mr. Chandler, it's a simple question. It requires a *yes* or *no* response. Do you love your wife?"

"Yes, absolutely. I'd die for her."

"That's an interesting answer. Would you also kill for her?"

"What? No!"

"Okay, Mr. Chandler." Detective London removed an inkpad from his box. "I'm going to need to collect your fingerprints."

The rattling handcuffs bit into William's wrists with each roll of his fingers, but London didn't care. He jerked on William's hands and rolled each print onto a fingerprint card. When he was done, he held the card up to the light. "Ah, these are great." He shoved the card into his notebook and nodded down at William. "Thank you for your cooperation and patience. I'll be in touch shortly."

William spent the remainder of the morning musing over his conversation with Detective London. *Who in the hell was murdered and what do I have to do with it?* Suddenly, his eyes watered. *What if they're calling what happened to Gracie a murder because of neglect?*

1:15 P.M.

"Time to rise and shine, Mr. Chandler."

William opened his eyes when he heard the familiar voice. Detective London was seated on the sofa chair. There was a box beside the chair and a stack of papers in his lap.

"How long have I slept?" William tried to wipe the sleep from his eyes, but the cuffs didn't allow for it.

"I've been spending the day doing my job—investigating—so I don't know what you've been doing over here in this hospital room. Are you ready to talk some more?"

William shrugged.

"Very good. Now, you do remember your rights, don't you?"

William hesitated.

London waved a dismissive hand. "Sure you do. You watch television. Let's get into the day you discovered your daughter dead. What day was that?"

"Everything happened Saturday night."

"Are you saying that you discovered your daughter's death on Saturday?"

"That's exactly what I'm saying. I came back from pulling Claire out of the river and we found . . . found Gracie . . . um . . . dead."

"I had a very interesting conversation with your wife—"

"Claire's awake?" William jerked his head off the pillow. "She's out of the coma?"

"Not only is she out of the coma, but she's also talking. She's very intuitive, that one. She could be a detective."

William thought he saw London smile. "I want to talk to my wife!"

"That won't be possible for some time. Let's get back to you. Tell me about the other time you became angry at the soldier."

"I didn't."

"You alluded to it earlier and your wife confirmed it." London flipped back in his notebook. "Ah, here it is; *Will,* she was referring to you, *yelled up at the soldier, 'Get the hell out of here before I kill you, you sick bastard.'* That's what she said. Does that bring the moment back to you?"

"I said that because he was peeping at us while we were swimming in the water. Claire had decided to take her shirt off and he was staring."

"Mr. Chandler, the forest is not your home. If you run around nude you're going to get looked at. That's no reason to threaten someone's life." London leaned back in the chair. "Seems a bit excessive, don't you think?"

"Excessive? I didn't do anything. I only yelled up at him."

"Do you own a knife?"

"A bunch of them."

"Do you own a Cold Steel Tanto?"

William squinted and wondered what Detective London was getting at. "Yes, I do."

"Where is it?"

"I don't know."

"That's a convenient answer."

"Last I saw, it was at the campsite."

Detective London scribbled in his notebook and flipped through the pages for several minutes. Finally, he spoke again. "You said earlier in your statement that you found Gracie dead Friday night. What time was that?"

"I said *Saturday* night. And I don't know what time it was. It was after I pulled Claire from the river. She almost drowned. I had to give her CPR. I was not thinking about what time it was."

"How often did Gracie sleep with you and your wife in the same bed?"

"Never. Claire was too worried about rolling on her."

"How often did you or Claire lie next to your baby and fall asleep?"

William shook his head. "Never. Claire did a lot of reading about babies and she always took every precaution."

"If I'm hearing you right, there was never a time when Gracie was in danger of being accidentally suffocated by you or Claire?"

"Never."

"Are you sure?"

"I'm absolutely positive."

"What happened three Sundays ago?"

William stared down at the foot of the bed. He didn't say anything.

"Let me refresh your memory." London glanced down at his notebook. "San Diego's kicking the shit out of the Saints. What was the final score again? 43 to 17?" London nodded. "Yep, that was it. Missed field goals, holding penalties—the usual with this Saints team."

"Sir, my daughter is dead because of a deranged soldier. Had he not attacked Claire, Gracie would be here today. While you're sitting here talking about football, he's out there getting away with—"

"Away with what? Are you still stuck on him pushing your wife? Let's talk about that for a minute. Why would some random soldier push your wife into the raging waters of Sky-bald River?"

William stared down at his shackled hands. "I've been asking myself that question for days."

"Why would he cut your brake lines so that you and your family might run off a cliff and be killed? Did he also make you drive at an estimated seventy miles per hour? Did he know you would be so reckless?"

William gritted his teeth.

"Tell me, what was the soldier's motive for all of this?"

"I have no idea," William said.

"Right, it doesn't make sense. What *does* make sense is that you—"

"Look, get out there and do your job. Investigate. Find Gaby and Jake. They'll verify everything I've said."

Detective London flipped through his notebook. "When did you say this couple—this Jake and Gaby Arthur—left the Sky-bald National Forest?"

"Saturday morning."

"Then how can they verify *every* thing you've said?"

"Jesus Christ, man! You don't quit, do you? Did it ever occur to you that I might be innocent? And if I'm innocent, don't you think I've been through enough?"

"What did occur to me is that you have a problem with anger.

This makes it a manslaughter case, as opposed to a murder."

"Look, for the last time, I had to leave Gracie to save Claire." Tears welled up in William's eyes, but he fought to quell the tide. "I love my little girl more than I love my own life. I wish it were me lying dead instead of her."

"I never for a minute thought you intended to do what you did. Sometimes, when a person loves someone, they do crazy things. Maybe she wouldn't stop crying. You tried to rock her and it didn't work. You gave her a bottle and still she cried. You tried playing with her, tried everything you could think of, but nothing seemed to help. So you held her. You held her because you loved her. You squeezed her to your chest; squeezed her too hard. Not intentionally, but you squeezed her too hard. She stopped crying . . . and she stopped breathing. When you re-alized what you had done, you had to make a plan. You had to get a story together and you had to involve your wife. She didn't want to go along so you push her—"

"What on earth are you talking about? Are you trying to mind-fuck me? Is that what they taught you in the police academy? Haven't you listened to a word I've said?"

Detective London dipped his head in a slow nod. "Let's get back to the Saints–Chargers game. Where was Claire while you watched the game?"

William was silent for several minutes. Finally, he spoke in a quiet voice. "What does that have to do with anything?"

"Just humor me, if you would."

William exhaled. "Uh, she was gone. I think she was shop-ping or something."

"Who was watching Gracie?"

"I was."

"What happened when Claire returned home?"

William leaned back and stared at the ceiling. His heart pounded in his chest as he realized what was happening.

"Well?"

"I have nothing to say."

"It's funny how you clam up when you get caught in a lie."

William turned and stared ice picks into Detective London's eyes. "I didn't lie."

"You said you never fell asleep with Gracie. That was a lie. Claire tells me she came home that Sunday and found you passed out in your recliner with Gracie on your chest. She climbed all over your ass. Remember that?"

"I wasn't passed out. I was sleeping."

"Sleeping." London glanced down at his notes. "And a minute ago you said you never fell asleep with Gracie."

"That's not what I said."

"Sure it is. You lied. Why? What are you hiding?"

"You're trying to confuse me!"

"There's nothing confusing about the truth."

"That's it! I'm not saying another word until I see my wife. And I want a goddamn lawyer!"

"Oh, I don't think your wife is in the mood to talk to you—ever." Detective London held up a clear plastic bag containing a Cold Steel Tanto.

William's eyes opened wide and his heart slowed to barely a tick when he saw dried blood streaked along the blade.

"I see you recognize your knife. You want to guess whose fingerprints I found on the handle?"

"Of course my prints are on it; it's my knife. But what's that got to do with anything?"

Detective London smiled, an evil glint in his eyes. "You know."

William's jaw slackened.

"An observant soldier is in the woods with you. He sees what you did to your baby, he sees you push your wife. He moves in to stop you and what do you do?" London tossed a picture on William's stomach. "You snap!"

William stared in horror at the picture on his stomach. The soldier lay on his back along a wooded trail. William's Tanto was buried deep in his chest. The pit bull was a few feet away, bloodied and swollen. "I didn't do this!"

"You attacked this old, defenseless soldier and you buried your knife to the hilt in his chest! And when his loyal dog moves in to defend him, you kill it too!" London stood. "And you did all of that to cover up the murder of your daughter."

CHAPTER SEVENTEEN

Wednesday, November 24, 2004

Magnolia Parish Sheriff's Office Substation

Dawn was standing outside the substation when I drove up. She slipped into the front passenger's seat and eyed me up and down. "Brandon, you're dressed like you're going to work."

I looked down at my Dockers, shirt, and tie. "What's wrong with what I'm wearing?"

She leaned over to loosen my tie, jerked it off, and freed my top button. "Here, now you look less like you're going to a funeral and more like you're going to church."

I grunted and backed out the driveway. It only took five minutes to drive the four miles to the Magnolia Faith Church. I stopped on the highway and surveyed the parking lot.

"There's no place to park," Dawn said.

There had to be two hundred cars crammed into the paved lot. "I can't believe the number of people in here."

"Imagine if everyone gave forty dollars per week."

"Some might give more. Look at the expensive cars in there. Rosalie didn't even have one and look how much she gave."

Dawn grunted. "Maybe that's why she didn't have one; she couldn't afford it."

I parked my unmarked cruiser off the shoulder of the road. "I wonder what this guy's selling."

"What do you mean?"

"Look at this place. The people here give Isaac a lot of money. Why? There has to be a reason."

"Why does there have to be a reason?"

"Nobody gives for nothing. Whether it's a guarantee that they'll go to Heaven or some other feel-good reason, they're paying for something."

"Maybe they give money to the church because the Bible says they're supposed to."

"And here I thought Jesus said to give to the poor." When there was no traffic, Dawn and I jogged across the highway.

"What'll we do once we're inside?" Dawn asked.

I shrugged. "I've never gone undercover in a church before."

"What if Isaac asks us to leave?"

"He can't. He already told us the assembly room is open to the public during—what words did he use?"

"Prayer and worship."

"Yeah, that." We ascended the wide cement steps. I looked at Dawn before opening the door. "Here goes nothing."

When we stepped inside, the deafening sound of hundreds of voices trying to talk over each other greeted us. There were people everywhere. Some stood in the aisles, some sat in the long solid oak pews. We jostled through the crowd, with Dawn leading the way. She stopped at one point and turned to speak. I shook my head to let her know I couldn't hear a word she said. She wrapped a hand around my neck and pulled my ear to her mouth. "Let's try to get a seat!"

The vibration of her voice made my ear ring. I nodded and followed her down the narrow aisles that separated the pews. We squeezed between an elderly couple and a family of six. Dawn leaned into the elderly couple and began talking to them. I surveyed the room. I recognized some faces from town, but most of the people were strangers to me. There were smiles everywhere. Whatever Isaac was selling, it sure made his parishioners happy.

Suddenly, there was a loud squeak and then a voice came over the microphone.

"Are you ready to celebrate *Jesus*?" the voice screamed. There were cheers from the crowd and people scrambled to their seats. "Are you ready to celebrate *life*?" Someone began strumming an electric guitar and another guy began beating a set of acoustic drums. Everyone rose to their feet and began swaying side to side, singing out loud, in unison.

Dawn and I stood and were rocked into each other by the people on either side of us. I thought about shoving the guy to my right, but decided against it. The church members clapped and belted out song after song. Some folks even danced in the narrow spaces between the pews and one guy ran up and down the aisles screaming something I couldn't understand. Through the swaying crowd I caught glimpses of Isaac Stewart on the stage. At one point he hopped along the stage on one leg, one arm pointing to the ceiling and the other arm slapping his chest. I glanced down at Dawn. She stared about, her chin nearly resting against her chest in awe. I had to admit; I'd never seen anything quite like it myself.

After nearly a solid hour of celebrating, the music stopped and Isaac's familiar voice came over the microphone. "What a marvelous day this is! Hallelujah!" The parishioners screamed in accord. Isaac raised his arms and the noise level dropped immediately to complete and utter silence. Everyone sat in hushed fashion.

I leaned over and whispered in Dawn's ear. "These people treat him like he's a rock star."

"Quiet!" hissed the man next to me.

I stared daggers into his eyeballs. He gulped and quickly looked back toward Isaac, who stood at a gold lectern. His head was bowed. Only his lips moved. When he looked up, he blew forcefully out over the crowd. "Through me, the Lord will breathe life back into those who believe. In order to receive life, you must believe. In order to receive healing, you must believe. My faith in the power of the Lord is strong, but I cannot give you my faith. I cannot say to you, *Here, borrow my faith for the day.* God will grant you the answers to your prayers based on your faith, so be wary, lest your faith not be strong enough!"

Several people said, "Amen." I stared at the faces in the room. All eyes were fixated on Isaac Stewart, from the oldest to the youngest. *How can one man brainwash so many people?*

Isaac moved forward to the edge of the stage and stopped. He pursed his lips and stared at the floor. When he looked up, tears flowed from his eyes. *Nice touch,* I thought.

"Good brethren and sisters, just recently one of our very own sisters set upon a journey of trial and tribulation."

My curiosity mounting, I leaned forward in my chair. Isaac's eyes honed in on my position. Our eyes locked. He hesitated and then abruptly returned to the lectern. When he spoke, his voice was forceful. "Brothers and sisters in the Lord, what becomes of a man who challenges God's messenger?"

"God will devour him!" a lady on the front row called.

"Open up your Bibles to Romans thirteen, verse four." Isaac paused while Bible pages flapped like hundreds of birds' wings. "It says, *For he is the minister of God to thee for good. But if thou do that which is evil, be afraid; for he beareth not the sword in vain: for he is the minister of God, a revenger to execute wrath upon him that doeth evil.*"

Isaac raised both hands high in the air and looked directly into my eyes. "I am an agent of God! If you come against me, you're coming against God and the Lord will devour your flesh!" He spun and waved a hand over the congregation. "Brothers and sisters, we have imposters in our midst. People who would want to do harm to the children of God. Let us rise up and pray now that these people, these evildoers, be dealt with according to the laws of *God!*"

Everyone jumped to their feet and began chanting in a language I couldn't understand. Dawn clutched my arm and screamed into my ear, "What is happening?"

"We've been made," I called back. The chanting became louder and louder. I'd always heard of people speaking in tongues, but I'd never witnessed it. The crowd turned to face us. They extended their hands toward us and, with eyes squeezed shut, bellowed their prayers. I clutched Dawn's hand and pressed my lips against her ear. "Stay close to me!"

I moved forward through the crowd, pulling Dawn along behind me. People clutched out at us as we pushed through. I neared the end of the crowd and the door came into sight. A large man stepped in my path. He braced himself and screamed his prayers. I shoved him aside with my shoulder and pulled Dawn past. I guided her ahead of me and out the door. The door slammed shut behind us with a force that sent us stumbling down the steps. I steadied Dawn and we listened. The chanting droned through the walls. After several minutes, we walked across the parking lot.

When we reached my unmarked car, Dawn shuddered. "Jesus Christ! Those people are crazy!"

"Yeah, that was a bit weird." We got in the unmarked and I drove off. "Isaac's not running a church, he's running a cult."

"Yeah," Dawn agreed. "I wouldn't be surprised if we walked in one day and found them all dead, their bellies full of fruit juice."

"When he started talking about their *sister* in the Lord, I could've sworn he was about to mention Rosalie's name." I rubbed the prickles on my chin. "I wonder what he meant by *breathing life back into those who believe.*"

Dawn turned in her seat. There was excitement in her eyes.

"Oh, he was talking about bringing people back to life!"

"Is he crazy?"

"The lady I was sitting next to—the elderly one with the beehive hairdo—she said he's already brought one person back to life."

"That's impossible."

"According to her, not only does he bring people back to life, but he heals people who are sick."

"What about Rosalie? Did he try to heal her?"

Dawn shook her head. "When I mentioned Rosalie's name, the lady shut down. She started asking me for my name and asked if I was a member."

"What did you tell her?"

"I didn't have to say anything, the music saved me."

"We need to find out who called him about Rosalie . . ."

I dropped Dawn at the substation at 7:00 P.M. "See you tomorrow night, then?"

She nodded. "Guess so. It sucks being alone on Thanksgiving."

CHAPTER EIGHTEEN

November 2004
Cote Blanche General Hospital
William lost track of time. Each day brought more of the same
. . . breakfast, lunch, and supper, with visits from the nurse in
between. Although he was chained to the bed and his left leg
trapped in a cast, the uniformed guards were a constant at the
door to his room. They removed the chains and forced him to
get up and shuffle around the room three times each day. "Have
to keep the circulation going," one of the guards had com-
mented. "We need to keep you healthy so we can get you
sentenced to death."

"Dying might not be so bad," William had said. "Maybe then
the itching in my leg would stop."

William tried to make conversation with his nurses and some
of the friendlier-looking guards, but no one wanted to be his
buddy. Nearly every day he asked about his wife and nearly
every answer was the same: "Prisoners can't communicate with
one another."

Morning
Monday, December 20, 2004
William set the breakfast tray aside. A guard stepped up and
William held out his arm to be cuffed. When the guard was
gone he settled back and stared at the ceiling. Within minutes
his eyelids began to droop. After an hour of battling sleep, the

door opened.

"There's a woman here to see you," the guard announced.

"Claire?" William's heart raced. He watched the door with anxious eyes. Heels clattered against the hard floor . . . closer . . . closer. A shadow fell across the floor and an image appeared in the doorway. William's imaginary hot-air balloon deflated and crashed to the ground, killing everyone onboard. *Damn it!*

The woman wore a brown faded business suit. She carried a black satchel with an antique flavor to it. Her hair was short, blonde, and damaged, and the centers of her eyeglasses were held together with clear plastic tape.

"Mr. Chandler?" The woman's face seemed to crack as she spoke and her voice squeaked.

"That would be me."

The woman shuffled to the bedside sofa and dropped onto it. "Whew, I've been driving all day." She unbuckled the strap on her satchel and removed a file. "Okay, I'm here to talk to you about your case."

"Who are you?"

"Oops, I guess I need to introduce myself." The woman stood and held out a wrinkled hand. "Esther Diebold, Cote Blanche Indigent Defender's Office. I'm your lawyer."

"Don't I get to pick my lawyer?"

"Well, seeing how a grand jury indicted you on first-degree murder charges and the judge refused to set bail, you won't be able to afford to pick your lawyer. Unless you have a pile of money in the bank, but I'm guessing *no.*"

"First-degree murder? What's the difference between that and regular murder?"

Esther Diebold frowned. "The difference is life and death."

"What's that mean?"

"If you're convicted of first-degree murder you'll get the

death penalty. If you get convicted of the lesser crime of second-degree murder you'll get life in prison."

"But I didn't kill anyone! I shouldn't even be here!"

"Sir, I read the statement you gave the police detective. You claim a bear killed your daughter while you were rescuing your wife because a dead man pushed her in the river—a dead man you killed. Not exactly the best defense."

William's eyes found the grooves they had burrowed into the ceiling over the previous weeks. "How can you defend me if you don't even believe me?"

"It's not my job to believe you. It's my job to do my best to ensure that you have a fair trial."

"What about my wife? Are you representing her, too?"

"Hasn't anyone told you?"

William's head jerked around. "Told me what?"

"Your wife struck a deal with the prosecutors. She agreed to testify against you in exchange for her release from jail."

"Testify against me?" William's chest ached. "But she knows I didn't do what they're saying. She would never—"

"Regardless of what you might think she knows, or how loyal you might think she is to you, she's testifying against you. So we need to prepare for what she might say." Esther flipped her notebook open to a fresh page. "Is there anything in your past that she could use against us?"

"But wait, I want to know—"

"Look, son, I get one hour with you. Let's not waste it getting to know each other. Is there anything in your past she can use?"

William was confused. "Like what?"

"Have you ever been arrested for anything?"

"No. Never."

"You answered that too fast. Take your time and think about it before you answer."

"Run my rap sheet if you don't believe me."

"The cops already did. It's clean, but rap sheets aren't always complete. I once defended a man who had a clean rap sheet. I let him take the witness stand in his own defense and everything went good . . . until the prosecutor asked if he'd ever been arrested. He said *no.*" Esther shook her head. "I should've known something was up when the prosecutor pitched a tent. He jumped to his feet and produced a document from some courthouse out in the sticks where my client had been found guilty of perjury. Do you think the jury believed anything he said? No sir. So, once more, have you ever been arrested for anything at all?"

"I already answered your question."

"Have you ever abused your wife in any way?"

"No."

"Ever hit her?"

"No."

"Ever leave a mark on her?"

"Well, I mean, we've wrestled around on the ground before, you know, play fighting and stuff. She gets bruised kind of easy."

"So, you have left a mark on her?"

"Yeah, but like I said, we were playing around."

Esther scribbled in her notebook. "Have you guys had any marital problems?"

"No more than the next couple, probably less than most."

"You guys ever argue?"

"Sure, every now and then."

"About what?"

"Look, none of this has anything to do with what happened to Gracie."

"Everything has to do with this case. You're on trial for first-degree murder and the state's star witness is your wife. She's been talking with them for weeks and I don't know what she's told them. I don't want to be neck deep in the trial and get caught with my skirt up on some issue because you failed to tell me things that might be crucial. You need to tell me everything. Let's start with the day you arrived at the forest. What happened?"

William told Esther everything, from beginning to end, just like he'd told Detective London. Esther stopped him often to complain about how fast he talked. "You need to slow down so my hand can catch up."

He couldn't help but wonder why she didn't have a tape recorder, but he didn't ask.

When William was done, Esther left the room and returned with a soda can. She popped the top and held the can to his mouth so he could drink. When she was seated again, she said, "Now tell me everything the detective asked you. It might help me get an angle on where he's taking this case."

William told her what he remembered of the interrogation.

"He suggested you smothered your baby?"

William nodded.

"Did he say why he thought this?"

"That detective was saying all kinds of things that didn't make sense. Look, you have to find Jake and Gaby Arthur. They can verify everything I've said."

"Where are they from?"

William was thoughtful. "They never said—to me, at least. Gaby might've told Claire."

"Well, we can't rely on Claire for anything. Whatever we get, it'll have to come from somewhere else."

"I don't believe what that detective said about my wife. I want to talk to her. You have to find out where she is and get her in here."

"I'll try, but I can't promise you anything." Esther gathered up her files and stood to go. "Your doctor told me the authorities are going to move you to the detention center as soon as the cast is removed from your leg."

"When will that be?"

"They're thinking two more weeks. Your arraignment had been scheduled for today, but I got a continuance. It'll be in four weeks. Meanwhile, I'll file a motion for discovery and find out exactly what kind of case the prosecutor has against you." Esther walked to the door and stopped. "Oh, try to have a Merry Christmas."

William only grunted.

"I'll bring you some Christmas dinner."

"I appreciate the gesture, but don't bother. All I want is to see my wife."

9:00 A.M.
Monday, January 3, 2005
Cote Blanche General Hospital

"Are you ready to go to your new home?"

William looked up. Two Cote Blanche deputies—one a young kid in an oversized uniform and the other an overweight old-timer—entered the hospital room carrying leg shackles and handcuffs attached to a length of chain. When they released him from the hospital bed they directed him to stand. He grimaced when he put weight on his left leg. It was pale and atrophied. He limped to the wall and placed his hands against it.

The officers shackled his legs together. They gave no indication they cared about his recent injury. The kid wrapped the chain belt around William's waist, pulled it snug, and attached the opposite links together with a padlock. He then clicked the cuffs around William's wrists.

The old-timer pointed to the door. "Walk."

William stared down at the light blue hospital gown he wore. "Where are y'all taking me?"

"The prom." The young kid laughed uncontrollably at his own joke. He slapped the old-timer's back. "Did you hear what I said? I said, *the prom!*"

William shook his head and shuffled to the door. The metal from the shackles bit into his ankles each time he flexed his foot. His left leg ached with each step. When the trio made their way through the exit and into the brilliant outdoors a sea of reporters converged on them and blocked the walkway to the prison van.

"Why did you kill your baby?" one of them screamed.

"Did you know the man you killed was a homeless Vietnam War hero?" another asked.

"Was your wife in on the plot?" still another wanted to know.

William looked straight at the ground. His eyes smarted at the mention of his wife. He had spent weeks in the hospital and she hadn't visited once. He knew she was out of jail. He'd seen her when he went before the magistrate. She was in the audience with her parents.

What did Detective London mean when he said she wasn't in the mood to speak to me? Did that cop have her believing I was responsible for Gracie's death? William shook his head to clear it.

The corrections officers led him into the van and slammed the sliding door shut, providing William relief from the frenzied media.

"Not every day we get a murder around here," the old-timer said when he was seated in the driver's seat.

"Especially one where the daddy kills his baby," said the young kid.

William sat quiet on the metal bench and stared at a spot of dirt on the floor. He didn't look up until they arrived at the parish prison and the old-timer opened the van door for him to step out. He followed the officers down a long musky corridor that was lined with prison cells. As they walked, inmates hollered at William. Some cursed him, some threatened him, and some praised him. But one thing was clear; they all seemed to know him.

The officers stopped outside a door that read *Booking Room*. They removed William's handcuffs and turned him over to a strapping woman. "She'll process you," the young kid said. He then pointed to the corridor. "And they'll eat you." He doubled over in laughter. His face red and tears streaming down his cheeks, he asked the strapping woman if she'd heard what he said.

The woman glared at him. "Ashley, go find something to do."

The kid abruptly stopped laughing and walked off.

"Thank you," William said, grateful to be rid of the annoying officer.

"Don't thank me." She slammed a thick palm on the booking desk. "Don't you ever thank me, you murdering piece of shit! I hope they kill you in here before you can make it to court. You don't deserve a trial. Trials are reserved for the bad people in this country. You, you're not even human. You killed your own child and then you killed an old defenseless man! Hell, they ought to torture your ass and kill you slow!"

William stared wide-eyed at the booking officer. He wanted to tell her he was innocent, but he dared not. He sat quiet until she completed her paperwork. When she was done, she sent him into a small room where a male guard was waiting.

"Take off your dress and place it in this bag," the guard said. He handed William a yellow plastic bag. The word *Property* was printed in large black letters across the front.

William scooted to a corner and turned his back to the guard. He slowly removed the hospital gown and dropped it into the bag.

"The sandals, too."

William pulled the sandals off and stepped gingerly on the

cold damp floor. His face reddened when the guard told him to bend over and spread his cheeks. He did as ordered, keeping his eyes trained on the floor.

"Okay, now turn around and lift your balls," the guard ordered.

"Excuse me?"

"Look, it'll be more embarrassing if I gotta walk over there and do it myself."

William stared at the wall to his left as he followed the guard's orders. When he was finished the guard threw an orange coverall in his direction. "Put this on."

Grateful to be back in clothes, William squeezed into the undersized coverall and tried to zip it up. He had to suck in his stomach to get the zipper up to his chest. "Sir, it's a bit small."

"Like your baby? That didn't keep you from—"

"Leave Gracie out of this!"

The door flung open and the female officer stepped in. "Is there a problem with the child murderer?"

The guard shook his head. "Everything's under control." He grabbed the front of William's coverall and jerked him forward and toward the doorway. The female officer handed him a blanket as he stumbled past her. He clutched it and stumbled in the direction the guard pointed—toward the corridor of cells where the other prisoners waited.

The guard opened one of the cells and shoved William into it. William lost his balance and fell against one of the prisoners who sat on the bottom bunk of one of the beds. The prisoner shoved William and hollered, "Get the fuck off me, Fish!"

William fell hard and slid across the cement floor. A stainless steel object mounted against the far wall brought his slide to an abrupt halt. He recoiled when he realized the object was the community crapper. Shaken, he picked himself up off the floor and moved to the far side of the cell, to the only available bed among the eight bunks crammed into the tiny room. He crawled onto the bottom bunk and curled up on the hard plastic mattress. Pulling the cover over his head, he cried in silence. His nose leaked. His throat burned. When he could no longer breathe as a result of his stuffed nose, he sniffed as quietly as he could.

Someone laughed.

"He's crying," a raspy voice called out. "Look, he's balled up like a little bitty baby."

"You gonna try and say you didn't cry your first time in the joint?" said another prisoner.

"Beaver, why you always tryin' to take up for the new fish?" asked Raspy Voice.

"So he can have him some fresh booty," another prisoner joined in.

William squeezed his eyes shut. He imagined the blanket was a wall. That it shielded him from the evil surrounding him. The voices became muffled and began to fade. Somehow he managed to drift off to sleep.

When William opened his eyes it was dark. He heard whispers from the corner of the cell. Bare feet padded toward him. He held his breath and strained to hear what was being said. He pulled himself to an elbow just in time to see a dark shadow loom in front of him. Suddenly, someone draped a blanket over his chest and arms. It was pulled tight, pinning him to the bed. He struggled and opened his mouth to protest, but someone shoved a pillow over his face. He tried to kick but a body dove onto his legs, crushing his recent injury.

William screamed inside the pillow. He moaned and struggled, but it was no use. There were too many of them and they were too strong. Something smashed into his ribs. Pain shot through to his liver. He gasped and tried to suck air through the plastic pillow. More blows rained down on him—his head, his ribs, his legs. The blows continued for what felt like days.

William's body became numb. He felt himself jerk with the impact of each blow, but he no longer felt the pain. His body was totally limp. His mind whirled. After a long eternity, the blows stopped. Someone tugged at his jumpsuit and it slid from his body. Rough hands flipped him onto his stomach.

William squeezed his eyes shut and screamed a silent cry.

CHAPTER NINETEEN

9:30 A.M.
Tuesday, January 4, 2005
Magnolia Parish, Southeastern Louisiana

It wasn't until the first week of January that Dawn received a fax from the phone company. "Look," she said, showing me a long list of telephone numbers. "These are all the calls made to the church. Of them all, this number keeps repeating the most, 555-3085."

"Any calls to the church on the Thursday night?"

Dawn moved her finger up and down the pages. "No. The latest call on Thursday is at 4:55 P.M. In fact, there are no calls to the church after 5:00 P.M., so that must be the time God shuts down for the day." Dawn ran a reverse look-up on the number. "It's not a land line. Gotta be a cell number."

"How're we going to trace it?"

Dawn shrugged. "Call it."

I pulled my cell phone from my pocket and flipped it open. I punched in the number and waited. After the sixth ring, the voicemail picked up. *"A Blessed day to you. You have reached the voicemail of Father Isaac Stewart . . ."* I snapped my phone shut. "Get on the horn and get a subpoena for that number; it's Isaac's cell."

"What company do we send it to?"

"It looks like a MagnoTele number."

Dawn snatched up the receiver and called the local Magno-

144

Tele office. A clerk confirmed that the prefix was one assigned to their phones. "Bingo, you're good," Dawn said. She then called Laci at the District Attorney's Office. After a brief conversation, she turned to me. "She'll have it done this afternoon and fax it over to MagnoTele."

I studied the list of numbers. "We need to call these numbers and speak to everyone who called the church."

"Why?"

"To find out whatever we can about this cult and that dead girl."

Dawn and I categorized all the numbers on the sheet and found that there were a total of twenty-two different numbers. We ran reverse look-ups on each of the numbers. None of them were listed in the phone directory.

"These aren't all cell numbers," Dawn said. "So what's the deal?"

"Isaac seems very secretive."

"Maybe he requires his parishioners to keep their numbers unlisted."

"You could be right." I tore the sheet in half. "You call the numbers on the top and I'll take the bottom."

"And say what?"

"Get as much information as you can about the church and Isaac. See if they'll agree to speak to us in person." I took my list into a neighboring office and settled in for the day. I made call after call and met with the same results—a relentless unwillingness to talk. My stomach began to growl and I checked the clock. 1:30 P.M. I walked into our office and found Dawn on the phone. "But ma'am," she was saying, "someone in your home called that number . . . I understand, but your number is on the phone records from the church . . . right, that means the call came from your house." Dawn rolled her eyes at me and pursed her lips. "Okay, well, thanks anyway, ma'am." She smashed the phone down. "These people are brainwashed like you wouldn't believe!"

"I guess Isaac has them scared into thinking if they say anything about him they'll go to hell." I dropped my half of the list on the desk. "Let's go to lunch."

8:45 A.M.
Friday, January 21, 2005
Magnolia Parish, Southeastern Louisiana
Dawn danced into the office and held a fax from MagnoTele high in the air. "Victory is mine!"

I turned away from the computer. "Please don't make me beg again."

"I won't." She plopped into a chair and smoothed the phone record on the desk. "Okay, on Thursday, November 18, 2004, at 8:47 P.M., someone called Isaac's cellular phone from 555-0066. I ran a reverse look-up. Do you want to know if I got a hit on the number?"

"Any day now."

"I did—Ray Broussard. He lives up in Château, at 1704 Ditch Blvd."

"Ray Broussard? Isn't he the guard at the courthouse?"

Dawn walked around the desk and leaned over me. The fragrance on her neck tickled my nostrils. She accessed the employee information file on our sheriff's office computer and searched for Ray Broussard. His name appeared, along with the same number and address as the Ray in question. She whistled. "It is the same Ray."

"Let's drive up and have a visit with him."

CHAPTER TWENTY

6:30 A.M.
Tuesday, January 4, 2005
Cote Blanche Detention Center

William lay in a heap on his bunk. His throat burned and the sour smell of vomit clung to the air. Someone had draped a blanket over his nude body. He didn't have the strength to pull his jumpsuit back on. The very thought of moving caused his entire body to scream with pain. He stared unblinking into the darkness. He tried to think, but couldn't. His mind was numb. He couldn't focus. He wanted to fade away . . . to just die.

William was still in that position the next morning when the guard opened the cell door and announced it was time for breakfast. William didn't move.

"Hey, you—get up." The guard nudged William. William groaned. The guard pulled the cover away from William and recoiled in horror. "Jesus Christ!"

William's eyes didn't move, didn't blink. They were dry and empty. The guard spun around and pointed a finger at the fifteen prisoners who stood against the bars. "Who's responsible for this?"

William heard a chorus of *I don't know*s. Someone snickered. The guard called for a medic over his radio and within seconds one rushed in carrying a satchel.

"What happened?" the medic asked.

"I don't know. Just found him here, covered in bruises, blood, and vomit. He hasn't moved and he's just been . . . like . . . he's just staring."

The medic shined a light in William's face. He asked William if he knew where he was. William just stared. The medic's voice was muffled and he moved in slow motion.

"He's in shock," the medic said. "We need to get him back to the hospital."

Several guards entered the room and escorted the other prisoners out. Two guards stood by until ambulance personnel rolled a stretcher into the cell. William whimpered when they slid him onto a spine board and then placed him on the stretcher.

He groaned with every jostle of the ambulance as they sped toward the hospital. When they arrived, the back doors flung open and the medics released the stretcher from the clamps that secured it. They slid it out. The metal legs opened with a clank and there was a slight jerk as the wheels came to rest on the ground.

William's head spun. His breath came in gasps. Sweat oozed from his body like a saturated sponge being stepped on. He stared at the bright sky until the ceiling of the hospital came into view. Florescent lights flashed by and the wheels rattled as the nurses rushed William down the long hallway. His body trembled. Someone stabbed a needle into his arm. He felt a burning sensation as the injection entered his skin. His eyelids began to sink. They grated against his dry eyeballs. He fought to keep them open. More and more weight piled atop them and they slowly clanked shut. The voices and beeping of equipment became a drone. He felt himself slipping . . .

★ ★ ★ ★ ★

8:17 A.M.
Tuesday, January 18, 2005
Cote Blanche General Hospital

Two weeks after he had been hospitalized a nurse walked in the hospital room and approached William's bedside. He turned away, shamefaced.

"Are you okay?" she asked in a soothing voice.

William stared at the wall and didn't answer.

The nurse moved the handcuffs and gently massaged his wrists. She then moved to his legs. "How's that? Does that feel better?"

William didn't speak.

The doctor walked in and dropped a clipboard in William's lap. "Okay, you're ready to go. Just sign here."

William took the pen and scribbled his signature. The nurse motioned with her head and the doctor followed her to a corner of the room. Her voice was low, but William could hear everything she said.

"Doctor, I don't think he's ready. He hasn't spoken a word since he got here."

The doctor shrugged his shoulders. "I wouldn't talk either if I were in his shoes. We've done our job. He's healed up great, he's eating again, and his strength is returning. There's no reason to keep him here any longer. Besides, he's due in court on Friday."

"I think maybe he needs some mental help, some emotional support. He hasn't fully recovered from his ordeal. He's been through a lot, you know."

The doctor walked away. "Why don't you find a stray puppy to adopt," he called over his shoulder, "and leave the murderers to the police?"

★ ★ ★ ★ ★

Two hours later, William leaned over and stepped out of the prison van. Chains and shackles clanked with each move he made. He hesitated outside the van and stared at the entrance to the jail. Just the sight of the place spawned a sickening feeling in the pit of his stomach. The guard gave him a shove. "Get inside."

They led him down the same corridor. He trembled uncontrollably. Sweat poured from his palms and splashed to the floor. He kept his eyes fixed on his feet and didn't look up until the guard in front of him opened a door. They led him into a plush office. Thick carpet covered the cement floor and a large oak desk squatted at the center of the room. A mammoth of a man sat behind the desk, arms crossed, eyes piercing. "Sit down, Mr. Chandler."

William sat across from the large man. His legs jumped. He tried to quell the fear that flooded his body with every beat of his heart.

"I'm Warden Bouzigard. I want you to know that I personally investigated the incident that occurred in your cell. I interviewed every prisoner in there, but no one confessed and no one saw anything." He slid a piece of paper toward William. "Do you care to write a statement about what happened?"

William just stared down at the paper. Several minutes went by.

"Okay, I guess that means no." The warden stood and motioned for the guard. "Get him out of here."

William stood to his feet and the guards led him to a six-by-eight solid cell with a single bed in the corner. There was a small stainless-steel toilet at one end. "You'll be in solitary for most of your stay here. The only time you'll be exposed to other prisoners is during chow and showers."

William stood while the guards released his hands and feet.

He jumped in his skin when the door clanked shut behind him. He sank to the bed and lay trembling for hours. In the distance, loud laughter echoed throughout the prison. Someone screamed. Metal clanked against metal. Each sound caused him to jerk and each time he closed his eyes he expected someone to strap him down. Somewhere in the darkness, he finally faded into slumber . . .

He was in the forest. There stood his dad, unaware, just beneath the killer tree. He screamed for his dad to move, but nothing came out. His dad smiled. Just as the tree fell to the ground, William was transformed to the inside of his Thunderbird and plunged over the cliff. He was trapped. He heard laughter. Whispers. A voice whispered in his ear. It was a familiar voice. It said over and over, "You ready, Will?"

William jerked to a seated position in his bed. Although it was cool in the cell, his jumpsuit was drenched. He felt his crotch area and realized he had wet himself. With hands that trembled, William removed his jumpsuit and washed it in the toilet water. He wrung it out and squeezed back into it, then crawled back into bed.

Some hours later, a guard opened the door and motioned for him to exit. "Time for your shower."

The guard handed William a fresh bar of soap, fresh jumpsuit, washcloth, and a large cotton towel.

William inched his way into the steamy shower room. There were men everywhere. The noise was deafening. He stared at the ground and moved through the fog to a showerhead that was unoccupied. He slowly removed his jumpsuit and scrubbed his body down. He didn't avert his eyes from the aqua-colored ceramic tiles.

William had been so preoccupied with scrubbing that he hadn't noticed someone was behind him until he felt a hand on his shoulder. He jerked around and felt the blood drain from his face. Beaver was standing there with a towel wrapped around his waist. His long, black hair was wet and plastered against his head. The scar on his face glistened. William shrunk back.

Beaver raised his hands. "I'm here to apologize about what happened." He looked around. "Jed Clement is the one who set this thing in motion against you. He's the bad ass in this place. The other guys, they just went along because they're scared of Jed."

William grabbed his towel and dried off. He stepped to the side and pulled on his jumpsuit. Beaver followed him. "Watch your back. Jed's saying he ain't done with you. Said he's gonna make you his permanent bitch. You see," he paused long enough for one of the prisoners to walk past, "there's a code among convicts. Anyone who hurts children and women, they get it in the joint. I've seen a lot of those types in my day, even hurt a few of them myself, but you . . . you don't look like that type."

William hurried out of the shower and into the safety of the guard's presence. The guard led him back to his cell and he crawled into bed to stare wide-eyed into the darkness.

9:20 A.M.
Friday, January 21, 2005
Cote Blanche Detention Center
The guard unlocked the door to the cell. "Get up. You have court this morning."

William stood and went through the routine. The guard escorted him to the corridor where a dozen other prisoners were shackled and ready to be transported to the courthouse. Jed Clement leaned against the wall and winked as he passed. William dropped his head. The chains that bound him rattled as his entire body trembled.

Thunder sounded outside and lightning flashed through the

wired windows that lined the upper walls of the corridor. The guards shuffled the prisoners through the rain and into the prison van. William slid into one of the seats and scooted against the window. Several prisoners stacked into the seat and smashed against him. Cool water dripped from his hair and down his face. He wiped his eyes with his sleeve and buried his nose there to mask the musky steam of too many filthy and wet prisoners being crammed into a confined space.

As William waited, someone behind him whispered. At first, he couldn't make out what the person was saying, but then the familiar sound caused the hair on his neck to stand up. His bladder burned with anxiety.

"You ready, Will?"

William stared at the floor and tried to block out the sound. It was no use. Over and over he whispered. Other prisoners hollered and jostled each other, the van's engine roared, and the weather outside added its own noise to the mix, but that whisper cut through it all and stabbed at his manhood.

William breathed a sigh of relief when they reached the courthouse and he was able to slide out of that corner. The rain had ceased. All the prisoners were led along a wet sidewalk to a door at the back of the courthouse. Six prison guards performed the escort, while two other guards kept onlookers back and cleared the way to the courthouse. Once inside, the prisoners were cramped into an elevator and brought to the second floor. They were then shuffled into a large courtroom and seated in the jury box.

One by one the prisoners were called before the court to enter their plea. William shivered when some of the charges were announced. There were several murderers, two drug dealers, and a few burglars. Beaver was in for growing marijuana. He pled not guilty and strode back to the jury box to reclaim his seat. He nodded at William. William looked away.

The bailiff called out William's name next. He stood and shuffled up to the microphone stand that was positioned in front of the judge's bench.

"In the matter of State of Louisiana versus William Chandler, you're charged with first-degree murder. How do you plead?"

William stared across the courtroom at the clerk. She was tall with dark hair and she wore a long dress. She read from a legal-looking paper that she held with painted fingers. Bright red . . . like the color of blood. William glanced at Esther Diebold, who had moved beside him. She pursed her lips and signaled with a solemn nod. "Go on, you need to say it."

William leaned close to the microphone. He opened his mouth to speak, but nothing came out. He tried a second time, but still nothing. Esther stepped forward. "My client pleads not guilty, Your Honor."

"Your client needs to say it."

William cleared his throat. "Not . . . not guilty."

Judge Raymond Rudolph shuffled some papers around and leaned to one side to retrieve a calendar. The robe he wore floated over his tiny frame. His black hair was speckled with silver and his dark eyes were sunken. Although his face was pale and he appeared frail, there was a fire in his eyes that William believed could burn a forest to the ground.

"Okay, my next trial month is June. We'll fix this matter for trial on Tuesday, June 21." Judge Rudolph handed the calendar to his clerk. "Give notice to the prisoner." He turned to William. "Take your notice and have a seat in the jury box with the rest of the prisoners."

William shuffled to the clerk and took the piece of paper she handed him. He turned and shuffled back to the jury box. He squeezed between two of the prisoners and glanced out at the audience. His heart thumped like a battle drum in his chest when he saw her. She sat between her mother and father in a pew located at the back of the large courtroom. Her eyes were aimed at the floor in front of her. During the rest of his time there, he never took his eyes off her and she never took her eyes off the floor—until the clerk called her name.

"Claire Chandler."

Claire stood and walked down the opening between the long row of pews and the far wall of the courthouse. An older man waited for her at the end of that long walk. He wore a dark suit and had a thick file tucked under his arm. He held open the small gate that separated the general audience from the proceedings area and Claire walked through. He invited her to take a seat beside him at the lawyers' table.

Emotions flooded William's every fiber. *Why won't she look at me?*

The prosecutor stood. He was tall with bushy eyebrows. A permanent scowl was etched into his weather-beaten face. His paunchy belly pushed the front of his coat open. "Your Honor, pursuant to an agreement between the State and Mrs. Chandler and her attorney, Mr. Wyatt, we would move to continue this matter without date."

The judge glanced at Claire's attorney. "Any objection, Mr. Wyatt?"

Mr. Wyatt stood. "None, Your Honor. My client intends to cooperate fully with the district attorney's office and, in exchange for her truthful testimony, they agree to dismiss all charges against her."

"Very well. Next."

William's jaw dropped. He watched through watery eyes as Claire and her lawyer walked to the back of the courthouse. Her parents rose from their seats and followed them out the door. William's eyes remained fixed on the door long after it was shut. A tear dripped from his eye and he quickly rubbed his face on the shoulder of his jumpsuit.

Just as he turned away from the door, it burst open again. Claire's lawyer walked in carrying some papers. He walked up to the bailiff and gave the papers to him. He spoke quietly to the bailiff and pointed at William before turning to leave.

William's pulse quickened as the bailiff approached. *Was this a message from Claire?* How he longed to hear from his wife, to hear her say everything was okay, that she loved him. He shook his mournful head to dismiss the last words she'd spoken to him, *Slow down! You're going to kill us!*

The bailiff handed William the papers and said, "You've been served."

William cast a curious glance at the papers in his hand and then jumped to his feet. "What the hell is this?"

The judge smashed his gavel down. There was venom in his eyes. "Sit down!"

William sank to his seat. "Sorry, sir."

"Another outburst like that and I'll find you in contempt!"

William nodded, but he wasn't listening. He scanned the divorce papers, searching for a reason. His heart sank when he found it: *adultery.*

CHAPTER TWENTY-ONE

Friday, January 21, 2005
Magnolia Parish Courthouse

Dawn and I drove to the courthouse and found Ray Broussard seated near the metal detectors. He rose when we walked up. "Hi, detectives. It's a pleasure to see y'all."

"Hey, Ray." I shook his hand. "Been busy?"

He smiled. "We're never busy on Fridays. What division are y'all heading to?"

"Actually, Ray, we need to speak with you."

Ray's face paled. He wrung his hands and glanced about. "Well, I can't leave my post."

"It's okay," Dawn said, "we've already called your supervisor. They're sending someone to replace you."

Ray's replacement arrived five minutes later. We secured his revolver in the lockbox and walked to a private office in the courthouse. When we were seated around the table, Dawn led the interview. She pulled out a *Miranda* rights form and read Ray his rights.

"Am I being arrested?" There was a tremor in Ray's voice.

"At the moment, we only need to ask you some questions."

"Sure, you know I'll cooperate in any way I can. What are the questions about?"

Dawn leaned forward. "Do you know Rosalie McKenzie?"

"Is that what this is about?"

"Yes, sir."

Ray nodded. "It's sad, really."

"What do you mean?"

"She thought she was ready, she thought her faith was strong enough."

"Strong enough for what?"

"To be healed."

"Healed? What was wrong with her?"

"You see, the church I belong to—"

"Magnolia Faith?" I asked.

Ray smiled. "That's it. Father Isaac is a wonderful man of God. He preaches faith healing. His prayers have healed many people. He even brought one person back to life. Rosalie got sick and she wanted to believe in the Lord for her recovery."

"Wait, let's back up," Dawn said. "You said he brought someone back to life. Who?"

Ray shook his head. "No one really knows. Father Isaac is big into confidentiality."

"Let's get back to Rosalie. Did she die under Father Isaac's care?"

Ray hung his head. "No. Father Isaac was out of town on business. Had he been here, there's no doubt in my mind he would've healed Rosalie."

"Ray," I said, "you expect us to believe that this Isaac Stewart heals people?"

"Well, God is doing the healing, but he's using Father Isaac. They work together like doctors and medicine."

"Isaac's a fraud and he's brainwashing all of you. He's nothing more than a common thief."

Ray's eyes were wide. "Please, Detective, don't mock Father Isaac. He's a man of God and God will—"

"I know, I know . . . devour my flesh. Bullshit. You're a law enforcement officer, Ray. You hold a position of public trust.

How'd you get sucked into this scam?"

Tears welled up in Ray's eyes and streamed down his face. "Oh, Detective, you're a good man. Why are you saying this?"

"Because it's true," Dawn said. "Were you at the church several Wednesdays ago when Brandon and I went? It's like they were putting a hex on us or something."

"That was y'all?" Ray wiped his face with a stained sleeve. "I heard about it. I wasn't there because I work every Wednesday. They weren't putting a hex on y'all. They were praying for y'all."

I shook my head. "Look, Ray, just start from the top and tell us what happened regarding Rosalie McKenzie."

"Sure, Detective. Rosalie moved to Seasville at the beginning of the year. One day, she visited the church and she liked the atmosphere. She became a regular. Then, back about two weeks before she died, she became very ill. Father Isaac had been going back and forth from here to a church he was helping to form up north, so he left Brother Reggie in charge. We met with Rosalie and asked her if she wanted to go to the hospital. She said no. We even called an ambulance and she refused medical service." Ray pointed to the phone that hung near the door. "You can call them and check their records. They said if she refused medical treatment there was nothing they could do for her."

"What about her family?" Dawn asked.

"She didn't have any. We took turns praying for her. She was never alone. And then, I think it was Thursday afternoon, the Lord took her home."

"Where was Father Isaac when she died?" I asked.

"He was up north. I called him on his cell phone Thursday night and told him that Rosalie had died. He said he had to go back up north on Saturday, but that he would return on Sunday and pray to God to raise her from the dead. Before he could get here, y'all had already gotten there and took her body."

I raised a finger. "First off, who was with you at the house Thursday night?"

"Brother Reggie."

"Second, what were y'all taking out of the trailer?"

"Her personal belongings. She didn't have the faith to be healed, so we wanted to remove any signs of negativity. You see, once a person dies, it's no longer their faith that counts, but the faith of those who are praying for them. But if you leave anything that might possess her negative spirits, that could interfere with the prayers of the faithful."

"When y'all left the trailer Thursday, did anyone go back?"

"No."

I scrubbed my stubble until it burned. "Ray, if what you're saying is true, y'all were going to leave that girl lying dead in that trailer for three days before trying to bring her back from the dead. Don't you think that's a bit long?"

"Father Isaac said it could be done. He said he could raise a body from the grave even."

"Why didn't y'all bring Rosalie's body with y'all to the church, or someplace else?"

"We can't move a dead body—that would be against the law."

"But it's okay to let her die?"

"Detective, we have a right to our beliefs. If I choose faith healing as a means of medicine, no one can force me to do otherwise."

I nodded. "Okay, Ray. We're going to need a list of names and phone numbers of anyone who knew anything about Rosalie McKenzie's death."

Ray wrung his shaking hands. "I . . . I can't give out any information. It's church policy."

"I don't give a shit about church policy," I said. "You need to give me the names of everyone who knew about that girl's death."

"I'll get kicked out of the church."

"You could get fired for not cooperating with our investigation."

Ray pursed his lips. "Detective, I only have a few years left until I retire. I really need the health insurance. If I get fired, it'll—"

"You will get fired if you don't provide the information," I said. "So, cough it up or pack your shit."

Ray hesitated, then sighed. "Okay, if you're saying I have to."

"Yes, we need to be sure that nothing illegal took place."

Ray pulled a tattered miniature notebook from his shirt pocket. He began scribbling names and addresses. "There were only eight of us who went to the house. We took turns praying for her."

"Is that why there was so much traffic down her street?" Dawn asked.

Ray looked up. "What do you mean?"

"The neighbors said cars would come in and out of there, like they were working shifts."

"I guess so. We would go two at a time and pray for Rosalie for about three hours. That way, we could cover a whole day, without her being left alone. She died while me and Brother Reggie were with her."

I stared down at Ray. Tears crept down his face. I couldn't help but feel sorry for this misguided mamma's boy. He was a nice man, easily manipulated, always seeing the best in everyone. I took the page that Ray tore from his notebook and stood to walk out. "Let's go, Dawn."

"Am . . . am I gonna get in trouble?"

I stopped by the door and turned to face Ray. "The district attorney will probably want to bring this before the grand jury.

As long as you cooperate with them, I don't think you'll have anything to worry about."

10:30 A.M.

Monday, February 4, 2005

Magnolia Parish Courthouse

Case file in hand, Dawn and I walked through the doors of the Hickory Five Six DC to give our testimony to the grand jury. When we were done, we camped out in the hallway and watched as the eight members of the Magnolia Faith Church that Ray identified filed through the door one at a time and gave their testimony.

"What do you think they're saying in there?" Dawn asked.

I shrugged and stood to walk to the door. Outside in the courtyard were a few dozen people. They carried Bibles and stood with hands raised and eyes closed. "Do you see this shit?" I asked.

Dawn walked beside me. "You think their prayers can save them?"

"It didn't work when they prayed for Rosalie, so I don't know how they think it'll work now."

Toward the end of the day, the bailiff exited the courtroom and walked outside. We heard him call for Isaac Stewart. Within a minute, Isaac ambled up the steps, glided through the metal detectors, and swaggered by us. He stopped and looked right into my eyes. "I am an agent of wrath. In accordance with God's law, I will execute wrath upon him that doeth evil." He bowed and then walked abruptly into the courtroom.

Dawn shuddered. "That guy gives me the creeps."

I laughed. "Don't worry about him."

An hour later, Isaac walked out of the courthouse. He was met by cheers from the ever-growing crowd that had gathered outside. The cheers were followed by jeers and I looked up. Ray

Broussard stepped cautiously through the door. I walked over and escorted him to the courtroom. I stopped him outside the door. "How are things?"

"I got excommunicated."

"What does that mean?"

"They kicked me out of the church. Father Isaac said I was doomed to spend eternity in hell."

"Don't worry about him."

"But the Bible says if you go against a man of God that—"

"Ray, the operative part of that passage is a *man of God*. Isaac is not a man of God, so you have nothing to worry about."

Ray didn't look one bit relieved as he walked through the doors.

4:45 P.M.

After an agonizing wait, Nelly Wainwright exited the courthouse. She walked over to where Dawn and I sat and frowned. "They returned a No True Bill."

I nodded my resignation. "Isaac will feel unstoppable now."

"He told the grand jury that only God can judge him." Nelly sighed. "I thought they would return an indictment just because of that comment, but . . ."

"Well, we knew there was nothing we could charge them with," I said.

"Yeah, but my boss wanted to bring it before the grand jury to be sure."

I turned to Dawn. "I guess we'll get back to the humdrum of working car burglaries and shoplifting."

Dawn smiled. "I like humdrum."

CHAPTER TWENTY-TWO

9:20 A.M.

Friday, January 21, 2005

Cote Blanche Detention Center

William clutched the divorce petition in his hands. When he was alone in his cell again, he spread it open on the bed. At the top of the document were three names. The first was Claire's, listed under *Petitioner.* The next was his, listed under *Respondent.* The third name was listed under *Co-Respondent.* When he read the name, a wave of acid welled up from his stomach and burned his throat. He crumpled the pages and threw the petition across the room. "That *bitch!*" he bellowed. Like a wild lion first introduced to its cage, he paced in his cell. His mind raced. How could he convince Claire that this was a lie? He walked to the door and banged his fists against the screened window. "Guard! Hello! Guard!"

A uniformed guard sauntered over and peered through the little rectangular window. "What, you wet your bed again?"

William felt his face flush. He took a deep breath. "No, sir. I would like to make a phone call."

The guard hesitated. "Okay, just hang tight. I'll be back in a minute."

When the guard returned, he unlocked the cell door and led William to a narrow room. A long table lined one wall and there were a dozen chairs pushed under it. About a dozen phones were mounted to the wall. "You get ten minutes," the guard said.

William picked up the phone. A sticker on the wall informed him that calls had to be made collect. He dialed his home number and waited. It rang a dozen times, but no one answered. He then dialed his in-laws. His mother-in-law answered and the operator announced, *"You have a collect call from William Chandler, do you accept the charges for this call?"*

William held his breath. He could hear his mother-in-law talking to someone in the background. Suddenly, his father-in-law came on the phone and told the operator he would not accept the charges. William smashed the phone down.

"Hey!" The guard glared at him. "You want to buy that phone?"

"Sorry," William mumbled. He stood and walked back to his cell. He requested paper and a pen, but the guard denied his request.

Shower time came quick that night. William stepped into the shower room with Claire on his mind. He had to find a way to reach her, to explain things to her. He showered without thought to anything else. When he was done, he toweled off and collected his washcloth and bar of soap. He walked across the wet tiles to where his clean jumpsuit was folded on a shelf. His eyes were on the floor, and he stopped when he saw someone blocking his path. He slowly looked up. Jed Clement.

"You ready, Will?" Jed asked in his southern drawl.

William began to shake. Four of Jed's friends stood in a semi-circle behind Jed.

"You get to pick," Jed said. "You can go easy or you can go hard. If you go easy, it won't hurt as bad."

William stared from Jed to his cronies. He looked past them to where the guard was supposed to be—he wasn't. Trembling, William slowly removed his towel and turned around.

"Now you're learning," Jed said. "After I'm done with you, I might have to go pay that little wife of yours a visit, since I heard you call out your address in court. I can tell her how I made you my bitch. If she's good, I might let her be my bitch, too."

William's blood began to boil. He held both ends of the towel in his right hand. He glanced down and realized it hung like a sling. In one deft motion, he dropped the heavy bar of soap into the crook of the towel. No one seemed to notice. Suddenly, he spun toward Jed. As he spun, he caught sight of Jed's unsuspecting face. Jed had taken a step forward, his face cracked into a wide, toothless grin. When Jed realized what was happening, it was too late. William whipped the towel toward Jed and the large bar of soap smashed against Jed's temple. William's spinning motion drove it with such force that the sickening thump was heard above the flowing water and rowdy talk in the steamy shower.

Jed fell without making a sound. William lifted the towel to strike again, but Jed lay motionless. The prisoners stared with mouths open. William took a cautious step forward and they made room for him. He dropped his towel in the clothes hamper near the doorway and quickly pulled his jumpsuit on. He took a deep breath to calm his nerves and hurried out of the shower room.

"Y'all didn't see *shit*!" he heard Beaver tell the other prisoners behind him.

William almost collided with the guard.

"Where you going in such a hurry?"

William pointed back over his shoulder. "They're fighting in there."

The guard rushed into the shower room. Seconds later, William heard him yelling for someone to call a medic. Guards converged on the area and ushered the prisoners into their respective cells. Minutes later, sirens sounded outside and ambulance personnel rushed down the corridor. William stood on tiptoes and watched through his window as they wheeled Jed out. Jed's neck was in a brace and his eyes were closed. The left side of his temple was swollen.

William backed to his bunk and dropped in it. Had he killed Jed? He began to shake. They already had him charged with two murders he didn't commit. This would be easy for them to put together.

Within the hour, metal scraped metal as a guard slid the key in the hole. The door squeaked open and two guards walked in. "Warden wants to see you."

William walked on shaky legs to the warden's office. He sat across the desk and tried to keep his face expressionless.

"What happened in the shower?" The Warden's voice was calm.

William wondered what he already knew. "I don't know. I heard someone arguing. It wasn't my business. I walked out and that's all I know."

"Who was arguing?"

"I don't know."

"Surely you saw something."

"Nothing. I was looking down."

"Would it surprise you to learn that the man who's lying on death's bed is the same man suspected of attacking you?"

"No."

The warden raised his left eyebrow. "What do you mean by *no*?"

"The guy's trouble, so I'm not surprised he was involved in a stabbing."

"Stabbing?"

William feigned ignorance. "You said somebody's about to die. I figured you meant they were stabbed. I've seen movies where prisoners make knives out of—"

The warden waved his hand. "Get him out of here. He doesn't know shit. Bring the next one in."

"That was the last of them, sir."

"Bullshit! Somebody must've seen something!"

William exhaled silently and relief flooded over him. The guard escorted him back down the hallway and when they passed the cell where William had spent his first night, he glanced over. The prisoners stared wide-eyed. His eyes met Beaver's, and Beaver nodded his approval.

11:00 A.M.
Sunday, November 13, 2005
Cote Blanche Detention Center
Esther Diebold visited William several times each week in the months following the arraignment. She had been able to get the trial date continued twice in order to buy some time to prepare a defense for him. She spent countless hours preparing him for the cross-examination that would ensue once he took the stand in his own defense. On her last visit, two days before the trial was to commence, she fired question after question at William, who seemed distracted.

"Come on, William! The trial starts on the fifteenth. Pay attention to my questions."

He stood from the table and walked around the prison library. "Are you sure you've mailed all the letters?"

Esther sighed. "Every last one of them."

William was thoughtful. "You think she read them?"

"Look, forget about Claire for the moment. You need to focus on this trial. If you're found guilty, there will be no Claire. Your only chance of getting her back is to win this trial—"

"I'm gonna win. There's no way they can convict an innocent man."

"William, how many times do I have to tell you? The state has a strong case against you. You have to take this serious."

"I've been in jail for almost twelve months. You don't think I'm taking this serious? Of course I'm taking it serious! I just believe in the justice system. I believe there's no way a jury of my peers will convict me for something I didn't do."

"Well, sit down so we can work on giving them a reasonable doubt. The judge denied my last motion for a continuance, so, ready or not, we go in two days."

"Two days until I'm free." William reclaimed his seat and leaned far back, crossing his hands behind his head. "You know, in nine days it'll mark a year since I've been in this dreaded place. A year since I've held my wife. A year since Gracie died. A year—"

"Will, I already told you; you need to prepare yourself in the event the jury returns a guilty verdict."

"Oh, I'm getting out." William pounded his fist on the table. "And when I do, I'll dedicate my life to seeing that Detective London pays for what he did to me!"

"For now, let's stick with the case. Okay, let's go over this again." Esther flipped through her notes and found the page she wanted. "Mr. Chandler, do you know Sarah Boudreaux?"

"Yep."

Esther glared at William with her cold, gray eyes.

"I know, I know, it's just hard calling you a sir."

"Focus. Now answer the question like I'm the prosecutor who wants to see you put to death for a crime you didn't commit."

"Yes, sir."

"How do you know Sarah Boudreaux?"

"I had an affair with her."

"Was she married at the time?"

"Yes, sir."

"Didn't you try to get Sarah to leave her husband?"

"Yes, sir."

"Did she ever leave him?"

"Not while we were seeing each other."

"Were you married at the time?"

"No, sir."

"Isn't it true that you met Claire while you were dating Sarah?"

"Yes, sir."

"Isn't it true that the only reason you became involved with Claire was to make Sarah jealous in hopes she would leave her husband for you?"

"No, sir."

"Oh, it's not? Well, isn't it also true that you lied to Claire about your relationship with Sarah?"

"I didn't tell her right away, but I didn't lie about it."

"Well, isn't that the same as lying?"

"When it looked like things were getting serious between me and Claire, I broke it off with Sarah and I told Claire everything."

"Right, and you and Claire went off and got married and lived happily ever after."

"Until you came along."

"William!"

William smiled. "I'm just messing with you, Esther. I like it when you get pissed."

"Just answer the question."

"Yes, Claire and I got married."

"How long have you two been married?"

"Just over eleven years."

"How long were you and Claire married before you started sleeping with Sarah again?"

"I didn't start sleeping with Sarah again."

"Oh, so you never stopped sleeping with Sarah?"

"Yes, sir, I stopped sleeping with Sarah when I met Claire. I've never been with her again."

Esther jumped up from her chair. "That's much better than the last time. Okay, let's continue. Uh, now you heard Sarah's testimony, right? Because you get to sit here and listen to everything that's going on."

"Yes, sir."

"You heard her say that you and she had an affair in October, just one month before you pushed your wife into Skybald River. Isn't that right?"

"Are you asking me if I heard her say that, or if it really happened?" William could see that Esther was pleased. He smiled to himself. *All her hard work is paying off.*

"Isn't it true that you and Sarah Boudreaux had an affair just one month before you pushed your wife into Skybald River?"

"No to both questions; I did not push my wife into Skybald River and I did not have an affair with Sarah Boudreaux one month before the incident."

"So, you deny meeting Sarah at the Shrimper's Lounge last October?"

"No, sir."

"Oh, so you did meet her there?"

"I didn't meet her there, like we would have planned it. I was there with some friends. She showed up later."

"Isn't it true that you called her to meet you there?"

"No, sir."

"So, if she said that, what, she's lying?"

"Yes, sir."

"What reason does Sarah Boudreaux have to come into court today and lie? I mean, we know your reason for lying . . ."

William sat there and stared up at Esther.

"Good," she praised. "I'm going to object when he does stuff like that. You just sit quiet. Okay, moving along . . . isn't it true that you and Sarah left the bar together?"

"No, sir."

"Well, didn't you hear the testimony of your friends, Wayne and Trevor, who testified that they saw you two leave the bar together?"

"I left and she followed me outside. When we got to the car—"

"Make sure you look at the jury when you're telling this part," Esther said.

William nodded. "When we got to the car, she stopped me and asked if I wanted to hang out. I told her no, that I was married and didn't do that sort of thing. She said I did it when she was married and that it wasn't fair—"

"Let's skip ahead. Didn't you two go back to her place and rekindle the old flame?"

"No, sir."

"Oh, so you're saying she's lying about that, too?"

"Yes, sir."

"Did you tell your wife you ran into Sarah Boudreaux?"

"No, sir."

"Why not?"

"It was nothing worth telling."

"Isn't it true that the reason you didn't tell her was because on that very night you went back to Sarah's house and had sex with her?"

"I already answered that question."

"Well, clear this up for me. On the night that you and Sarah met at the Shrimper's Lounge, was she married?"

"No, she was divorced."

"So, the only thing that now stood between you and Sarah being together was your wife, Claire, and your baby, Gracie—isn't that true?"

"No, sir."

"Well, isn't that why you murdered your helpless baby and pushed your wife into the killer rapids of Skybald River?"

"I didn't kill Gracie and I didn't push Claire into the river." William hung his head and a tear tugged at the corner of his eye. He sighed. "I'm ready for this to be over."

Esther walked over and patted his back. "That's enough for today. You'll do fine."

William wiped his eye. "Still not able to find Jake and Gaby Arthur?"

"Our investigator couldn't come up with anything, so I spoke with Detective London." Esther grunted. "At first he said he didn't need to talk to them. I told him we needed them, but he told me he wasn't going to do my work for me. Then he said he ran their names through his computer and couldn't find any such people. He also said he spoke with the Rangers and they said they have no record of a Jake or Gaby Arthur camping there."

"That's it!" William jumped to his feet. "They used aliases! We need to get out there and find out who they really are."

Esther sighed. "I'm sorry, Will, but there's just no time. We need to focus on what we have in front of us and hope for the best."

"I understand. Look, I appreciate all that you're doing. You're really a good lawyer."

Esther shrugged, started to say something, but paused.

"What is it?"

"I don't know." Esther pointed to the case file. "The prosecutor told me he's going to drop a bombshell during the trial. When I reminded him of our Open File Agreement, he told me I had everything he had, and that the information was right there in front of me."

William scowled. "I read every page of that file and I didn't notice anything we haven't covered yet."

"Neither did I."

"He's probably bluffing."

"I sure hope so."

William helped Esther pack up her files and then signaled to the guard that he was ready.

"Just in time for lunch," the guard said.

William waved to Esther and followed the guard to the cafeteria. He snatched up a tray and joined Beaver in the long line of red jumpsuits.

"I hear your trial's coming up," Beaver said.

"Yep. I just want the damn thing to be over."

"Don't forget about me when you're out in the free world."

"You know I won't."

They had almost made it to the food when Jed Clement shuffled past with his tray. His head was still bald and the large scar where the doctors had performed surgery to relieve the swelling in his brain was clearly visible. William nodded a greeting. Guilt tugged at his heart. "How you doing, Jed?"

"O'tay," Jed slurred in automatic fashion, like a child programmed to answer that sort of question. He shuffled past without looking up.

"You sure stopped that asshole's clock."

William shook his head. "I didn't mean for that to happen to him."

"To hell with him. He had it coming."

CHAPTER TWENTY-THREE

10:30 A.M.

Thursday, November 17, 2005

Magnolia Parish Sheriff's Office Substation

"Yes, ma'am, two adults and one child. That's correct, from November 18 to November 20. Thank you." I hung up the phone.

"Am I invited?" Dawn was stretched out on her stomach on the desk; propped up on her elbows, chin resting in her palms.

"Sorry, this isn't a business trip."

"Ah, pleasure trip—my favorite! I'll be packed in an hour."

"I'd love to have you come along, but this one's for my wife and daughter."

Dawn squinted her eyes and tapped her temple with a forefinger. "Let's see, what could be the occasion?"

I leaned back in my chair and crossed my arms. "Lunch says you can't guess it."

"Samantha's birthday?"

"Nope."

"How many guesses do I get?"

"One more."

Dawn rolled to her back and swung her legs over the edge of the desk. "Don't think for a second I don't know what's going on," she said. "You're scheduling a vacation for your anniversary."

"Does that make me a good husband?"

175

"Maybe."

"What?"

"Making the reservation doesn't make you a good husband. Keeping it does."

I nodded. "This year will be different. Nothing will stop me from keeping my plans."

Dawn struck a seductive pose. "Not even me?"

"Not even you."

She pouted. "You're really no good for my self-esteem."

I shook my head. "That's one thing you don't lack."

"Where're you going, anyway?"

"Gulf Shores, Alabama. That's where we met."

"Aren't they still rebuilding from Hurricane Katrina?"

"They've already restored the beach and there's this awesome new condo that overlooks the Gulf. I've reserved a room for three nights. It'll be great."

"When are you leaving?"

"Tomorrow after work."

"You staying there Sunday night, too?"

I nodded.

"What about work?"

"After tomorrow, I'm off until Tuesday."

"I'm jealous!"

11:00 A.M.

I drove home for lunch and found Debbie on the living room sofa. Her eyes were fixed on the television. She didn't even look up at me when I walked in. "What're you watching?"

Debbie pressed an index finger to her lips and pointed to the screen. "Listen."

A reporter stood in front of an old courthouse. The bubble at the bottom of the screen told me the location was Cote Blanche Parish. *"The trial began today for a Mississippi man accused of kill-*

ing his own baby and an aged Vietnam War veteran, who likely was a witness to the baby's murder. William Chandler faces the death penalty in connection with the murders, which occurred in a remote section of the Skybald National Forest, not far from where his father died twenty years prior. I spoke with a psychologist who said that returning to the location might have triggered feelings that were suppressed for many years and could have led to the killings. The first witness in the case was Chandler's wife, who was called to the witness stand by the prosecution. She remained on the witness stand throughout most of the morning and is expected to return to the stand after lunch, at which time she'll be cross-examined by her husband's attorney, Public Defender Esther Diebold."

"Oh my God, how could anyone kill their own child?" Debbie's eyes were moist.

"There're a lot of evil people in this world." I leaned over and pressed the power button on the remote.

"Why'd you turn it off?" Debbie protested.

I sat beside her and took her hands in mine. "Don't make plans for this weekend."

"Why not?"

"I already have. I need you to pack clothes for you and Samantha for three nights."

"Where are we going?"

"That's a surprise."

Debbie's eyes lit up, but a cloud of doubt cast a shadow across them. "What if you get called out to something?"

"I've already cleared it with the captain. We're leaving Friday night and not returning until Monday evening. He knows not to bother me."

"But what if some emergency arises?"

"They'll call out someone else."

"What if they have another murder?"

"Baby, we're leaving . . . period. I've already made the reservations."

"You made reservations last year, too."

"What happened last year will never happen again. If I have to, I'll quit my job to keep these reservations."

"You promise?"

"Cross my heart."

CHAPTER TWENTY-FOUR

Thursday, November 17, 2005
Cote Blanche Courthouse

Esther Diebold was right—it took all of three days to pick a jury. Finally, on Thursday, opening arguments began. William sat at the defendant's table beside Esther. She had purchased enough dress clothes for him to last two weeks. He wore a light blue shirt with black slacks. He smiled as he thought back to their conversation earlier in the week.

"These will make you look more presentable," she'd said. "Red jumpsuits don't look good on you."

"Compliments of the state?" William had asked when Esther handed him the hangers of clothes.

"Compliments of the 'I believe you're innocent fund.' "

"Thanks. That means a lot to me."

Esther had tried to ignore the moment. "I got you a belt, but they wouldn't let me give it to you. Regulations."

William glanced over his shoulder. Every seat in the courthouse was taken. Reporters were crammed into their seats, waiting with poised pens.

The prosecutor stood and walked to the lectern. He introduced himself as Assistant District Attorney Allen Crochet. While he offered his opening statement, William watched the jurors. There were eight men and six women. The average age had to be mid-forties. They listened attentively and a few of

179

them raised an eyebrow when Assistant Crochet mentioned William's fingerprints on the murder weapon.

When Assistant Crochet was done, he strolled over to where William sat. "And at the conclusion of the trial," he said, "you'll find that the state has met its burden and has proven beyond a reasonable doubt that *this* man"—he pointed in William's face—"committed the heinous crime of first-degree murder by smothering his very own daughter and the crime of second-degree murder by stabbing an innocent homeless man in the chest. Thank you." Crochet remained there and stared into William's eyes for a few long seconds before returning to his table.

Esther Diebold walked to the lectern. She introduced herself and then walked behind William. She placed both hands on William's shoulders. "Ladies and gentlemen, my client and I don't have to prove or disprove anything. The state has the burden of proving every element of each crime for which they have Mr. Chandler charged. Additionally, it's Mr. Chandler's right not to take the witness stand. In most cases, defendants don't take the witness stand and jurors can't hold that against them because it's their right not to. Now, why don't defendants take the witness stand?"

Esther moved back to the lectern. "There could be a number of reasons why a defendant wouldn't take the witness stand, and every one of those reasons would ultimately point back to one main reason: that in taking the witness stand, they subject themselves to cross-examination by the state's prosecutors. And Assistant District Attorney Allen Crochet is a fine prosecutor. He is absolutely a prosecutor to be feared." Esther held an open hand in William's direction. "Ladies and gentlemen, you will hear from Mr. Chandler during the course of this trial. The reason is simple . . . he has nothing to hide. He's not worried about being cross-examined by the feared prosecutor because he has nothing to hide. You can't distort the truth, ladies and gentlemen! The state will try, but at the end of the day you will all realize that a grave miscarriage of justice has occurred. You will find that there has been a rush to judgment, both on the part of the police who investigated the crime, and on the part of the district attorney's office. There's no doubt in my mind you'll find that my client is not guilty and you'll force the police to get out there and do their jobs and find the real person responsible for this horrible crime."

When Esther was back beside William, Judge Rudolph turned to Assistant Crochet. "State, rebuttal?"

"Briefly, Your Honor. Ladies and gentlemen, there is only one killer and he's sitting right there in front of you. Of course they're going to try to say there's someone else. They have to. I mean, what else could they say? Use your common sense while listening to the testimony and examining the evidence that will be presented in this trial. Don't be fooled by their tactics. That's all."

William leaned over and whispered in Esther's ear. "It doesn't look good for us."

"Relax," Esther whispered back. "The opening statements aren't evidence."

Judge Rudolph asked Crochet if he was ready to call his first witness.

"We are, Your Honor. State calls Claire Chandler to the stand."

William's heart began to race. He looked to the back of the courtroom and watched as the door opened and his wife entered. She wore her navy blue business suit. It was tailored and fit her smooth curves like a latex glove. The last time she'd worn that suit was over two years ago, when she and William had gone to supper and she announced she was pregnant. *What is she trying to tell me?* His eyes remained fixed on her. She stopped to be sworn by the clerk and then sat in the witness chair.

Allen Crochet made her say her name and address. He then questioned her about their reason for going camping and what happened out at the campsite. Claire stayed on the witness stand up until noon, recounting every detail and horror of that fateful camping trip.

"I tender the witness," Crochet said when a tired Claire answered his last question.

"We're going to break for lunch and when we return, Mrs. Diebold, you can cross-examine the witness. Court's in recess until one-thirty."

Everyone stood while the jury walked out. William's eyes remained on Claire until she left the courtroom. He sank to his chair. Not once during her testimony had Claire looked at him. She seemed so cold.

The young jailer, Ashley, and the old-timer walked up to him.

"Time to go to lunch," the old-timer said.

"I'm not hungry."

"We gotta bring you back to the jail. You can eat or not once we get there."

William stood and Ashley put the chain belt around his waist. "Lost your appetite, did you? Yeah, I don't think I could eat if I were facing the death penalty."

William stared straight ahead when they walked out into the hallway. The old-timer cleared the elevator while William stood alone in the hallway with Ashley. There was a window at the end of the hallway and William could see that it was getting overcast. When the old timer gave the thumbs-up, Ashley pushed William into the elevator and they rode down to the first floor.

When the elevator doors opened, William and the guards were met with a bombardment of newspaper reporters and television crews. They shoved one another and jockeyed for position. Ashley smashed the close button and called for assistance. They remained in the elevator until the guards on the outside radioed and told Ashley that they had created an opening through the crowd. Ashley opened the door once again and they bustled through the narrow crack in the human wall to a doorway that led to the garage where the prison van was parked.

The old-timer secured William in the back seat while Ashley snatched the keys from under the floor mat. When they were set, Ashley pressed the remote garage door opener that was clipped to the sun visor. They sped out onto the street and toward the jail. News reporters ran beside the van and screamed their questions until they were lost in its wake. Television crews aimed their cameras at the van and tracked it until it was out of sight.

"Damn, you're a famous man," Ashley said.

"They know I'm innocent."

Ashley threw his head back and laughed.

"Watch the road, boy," the old-timer cautioned. "I got three years left until retirement. I don't want to end my career wrapped around a tree with your silly ass."

There were more camera crews and reporters at the prison. When they finally made their way inside, William went to the cafeteria and found Beaver. "Hey, you ever heard of somebody getting convicted of a crime they didn't commit?"

"Losing faith?"

"I'm just trying to figure what my chances are. My own wife testified that she thinks I pushed her into the water." He shook his head. "I can't believe she thinks I did this."

"Look, innocent people do get convicted sometimes, but it won't happen to you."

"How can you be so sure?"

"You don't look like a killer."

"Beaver, my fingerprints are on the murder weapon—a murder weapon that I own!"

"Don't lose faith, kid. That lawyer of yours is going to figure something out."

"I sure hope so."

The clock on the cafeteria wall read one o'clock when Ashley summoned William. "Time to go back into the sea of media." He smiled big. "Will you mention me in your book?"

"I already forgot you," William said and held his arms out to be cuffed.

It was right at one-thirty by the time they parked and made it through the crowded hallways. Ashley removed William's chains just outside the doorway to the courtroom, so as not to prejudice the jury against him. "Don't try anything stupid. We got orders to shoot to kill."

"Don't you get tired of saying that?" William asked before walking to the defendant's table and sitting beside Esther.

Esther leaned close and stared into William's eyes. Her breath smelled of wintergreen. "I'm going to cross-examine Claire. I know you love her, but if I have to get rough with her, I don't want any shit from you in front of this jury. Understand?"

William nodded. They stood when the jury entered. Claire returned to the witness stand and Esther greeted her. "Let's get right to it, Mrs. Chandler. Has your husband ever hit you or abused you in any way?"

"No."

"What kind of father was he?"

"He was a great father. He loved Gracie from the moment she was born."

"Has he ever done anything at all that would ever lead you to believe he would harm you or Gracie in any way?"

Claire shook her head.

"Could you please answer out loud, so the court reporter can record your answer?"

"Uh, sorry. No."

"Then why would you think your husband pushed you into the river?"

"Well, there was no one else out there."

Esther grabbed her notebook and walked around to the front of the defendant's table. "Wasn't there another couple in the forest? A Jake and Gaby Arthur?"

"They left earlier that morning."

"Did you see them drive away?"

Claire thought for a moment. "Well, not really."

"So, isn't it possible they were still lurking around in the woods?"

"I don't think they were."

"But isn't it possible?"

"I guess so."

"What about the other families who were camped near the parking lot? Couldn't it have been one of those people?"

"I don't think they—"

"What about this army fellow that was out in the jungle? Isn't it possible that he pushed you in the water?"

"He was dead."

"Dead? How do you know that?"

"What do you mean?"

"How did you know the guy was dead?"

"I mean, I didn't know it at the time."

"Well, when did you first find out he was dead?"

"When the detective told me."

Esther looked at the jury and then at Claire. "So, at the time you were in the woods, you didn't know the army man was dead, isn't that correct?"

"Yes, ma'am."

"So, isn't it possible that the army guy pushed you into the water?"

"I guess so."

"Isn't it also possible that you just slipped and fell into the water, that no one pushed you?"

"I . . . it . . . someone pushed me."

"Are you absolutely positive?"

Claire glanced at the prosecutor and then at Esther. "I . . . I mean, I felt someone push me."

"Let me ask you this: What condition was Gracie in when you fell into the water?"

"I don't know. William said he put her down in the tent."

"Any reason not to believe him?"

"No."

"Did you hear anything unusual in the tent when he put her down?"

"No."

"Did it take an unusual amount of time for him to put Gracie to bed?"

"No."

"Who rescued you from certain death by drowning?"

Claire looked down and answered in a low voice. "William."

"Who performed CPR on you as you lay on the banks of the raging river, not breathing and with no pulse?"

Without looking up, Claire pointed to William.

Esther paused for a moment to allow the information to sink into the minds of the jury. "Okay, how long after you fell in the water did it take for William to come to your aid?"

"Well, it was kind of quick. I mean, the water dragged me pretty fast and it seemed he was right there, right quick. That's another reason I thought it was him who pushed me."

"Well, if he was right there pushing you, then who smothered Gracie?"

Claire stared, a blank expression pasted on her face.

"And if William was up by the tent smothering Gracie, then who pushed you?"

"I . . . I . . . don't know."

"And that's the gist of it, isn't it? That you don't know?"

"Ma'am?"

"Well, as you and William drove off with your baby girl lying lifeless in your lap, did you say to yourself, *I need to call the cops and report that William pushed me in the raging water?* Or, did you say to yourself, *I need to report William for killing my baby girl?*"

"No, I thought the bear had killed her."

"Why did you think the bear killed your baby girl?"

"Because it . . . it . . ." Claire lowered her head and tears streamed down her face. "Because I saw what it did to her."

"So, if the bear killed Gracie, and you saw the wounds, how on earth could William have smothered her?"

"I don't know. Detective London said that's how it happened."

"Right. And it wasn't until you spoke with Detective London that you began suspecting your husband of these awful crimes, right?"

"I guess so."

"Actually, you didn't start suspecting your husband of murder until Detective London told you that he'd had an affair with a former lover, isn't that correct?"

Claire's face paled. She stared wide-eyed at William. "That's correct," she said in a weak voice.

"Do you have any evidence or any knowledge to suggest that your husband killed your daughter?"

"No."

"What condition was Gracie in just before William put her down to sleep?"

"She was fine."

"And when was this?"

"Saturday night."

"So, on Saturday night, at the time William put Gracie down, there was nothing wrong with her?"

"No, there was nothing wrong with her at that time."

"You mentioned William threatening the army soldier. Why did he say what you claim he said?"

"Because he was mad that the man was looking at me."

"So, basically, he made that statement in your honor, right?"

"Yes, I guess."

"Do you have any evidence or knowledge to suggest that your husband killed the soldier?"

"No."

"You mentioned under direct examination that William was out of your sight on one or two occasions. When he returned, did he ever have blood on his hands or clothes?"

"No."

"Was he out of breath at any time or did he ever appear to have been involved in a struggle?"

"No, ma'am."

"In fact, after you ended up in the water, didn't you both suspect the soldier of pushing you into Skybald River?"

"Yes."

"And what did William do after you two discovered that Gracie was badly injured?"

"He freaked out like I've never seen. He looked scared, helpless."

"Did he look like a man who had just brutally murdered his own child?"

"No, ma'am," Claire said in a low whisper.

"After y'all discovered Gracie in that condition, did William ever leave your sight?"

"No. That's when we left and the wreck happened."

Esther thumbed through her files and pulled out a report. "Mrs. Chandler, have you ever been arrested?"

"Only for this."

"Only for what?"

"For what happened with Gracie."

"Oh, so you were arrested for murder, also?"

Claire nodded.

"Please answer—"

"Yes."

"Why aren't you on trial today?"

Allen Crochet jumped to his feet. "Objection, Your Honor. Relevance."

Judge Rudolph waved both attorneys to his bench. They whispered heatedly for several moments and when Esther returned to the defendant's table she winked at William. She turned to Claire. "Please answer the question, Mrs. Chandler. Why aren't you on trial today?"

Claire cast a nervous glance toward the Assistant District Attorney. "My lawyer told me if I testified against my husband I wouldn't be charged with the murder."

"And who told your lawyer you wouldn't be charged?"

"Mr. Crochet."

Esther sat down. "No more questions."

The judge looked at Crochet. "Redirect?"

"Mrs. Chandler, how long have you and William been married?"

"A little over eleven years."

"Is it difficult testifying in front of your husband today?"

"Yes, sir."

He pursed his lips and nodded. "No more questions."

★ ★ ★ ★ ★

10:00 A.M.
Friday, November 18, 2005
Cote Blanche Courthouse

William entered the courtroom with a bounce in his step. He dropped into his chair next to Esther and smiled. "You did great yesterday. In only an hour or so you unraveled several months of work on the part of the prosecution."

"Don't start celebrating just yet," Esther cautioned. "This trial is far from over."

"Yeah, but I could see in Claire's eyes that she realized the detective tricked her into thinking I did this."

"It doesn't matter what Claire thinks." Esther pointed to the empty jury box. "It only matters what they think."

William turned and surveyed the faces in the crowded courtroom. Other than several returned media personnel, he didn't recognize anyone. He wondered if Claire would be returning and wished his mother could be there. He sighed. At least she had lived long enough to see Gracie born.

Judge Rudolph walked in and met with Crochet and Diebold in private. After the meeting, the bailiff left through a side door and returned with the jury. "All rise," he bellowed.

Everyone stood to their feet and waited for the jury to be seated. William tried to catch the eyes of several of the jurors, but they refused to make eye contact with him.

"State, call your next witness," Judge Rudolph said.

Allen Crochet stood. "Your Honor, we call Dr. Beth Snyder."

The bailiff exited the courtroom and returned with an elderly woman who wore scrubs and carried a clipboard. After she was sworn, she took the witness stand and pulled on a dark-rimmed pair of reading glasses.

"State your name and occupation, please," Allen Crochet said.

"I'm Beth Snyder, medical doctor. I'm the assistant coroner."

"Did you have the occasion to perform an autopsy on one Jeremy McAllister?"

"Yes, I did."

"What did you determine the cause of death to be?"

"Multiple stab wounds to the heart."

"And the manner of death?"

"Homicide."

"Did you also perform an autopsy on an infant, who was identified as Grace Chandler?"

"Yes, I did."

"What did you determine the infant's cause of death to be?"

"There was some indication that the baby might have been sick prior to her death, but, in my professional opinion, the chief cause of death was hypoxia."

"So the jury can understand?"

Dr. Snyder turned to the jury. "Basically, the baby died from a lack of oxygen to the brain."

"Is this consistent with, say, suffocating the baby by putting a pillow over her face?"

"Yes."

"In your profession, have you seen cases where a baby was crying, maybe from some sort of discomfort caused by an illness, and the parents did different things to try and make the baby stop crying?"

"Yes."

"Have you ever worked a case where a parent, out of frustration, has placed a pillow over the baby's face to make it stop crying?"

"Yes, I have."

"In that case, were your findings similar to what you found while performing the autopsy on Grace Chandler?"

"Yes, they were."

"What did you determine the manner of death to be in this case?"

"Homicide."

"Now, there were some severe wounds to the baby that could have been caused by a bear, isn't that correct?"

"There were some post-mortem lacerations consistent with a bear attack, yes."

"Could you explain to the jury what *post mortem* means?"

"It means the wounds occurred after the baby was already dead."

"Just to be clear, when the bear mauled little Grace Chandler in the tent she was already dead—had been so for some time. Isn't that correct?"

"Yes, it is."

"Thank you, Doctor. I tender the witness."

William leaned close to Esther and whispered, "Is this the bombshell the prosecutor was talking about? This is bullshit! Gracie was alive when I left her in that tent!"

Esther waved William silent and stood with an official-looking report in her hand. She walked around the defendant's table. "May I approach the witness?"

"You may," Judge Rudolph said.

Esther handed the report to Doctor Snyder. "Do you recognize the report I've handed you?"

"Yes."

"Please tell the jury what it is."

"My autopsy report for the infant, Grace Chandler."

"In it, you list the *probable* cause of death as hypoxia. Isn't that correct?"

"Yes, I do."

"So, you haven't been able to determine the cause of death to a medical certainty; isn't that correct?"

"That's correct."

"Is it sometimes difficult to determine the actual cause of death in infants?"

"Yes, it is."

"Does it also complicate matters when the infant has been dead for a couple of days before the body gets to you?"

"Certainly."

"And if I understand your testimony and the findings in your report, there is a possibility that the cause of death is something other than hypoxia, correct?"

"There's always that possibility."

"So, then it is possible the bear killed little Gracie, isn't that correct?"

"No, ma'am, that's not possible."

"But you just testified that it's possible the cause of death was something other than hypoxia."

"While I can't testify to a medical certainty that the victim died of hypoxia, I can certainly testify to a medical certainty that the infant was not killed by the bear. The wounds were inflicted postmortem, meaning they were inflicted after the baby died."

Esther studied her notes for several moments. Finally, she nodded. "Thank you. No more questions."

Allen Crochet stood. "Doctor, what is the most likely cause of death?"

"As I said earlier, a lack of oxygen to the brain."

"Did you find any evidence of some other cause of death?"

"No, sir."

"Nothing further. State calls Detective Oscar London."

William felt his pulse quicken as the Detective approached the witness stand. He wore a full three-piece suit with a thick tie. His shoes were shiny and they clanked with authority on the floor. His face was smooth and his hair slicked back. There was a large three-ring binder in his hand. He stood before the red-nailed clerk and placed his left hand on the Bible.

"Do you swear to tell the truth and nothing but the truth, so help you God?"

Detective London nodded. "I do."

Assistant District Attorney Allen Crochet began cleverly building his case against William with Detective London's testimony. The longer Detective London stayed on the witness stand, the more confident Crochet became.

London first told of a career that spanned over two decades and was filled with accomplishments and awards.

William grunted to himself. *What is this,* he wondered, *a new reality show called "Who Wants to be an Award-Winning Detective"?*

At Crochet's prompting, Detective London presented professional and compelling testimony in support of the state's case. Using enlarged photographs and crime-scene sketches, he explained what he found out in the forest. He showed the jury aerial photographs and linked the different crime scenes to each other. He described the murder scene where the army veteran's body was found as bloody and described the murder as brutal. When he described the manner in which the pit bull had been killed, several members of the jury gasped and stared wide-eyed at William.

After Detective London finished describing the crime scenes, Crochet stood. "Did you recover any evidence at the scene of Jeremy McAllister's murder?"

"Yes, sir."

"Please tell the jury what you found."

"I found the murder weapon to be a Cold Steel Tanto."

"From where did you recover the murder weapon?"

"From the victim's chest. It was buried to the hand guard."

"Did you ascertain to whom the murder weapon belonged?"

"Yes, sir. It belongs to the defendant, Mr. William Chandler."

William saw some of the jurors glance in his direction.

"How was it that you were able to determine to whom the knife belonged?"

"Mr. Chandler and Mrs. Chandler both identified it as being his knife."

The prosecutor made a big show of taking the Tanto out of the evidence box and waving it around the courtroom. "Did you process the knife for prints?"

"Yes, sir."

"Were the defendant's prints on the knife?"

Esther jumped to her feet. "Objection! Leading."

"I'll rephrase, Your Honor. Detective, whose prints were on the knife?"

"William Chandler's."

William watched the jury. Several eyebrows were raised when the detective mentioned his prints being on the knife.

"Detective, when you processed the crime scene and the tent area, did you locate any evidence to suggest that anyone other than the defendant, William Chandler, committed the murders of Jeremy McAllister and infant Grace Chandler?"

"None whatsoever."

"Did you find any evidence to link Jeremy McAllister to the infant's murder?"

"No, sir. I recovered hair samples, fibers, fingerprints, and shoe impressions from the tent area and they all belonged to the defendant and his wife. There was no evidence whatsoever to suggest that Mr. McAllister was anything other than an innocent victim."

"Did you recover any foreign hair fibers on the infant's body?"

"Yes. They were matched to the defendant and his wife."

"Detective, through your investigation, was Mrs. Chandler ruled out as a suspect?"

"Yes, sir. It was determined that at the time of her daughter's murder, Claire Chandler was near the banks of Skybald River, cleaning the dishes from supper."

"Thank you, Detective."

Esther cleared her throat and walked to the jury box. She leaned against it and crossed her arms. "Detective, didn't you recover some unidentifiable prints on the murder weapon?"

"Yes, there was one print that I was not able to identify."

"Well, isn't it possible that someone else killed Jeremy McAllister and framed my client?"

"Anything's possible. It's possible that aliens exist and they killed Jeremy McAllister, but it's not reasonable and there's no evidence to support that theory."

Several jurors snickered.

"Detective, isn't it fair to say that once you had Mr. Chandler in custody, the investigation ceased?"

"Not at all. I processed the crime scenes *after* he was in custody. I recovered the hairs and prints *after* he was in custody. We actually didn't even find Mr. McAllister's body until long after the defendant was in custody."

"Other than my client's fingerprints, did you find any other evidence to link him to the scene where Mr. McAllister's body was located?"

"His prints were on the murder weapon, what more do you want?"

"Please answer the question."

"No, ma'am. The only thing we found were his fingerprints, which were all over the murder weapon that was still buried in the victim's chest."

"Detective, did you attempt to locate a Jake and Gaby Arthur?"

"Yes, ma'am. They do not exist."

"How can you say with certainty that they don't exist?"

"Because I ran a name inquiry on every data system available to law enforcement and their names did not register a single match."

"Well, I think it's more accurate to say you couldn't locate them. To say they don't exist is being a bit presumptuous, don't you think?"

"No, ma'am."

"Oh, really? Other than running a name inquiry, did you make any other attempts to locate these individuals?"

"No, ma'am."

"Why not?"

"Even if they do exist, they could add nothing to the investigation."

"Couldn't they have verified that Mr. McAllister was the one who cut the brake lines on the defendant's car?"

"They could have only testified that they saw him squatting near the vehicle. The brake lines weren't cut."

"Excuse me?"

"Another part of my investigation was to examine the undercarriage of the Chandler vehicle. The brake lines were not cut."

Esther walked over to William and whispered in his ear. "I thought you said the brake lines were cut?"

"They had to have been, because my brakes didn't work."

"Are you sure?"

"Positive."

Esther straightened. "Detective, did you check the fluid levels in the vehicle?"

Detective London hesitated ever so slightly. "No, ma'am."

"Don't you think that would've been an important part of this investigation?"

"The defendant claimed the brake lines were cut. I tried to verify that—"

"What else did you forget to do during this investigation?"

"Excuse me?"

"You didn't check the fluid levels, you didn't track down Jake and Gaby—"

Crochet stood. "Objection, Your Honor."

"Mrs. Diebold, if you have a question, please ask it."

"Detective, you just testified that you did not really try to locate Jake Arthur. Isn't it possible that the mystery fingerprint belonged to him, and that he was the killer?"

"He had no motive to kill Jeremy McAllister or Grace Chandler."

"How do you know if he had motive or not?"

"My investigation didn't reveal anything other than the defendant was responsible for the murders."

"Did you interview Jake Arthur?"

"No, ma'am."

"Do you know anything about Jake Arthur?"

"No, ma'am."

"Then how can you sit there, under oath, and say he did not have motive to kill Jeremy McAllister or Grace Chandler?"

"Because my investigation—"

"I know, I know, your investigation." Esther flipped through her pages. She put down her notebook and scanned the arrest report. Finally, she looked up. "I have no more questions."

Crochet stood up. "Briefly, Detective. Whose fingerprints were on the knife that killed Mr. McAllister?"

"The defendant's . . . Mr. William Chandler."

"Is there any doubt about that?"

"Absolutely none."

"Is there any evidence that anyone other than the defendant and his wife came into contact with the infant, Grace Chandler?"

"None whatsoever."

"Did you find any shoe prints in the area of the tent that you have not been able to positively identify?"

"No, sir. The only shoe prints at the scene were matched to the shoes we removed from Mr. and Mrs. Chandler after their automobile accident."

"Through your investigation, were you able to determine that the two murders were committed by the same person?"

"Yes, sir."

"Did you conduct a thorough investigation into these two murders?"

"Yes, sir."

"Did you find any evidence that someone other than that man," Crochet pointed an accusing finger at William, "committed these two murders?"

"No, sir."

Several jurors nodded at Detective London's final remarks. William slouched into his chair. "I'm dead."

"Shush," Esther whispered.

"Your Honor, that's all we have for Detective London."

"You're released, Detective." Judge Rudolph glanced at the clock on the far wall. It was five minutes until noon. "I guess this is a good time to take a break. Court will be adjourned until one-thirty."

Everyone stood while the jury exited the courtroom. When they were gone, William turned to Esther. "You have to find Jake. I know it was him who stole my knife. I had it Friday night. They came by Saturday morning and then it was gone. It had to be him—or her."

"William, I've exhausted all my resources trying to find them. They simply don't exist."

"That's because you've been looking for them under their fake names. Look, they stayed at that campsite for over a week. They had to fill out an envelope to stay there. Had to write their address, the city they were from, the dates they stayed there. If you run the license plate number on every vehicle out there during the week we were there, you'll find their real names." William licked his lips. "Look, if Gracie was dead before that bear attacked her, they killed her while I was rescuing Claire! You *have* to find them!"

Esther frowned. "William, it's too late for that. I need to concentrate on the state's next witness and on my closing. We need to get through this trial and pray for the best."

"Pray for the—" William slapped his forehead and walked in a circle. Several reporters who had lingered in the courtroom stared. He leaned close to Esther. "Listen, Jake did this! I have to find him. My life depends on it!"

"William, we're out of time. There's no way the judge will grant a stay in the middle of—"

"Damn it, Esther! You saw the way that jury looked at me! They're going to put me to death for something I didn't do and Jake's the only chance I've got left!" William grabbed Esther's shoulders and shook her. "You need to find him!"

Esther screamed and William caught movement in his peripheral vision. He spun in time to see Ashley swinging a police baton at his head. William raised his arm and took the brunt of the blow on the outside of his upper arm. He stepped close and punched Ashley as hard as he could. Ashley yelped and staggered backward. William rushed forward and grabbed Ashley's gun and jerked on it. It was stuck. William punched him again and fumbled with the snap. Something struck the back of William's neck and pain shot straight down to his toes. He buckled and nearly fell. He turned in time to see the gun descending again . . . this time his head was the target.

William slipped to the side and grabbed at the gun with both hands. The old-timer's grip was no match for his strength. He wrenched the revolver from the old-timer's grasp and stepped back. People screamed. The door burst open and other guards rushed in.

William stared wildly about like a hunted animal. Acting upon instinct, he grabbed Ashley, who was still dazed from the blow to the face. He pulled Ashley in front of him and placed the muzzle of the gun to his head. "Everybody back up!" he screamed. "Back up!"

The guards hesitated. Gun barrels pointed in William's direction. Fingers whitened around the triggers.

"William, please don't do this!" Esther wailed.

"Get back or I'll kill Ashley! Move! *Move!*" William pushed Ashley toward the door. The guards backed away, unsure of what to do. William continued to push forward and through the door and into the crowded hallway. People scrambled when they realized what was taking place. William pushed toward the elevator, keeping Ashley between him and the menacing gun barrels of the hesitant guards. "Push the button," he ordered.

Ashley fumbled with the button. When the doors opened, William backed into the empty elevator. "Stay back!" he hissed at the guards, who attempted to inch closer. "Close the door!"

Ashley mashed the button and the doors slid shut. He trembled in William's grasp. "Please don't kill me!"

The elevator came to rest on the first floor and the doors began to part. William fired a shot into the ceiling and the crowd of reporters stationed outside the elevator stampeded toward the exits. William rushed behind them, pushing Ashley ahead of him. He turned the corner and shoved Ashley through the opening to the garage. He slammed the door shut and pushed Ashley against it. "Unsnap your gun!"

With a hand that quivered, Ashley unsnapped his semi-automatic pistol. William jerked it from the holster and backed slowly away. "The keys still under the floor mat?"

Ashley nodded. "Please don't kill me."

William tucked Ashley's gun in his waistband and opened the van door with his left hand. He leaned over and felt on the floor. Tiny pieces of dirt rolled under his hand and he felt a bulge under the floor mat. He ripped the floor mat away and snatched up the keys. "Move to the front of the van." William kept the gun trained on Ashley's chest. Tears streamed down the young guard's face. He sidestepped, keeping his eyes on the floor, until he was in front of the van.

William jumped into the driver's seat and rolled the window down. When the engine roared to life, he pressed the remote garage opener. The rolling door began to rise. "Get out of the way!"

Ashley dove to the ground and rolled to the side. When the door was higher than the height of the van, William tossed the guns out the window and smashed the accelerator. The van shot forward and he sped out of the garage.

CHAPTER TWENTY-FIVE

11:00 A.M.

Friday, November 18, 2005

Magnolia Parish Sheriff's Office Substation

I was walking out of the office bathroom when my phone screamed in my pocket. I glanced at the display screen and flipped it open. "Hey, Debbie, what's up?"

"He escaped!"

"Who?"

"The guy from the TV."

I made it to my office and wiggled the mouse to wake up my computer. "What guy from TV?"

"You know, the one who killed his baby."

"Oh, from the news?"

"Yeah. He took a prison guard hostage and escaped from the courthouse. He even stole a police van."

"No kidding?"

Dawn walked into the office. "What's happening?"

"That guy who killed his baby at the Skybald National Park escaped."

"What? That's horrible!"

"Is that Dawn?" Debbie wanted to know.

"Yeah."

"Let me talk to her."

I handed Dawn the phone. "Deb wants you."

After they spoke for several minutes, Dawn slid my phone

across the desktop. "You'd better not let Debbie down this time."

I didn't look up from my computer. "Does that mean you'll take whatever comes?"

"You know it."

"Good. Now let me finish these reports so I can leave with a good heart."

Dawn walked out of the office and I drummed away at the keyboard. The burglary cases were piled knee-deep on my desk. I knew if I didn't get those reports done before leaving for the weekend, there would be double the work when I returned. Every time I completed one burglary case there were two more to take its place. Thankfully, the violent crime rate was low in our parish.

Just as my stomach started to growl, Dawn walked in with a plate lunch from a local mom-and-pop restaurant. "Thought you might want to work through lunch, so I picked up."

"You know me well."

"Too well. It's your favorite . . . shrimp spaghetti with garlic bread."

I flashed a grateful smile and flipped the plastic cover open. Dawn dropped a computer printout on the desk.

"What's that?" I asked between mouthfuls.

"A teletype BOLO from Cote Blanche Parish."

"For the child killer?"

"Yeah. Get this, he disarmed two prison guards, fired a round into the ceiling, and stole a prison van. He didn't hurt anyone and as he drove away, he tossed the guns. Does that sound like something a killer would do? I think not."

I shrugged. "Maybe he only kills when people give him a reason."

"What reason could a six-month-old give?"

"True." I swallowed a large swig of soda. "Regardless of what he did or didn't do during his escape, he was the last to see his baby alive and his fingerprints are on the knife that killed that old man."

"I know, I know. He just doesn't look like a killer."

"What does that mean? You've been doing this long enough to know that criminals don't have a particular look."

Dawn blushed. "Yeah, you're right. He's just too cute to be a killer."

I groaned. "I'm getting back to work. Thanks for the lunch."

CHAPTER TWENTY-SIX

12:45 P.M.
Friday, November 18, 2005
Downtown Cote Blanche
William drove straight into midday traffic. Cote Blanche was a rural parish, but its downtown was crowded. He glanced in the rearview mirror. Lights flashed back in the distance and he heard the faint scream of a siren. Traffic tried to inch toward the crowded sidewalks to allow the squad cars to get through. He tried to see past the line of cars ahead of him. He remembered seeing a shopping mall on the ride over from the prison. If he could only make it to that crowded building . . .

William suddenly realized that the car in front of him was trying to pull over to the sidewalk. He glanced in his rearview mirror. The squad cars were still a great distance behind him. He looked back to the front. The car had cleared a path for him to drive around. He mashed the pedal and accelerated around the car. Another car pulled over. Realization hit him like a bat to the skull—he was in a cop van! *These drivers think they're hearing my sirens!* He glanced down at the control panel on the console. One button read "lights" and the other read "siren." He flipped on both switches and sped ahead. Cars darted out of his path.

All of a sudden, a squad car swerved into the oncoming lane two blocks ahead. In a panic, William jerked the steering wheel to the right and shot down a one-way cross street. A truck swerved to avoid a head-on collision and William said a quiet prayer as he rounded a blind corner. All was clear ahead of him and the city street turned into a hilly parish road that was shouldered by tall pines and squat oaks. He raced down the bumpy road for several miles—the van swaying with the subtle changes in the road's surface—until he saw a sign that read, *Road Ends.* He skidded to a sudden stop when he reached an intersection at the end of the road. He glanced in the rearview mirror. The squad cars were gaining on him. A road sign told him the Skybald National Forest was six miles to the left and the town of Oaksterville was twenty-seven miles to the right. Thinking quickly, he headed toward Oaksterville and began looking for the right spot along the curvy road.

Tires cried out and the van rocked precariously as he negotiated the sharp curves at a speed that would make a racecar driver vomit. After miles of the same type of shoulder, he rounded a final curve and saw the perfect spot. The road to the left dropped off into a deep gully. He smashed the brakes and his body lurched forward as the van slowed dramatically.

William held the steering wheel steady with one hand and opened the door with his other. The van slowed to a mere roll and, just before it reached the edge of the cliff, William jumped to the ground and tumbled toward the cliff. A gasp ripped from his lips as he slid face-first to a stop at the very edge. The van rolled forward and plunged over the edge. The tires whined. It fell breathlessly. Metal crunched violently as it crashed to the rocks below.

William rushed to his feet and sprinted across the road. He dove into the bushes just as the first squad car screamed around the curve. It didn't stop. Another squad car sped by. William cried with relief. His cries turned to laughter. *It worked! God, Almighty, it worked!* He slowly stood to his feet. There was no time to waste. It wouldn't take the cops long to realize their mistake and find the van in the gully.

William faded deep into the trees and began the long trek toward the Skybald National Forest. He heard many sirens during his hike back to the intersection. When he reached the shoulder of the parish road, he peered cautiously out of the trees. All was clear. He darted across the roadway and plunged into the woods on the other side. Sweat drained from his pores. He stripped off his coat and draped it over his shoulder. Twigs snapped underfoot. Briars sliced at his legs. Spider webs clung to his face. He trudged on. There was only one thing he could do . . . find Jake Arthur. And the key to finding him was back at the Ranger Station. *What if the fingerprint on the knife doesn't match Jake's?* He shuddered. It had to match. It just had to.

Sometime near dark

The sun was well into its westward slide when William reached the fence that separated the Ranger Station from the thick forest. Nothing moved in the large clearing. A half dozen faded green forestry trucks squatted under a tin overhang. The buildings appeared empty. He looked at the sky. Still too much daylight. He'd have to wait until dark.

He shoveled pine needles into a natural mattress and lay in the evening shadows to wait. His stomach grumbled. He closed his eyes and dreamed of being home again . . .

He could smell Claire's fried shrimp and white beans cooking in the kitchen, could hear the soft music playing in the background, could feel her soft fingers caressing his neck, rubbing up and down his back, could taste—

William jerked awake. It was darker than the Devil's mood when he got kicked out of Heaven. He had to blink several times to ensure his eyes were open. When acclimated to the night, he scaled the cyclone fence with a soft touch and slinked across the open ground to the green building that stood lonely and silent against the backdrop of darkness. He felt his way around the building until he found the front door and he tried the handle. Locked. There was a window just to the right of the door. He pressed his face against the glass and peered inside. A faint glow came from the depths of the room.

William surveyed the surrounding darkness. There was nothing but the natural night music of the forest. An occasional twig snapped. A small animal rustled the bushes just beyond the fenced enclosure. With hands that shook, he wrapped his coat around his right elbow. After taking a deep breath, he smashed a hole in the window. Glass rained onto the cement floor and the sounds echoed through the tranquil night. He froze. It was as though someone had pressed the mute button on the forest's volume control. He didn't move, tried to silence his heavy breathing. After several minutes, the night creatures returned to their routines.

William reached through the hole he'd created and unlocked the deadbolt. He turned the knob and eased the door open. He tiptoed inside and made his way toward the glow. The deeper he walked into the building, the faster his heart raced. He paused often, listening. *What if Detective London called the Rangers? What if they're hiding just around the corner, waiting to take me back into custody?* There was no sound but the dull thump of his heart and the quiet hum of a computer somewhere in the building. He made his way through what looked to be a worker's lounge. A doorway to the right held the source of the glow: a computer monitor. The room appeared to be an office.

William walked to a large filing cabinet in the corner of the room. The center drawer was labeled, *Parking Pass Envelopes*. He tried the latch. Locked. He moved to the metal desk in the center of the room and rummaged through the drawers. A small box with a dozen sets of keys was in the bottom drawer. He dumped the box. Car keys. He scattered them on the desk, searching for a key that would unlock the filing cabinet. There was none. He walked to the filing cabinet and jerked on the drawer. The cabinet rattled on the cement floor, but the drawer didn't budge. He moved about the room, desperately searching for something, anything, to help break open the drawer. As he hurried past the desk, his foot slid on a small object and he fell hard, banging the back of his head on the floor.

"Shit!" William rolled to his stomach and was about to push off the floor when he saw what he'd slipped on . . . one of the sets of keys. An idea struck him and he snatched them up and hurried out of the office. A red light toward the back of the building marked the rear exit. He smashed through the door and ran across the clearing to the nearest truck. The key didn't fit. He scrambled to the next. Nothing. There were only two trucks left to check when his key finally turned in the lock. He jerked the door open and found the latch to release the driver's seat.

William felt in the dark until he found the tire iron. He snatched it and rushed back into the office. Stabbing the pointed end into the crack above the drawer, he gave it a violent jerk. The drawer labeled *Parking Passes* burst open and revealed a stack of hanging file folders. He grabbed a handful and threw them on the desk in front of the monitor. They were categorized by year and subcategorized by month. He thumbed through the files until he found November of the year 2004. He plucked the folder loose and pushed the other files to the floor.

Wiping sweat from his forehead, he took a deep breath and exhaled forcefully. "God, please let this be it!" He opened the folder. There were four stacks of day passes wrapped in rubber bands, all of a different color. He reached for the pink stack. Before he had time to thumb through them, a car door slammed in the distance. He froze, heart pounding against his sternum.

"Hey, I've got a broken window here!" a voice called from

just outside the building.

William snatched the stack of pink day passes and shoved them into his pocket. He grabbed the keys and crept to the doorway. He was about to peek out when a bright beam of light splashed against the doorframe. He jerked back and scrambled toward the far wall, searching for someplace to hide. Two men whispered to each other. Shoes squeaked against the slick cement floor and drew nearer.

William sucked in air when he heard the unmistakable racking of a shotgun. "Forest Rangers! Come out with your hands up or we're coming in shooting!"

William moved to a window and fumbled with the latch. His teeth chattered inside his mouth. He managed to unlock the window and was about to slide it up when a dark shadow appeared outside the glass. He dropped to the floor and pressed his body against the wall. A beam of light shot through the window and darted about the room. It searched for him with evil intentions. The beam stopped momentarily on the filing cabinet and then moved to the scattered keys atop the desk.

"He's going for the trucks!" the dark shadow yelled from outside.

Footsteps clattered in the hallway and a Ranger darted past the doorway. William heard the Ranger smash the release bar on the rear exit. The light beam disappeared and the dark shadow stomped off, his footsteps fading as he raced toward the tin overhang where the trucks were parked.

William bolted from his hiding spot and ran lightly from the office and down the hallway. When he reached the front door, he skidded to a halt. Headlights from a running truck flooded the open doorway. He shielded his eyes and tried to see through the brightness, but couldn't. He glanced back toward the depths of the Ranger Station. Loud voices emitted from the area of the tin overhang.

Eyes squeezed shut against the blinding headlights, William made a dash for freedom. He did not know what lay beyond those beams, but he had no other choice. Relief flooded over him when he punched through to the other side without being challenged. His legs pumped like pistons as he made a beeline for the deep forest. He was nearly there when it hit him—the truck was left unattended! He slid to a stop and turned to look back. Breathing heavy, he hunched over, rested his palms on his knees, and stared with indecision at the truck. It sat with doors open, inviting him over. The engine hummed a welcome tune. *What to do?* He looked back toward the forest. Gaby had said it was 251 miles from here to her front door. Too far to walk.

William sprinted back to the truck and slipped into the driver's seat. He pulled the shift into gear and stomped the accelerator. The back tires kicked dirt and loose gravel under the truck as it shot rearward. He jerked the steering wheel and whipped the truck around. Metal grinded against metal as he forced it into first. When it settled into gear, the truck jumped forward and the passenger's door slammed shut. He slowed when he reached the end of the driveway and turned right onto the forest road, heading toward the parish road that led to the interstate—and freedom.

As darkness closed in behind him, he began to relax. His heart slowed and his breathing leveled. "Thank God that's—"

Suddenly, there was an explosion behind him and the back glass propelled forward. Pieces of it stabbed into the back of his neck. William ducked his head. The truck jerked violently on the loose gravel. A second shot rang out. He struggled with the steering wheel. It took several wild seconds for him to bring the truck under control and point it toward his getaway. A third shot exploded and the passenger-side window was pulverized.

"Shit!" He ducked low in the seat and fought to keep the truck steadied on the rocky road. When he had put enough

distance between himself and the Rangers, he sat up in the seat and increased his speed. The truck bumped along the forest road. Trees flashed by in the darkness. After what seemed like an hour of driving, he finally reached the blacktopped parish road.

His mind raced. What to do next? He had to somehow figure out where Gaby and Jake lived. He drove for nearly thirty miles and slowed to a stop on the shoulder of the road when he saw the interstate looming ahead. He turned the inside light on and looked around the truck. The fuel gauge read a quarter of a tank. A police radio microphone was clipped to the dashboard. The radio was on. The seat was peppered with glass shards. He dusted it off. A clipboard on the seat beside him was also laden with glass. He lifted it and turned it over, dumping the glass to the floor. There was some kind of code sheet taped to the back of the clipboard. He held it close. The title of the sheet read "Ten Code." *Must be police junk,* he thought. He'd watched cop shows on television where they had said the ten-stuff over the police radio.

William took a cautious glance around and then pulled the pink envelopes from his pocket. He rifled through them and separated the envelopes that had been filled out prior to their arrival on the nineteenth of November. There were over a hundred of them. He tossed out all but the ones with cities in the states of Texas, Arkansas, and Louisiana. He grunted. Over fifty to choose from. He made stacks of the envelopes with the same vehicle information and different dates. Ten of the vehicles had been there for two days. One vehicle had been there only one day.

William's heart pounded in his chest. Two of the vehicles had been registered there for the same fourteen days. They both had departed on November 20, 2004.

"Okay, one of y'all has to be the Arthurs." William checked

the city box on the first set of envelopes. There was none. Just the license plate and state boxes were filled in; *123V1KR87, Louisiana*—one for each day they were at the campsite. He checked the other stack. No city, just license plate and state; *555N2DL43, Louisiana.* He scratched his head. "Which one are you?"

William shook his head. It didn't really matter. Without a city, there was nothing he could do. If only he had a map, he could figure which city was 251 miles from the Skybald National Forest. He pulled down the sun visor. Nothing. He opened the glove box and his eyes lit up. There was a map folded in a plastic wrapper. William jerked the map out and unfolded it with anxious fingers. He sighed when he discovered it was a map of the Skybald Forest. "Just my rotten—"

"Headquarters, R12."

William jumped when the loud voice came over the police radio speaker. He flicked the dome light off and stared wildly about.

"Headquarters, R12 and R14, are you guys Code 4?"

William fumbled for the radio switch and was about to turn it off when an idea crossed his desperate mind. He snatched up the clipboard and scanned the list of codes. Code 4 meant that all was well. He searched for the appropriate response. *Got it!* He grabbed the microphone and pressed the button on the side. Clearing his throat, he said, in as panic-ridden a voice as he could muster, and trying to imitate the accent of the Forest Ranger, "10-4, but there's been a break-in at the Ranger station."

"10-9; you're coming in scratchy."

That meant to repeat his traffic. "There's been a break-in at the Ranger station, the person got away on foot."

"10-4. Should I call the locals for back-up?"

"No . . . I mean 10-50. We just need a . . ." William searched the codes for license plate check. "10-28." He held his breath. There was a moment of silence.

"Go ahead with the license plate number, R12." The female dispatcher sounded impatient, like she had something better to do.

William fumbled with the envelopes. "Uh, 123V1KR87."

"Is that Victor, or Bravo?"

"What?" William glanced over the 10-code sheet, frantically searching for this special code about Victor or Bravo. There it was, up in the corner: it was the phonetic alphabet. "Oh, *Victor.*"

"Alright, stand by."

William waited for a long three minutes. Finally, the dispatcher came on and spat out a myriad of information. William searched frantically around the cab of the truck until he located an ink pen. "Uh, repeat that," he said.

"R12, are you ready to copy?"

William glanced at the ten-code page. "10-4, ready."

"The vehicle's a white 1999 Honda minivan, registered to Jacob Albert, of 129 Piped Lane in Seasville, LA. No 29. Need criminal history run?"

William scribbled the information on the back of the envelope and smiled to himself. Jake Arthur . . . Jacob Albert. He flipped the police radio switch to "off" and sped toward the interstate. Once there, he headed south. The road was empty as it cut through the wooded hillsides. From time to time, William glanced nervously at the gas gauge. Finally, after driving for nearly an hour, a fueling station came into view. It was nestled against the dark forest, its lights glowing like a small city against the utter blackness.

William pulled onto the shoulder of the road and surveyed the area carefully. All seemed clear. He sped across the northbound lane of the interstate and parked at the far edge of the parking lot. He could make out a young girl sitting at the counter. She was reading something and hadn't even looked up when the headlights from William's borrowed truck panned the front of the store.

Saying a silent thanks to Esther for buying normal clothes for court, William walked quickly through the cool night breeze and entered the store. He immediately spotted the magazine rack and ambled to it. The girl was busy reading and didn't take her eyes off the book in front of her. Hiding behind the rack, William slipped a Louisiana map into the front of his shirt and looked around the store. He spotted the bathroom at the back of the building. Once inside, he squatted on the floor and spread the map out. He searched the city index and found Seasville. It was a tiny blip. "Gaby was right, two hundred and fifty miles from Skybald." He shook his head. "Two hundred and fifty *long* miles to the south." At least he was headed in the right direction and it was interstate travel all the way. His hometown was east of Skybald. "Cops probably have every inch of that road covered," he mused aloud.

William refolded the map and shoved it back into his shirt. He flushed the toilet so the clerk wouldn't get suspicious and walked to the counter. "Can you turn the pump on?" he asked.

"Pay before you pump," the clerk said without looking up.

"Yeah, but I have to fill up, so I don't know how much it'll be."

The clerk grunted, put her book down, and flipped a switch located to the right of where she sat.

When William reached the truck, he snatched up the gasoline nozzle and began filling the tank. He tapped his foot nervously as the pump groaned and squirted fuel from the metal nostril. "Come on, come on," he urged. It would only be a matter of time before the police realized he had headed south instead of north. Finally, the handle clicked to indicate the tank was full. William shoved the nozzle into the slot and jerked the truck door open. When he did, a gust of wind blew in and snatched a handful of the pink envelopes from off the seat. He clutched wildly at the air, trying to catch them all, but the wind carried some of the tiny papers up and away. He shot a nervous glance toward the store. The girl was reading her book again and seemed totally engrossed. *To hell with it,* he thought and jumped into the truck.

He drove across the interstate and down a narrow parish road until he was out of sight. He turned off his headlights, spun around, and merged back onto the interstate, heading south. The headlights stayed off until he was sure the clerk and customer could no longer see the truck. Relaxing, he flicked them back on and settled into the long drive.

William drove for hours on the lonely interstate. He didn't see many cars except for the occasional eighteen-wheeler that sped past. The wind blew in through the gaping hole in the passenger window and made for a loud, but comfortable drive. His mind raced ahead, wondering what he would find in Seasville. What would he do once he confronted Jake Arthur, or Jacob Albert? What would happen to him once he was back in custody? No matter. Once he found Jacob Albert, he would gladly turn himself over to Detective London.

William grunted. "Detective London, you're going to owe my wife and me one big apology and you're going to have to thank me for solving this case for you!"

CHAPTER TWENTY-SEVEN

6:45 P.M.

Friday, November 18, 2005

Magnolia Parish Sheriff's Office Substation

Things were not going exactly as I had planned. It was a quarter to seven and I still had four reports to write before I could go home. I had been writing at a rate of about five words per minute, what with all the interruptions and phone calls.

"Wait until you get back to finish them," Dawn had suggested before leaving for the day.

"I can't," I'd told her. "The District Attorney's Office is expecting these reports by Monday for court, especially the looting cases."

"Why'd you wait so long to finish them?"

I'd only glared at her. She knew I had spent the better part of September and October helping out the New Orleans Police Department with the recovery efforts from Hurricane Katrina. Our own parish had been spared the direct brunt of the storm and we'd suffered only power outages, fallen trees, and minor roof and structural damages. A dozen of our parish's deputies and firemen had made the short trek east to assist with rescues and body recovery. I had never seen such widespread destruction and death. It was something that would stay with me forever.

I clicked the *save* button and called Debbie. "Baby, I'm running a little behind schedule."

"Yeah, I was starting to wonder if we were going at all."

"I'll be a couple more hours."

Debbie was silent for a minute and when she spoke I could tell she was trying to be upbeat. "Do you want to just wait and leave tomorrow?"

"Oh, no. We're leaving tonight, regardless of how late it is. Besides, I'd rather travel late at night—less traffic."

"Yeah, you're right. It's also cooler."

"Hey, did you catch anything more on the news about that baby killer?"

"They located the prison van he stole," Debbie said. "It was crashed over a cliff, but he was nowhere to be found. They tried to track him with dogs, but they didn't get anywhere. The last I heard they were putting out calls to Mississippi cops, because that's where he's from."

"I hope they catch that sick bastard."

"Me, too. I'm glad we don't have people like that around here."

"You never know who your neighbors are."

"Don't say that!" Debbie shrieked. "You know how scared I get when you work late."

"Yeah, well, I'll be home soon. Give Samantha a kiss for me and tell her I love her."

"Why don't I go get her, so you can tell her yourself?"

"No, that's okay. Let her play. I'll be home soon, anyway."

I dropped the phone and turned my tired eyes back to the computer screen.

11:55 P.M.

"Where *are* you?"

"I'm still at the office," I told Debbie. "I only have one report to go and I can leave with a clear conscience."

"But it's almost midnight!"

"I know, I know. I'll be home within the hour." I flipped my cell phone shut and turned back to the computer. Before I could touch the keyboard, the office phone rang. I stared suspiciously at it. The only time it rang at night was when there was work to be done. I thought about not answering, but then thought better. Maybe it was an emergency. I snatched it up and answered, trying not to sound reluctant.

"Hello," came an official-sounding voice, "I'm Detective Oscar London from the Cote Blanche Parish Sheriff's Office. I need to speak to a detective on the night squad."

Midway through my sigh, I froze, curiosity mounting. "Cote Blanche? Didn't y'all have a child-killer escape from court?"

"Yes, we did. May I speak to the night detective?"

"I'm sorry. I'm Detective Brandon Berger. I'm not on call, but I can get you whatever you need."

"I have reason to believe that William Chandler is en route to your parish."

"Here? What makes you think that?"

"After Chandler escaped, he broke into the Rangers Station at the national park. We later received a report of a gas drive-off not far from the entrance to the Skybald National Forest. When we responded to that location, we found some registration envelopes from the national park on the ground. We've checked them all and only one of the envelopes showed a registration that was filled out during the same week he was there when he killed his daughter."

"I still don't understand the connection."

"Well, there's some indication that he's trying to conduct his own investigation. At first he claimed this Jake Arthur was a witness, but right before his escape he told his lawyer he now thinks this guy stole his knife and that he's responsible for his daughter's death. He might think he's on some hunt for his daughter's killer. In the two interviews I've conducted with him, he mentioned the name Jake Arthur as a person he thinks killed his daughter. We ran the license plate number on the envelope registration we found at the gas station. It came back to Jacob Albert of 129 Piped Lane."

"You think there's any truth to what he said?"

"About what?"

"About this Jake Arthur being the one who killed his daughter."

"Absolutely not. I don't know how many murderers you've interviewed down there, but I've interviewed fifty-four in my career. I know when I'm looking into the eyes of a killer and William Chandler is as cold-blooded a killer as I've ever met. If you don't want to be working a murder in your parish, I'd suggest you get out to this address as soon as possible."

"Did you run them through directory for a phone number? I can give them a heads-up call in—"

"I tried that. The answering machine picked up, so I left a message. We might already be too late."

I glanced at the clock, scowled. "Didn't this guy escape before lunch today?"

"Yes. So?"

"So why didn't you call earlier?"

"When the rangers put out the BOLO for him, we concentrated all of our efforts on the roads to Mississippi, because that's where he's from. I never thought he would go on some wild goose chase."

I glanced at the clock again and shook my head, then sighed. "129 Piped Lane, right?"

"That's right."

"Give me your number so I can call you if we get him." I wrote down the number, clicked the hang-up button. Next, I called Dawn. "Get down here as fast as you can!"

"What?" Her voice was groggy, but sexy.

"That child-killer escaped. He's heading this way. Get to the office as quick as you can!"

"You mean you've decided to spend your night with me instead of Debbie?"

I slapped my forehead . . . *Shit! Debbie.*

CHAPTER TWENTY-EIGHT

Late into the night
Friday, November 18, 2005
Somewhere south of Cote Blanche Parish
The traffic was heavier through New Orleans, but once William turned onto I-310, the roads were left to him and the truckers once more. It was midnight when the *Welcome to Seasville* sign came into view. William spotted an all-night gas station off to the right. He drove past it and parked the ranger truck along the side of the road. He walked into the store and approached the clerk, a young pimple-faced boy who had *Nerd* tattooed to his forehead and who was busy reading the latest issue of some gaming magazine.

"Howdy," William greeted. "I'm looking for Piped Lane."

Only the nerd's eyes moved as he looked up through his eyebrows. "It ain't in here."

William's blood boiled. He thought about snatching the kid by the throat and drilling him through the cement floor. "Could you please tell me where to find it?"

The nerd exhaled forcefully and put down his magazine. He pointed a toothpick of a finger south. "Go down about six miles to the next bridge you see. Cross over to Highway 80 and keep going south for about four miles. It'll be on your left—because only the bayou's on your right."

William didn't even thank him as he hurried out of the store. He surveyed the area carefully before he approached the truck.

Everything looked safe. He had just put his hand on the doorknob when he heard sirens behind him. He dove headlong into a ditch beside the road and lay flat. The sirens moved rapidly closer and zipped past William's position. He raised his head and peered over the mound of dirt. An unmarked police car faded into the distance. Brilliant flashes of blue pierced the night air. *Shit!* That was the direction he needed to go.

William pulled himself from the ditch and dusted off his pants. *Esther, you're gonna be pissed when you see these clothes!* He pulled onto the highway and headed south. He made sure he maintained the thirty-five mile per hour speed limit. All he needed now was to get stopped for some bogus traffic violation.

He found the bridge like the nerd had promised, crossed, and then turned right. All of the street signs were green and numbered. The sign across from the bridge was East One-Eightieth and as he traveled south they increased in number. He drove the four miles and still hadn't found Piped Lane. He was about to turn the truck around when his eyes caught sight of a blue street sign in the distance. Relief flooded his body when he read the name in bold white letters, *Piped Lane.*

William drove past Piped Lane and searched for a place to hide the truck. It didn't take long to find a road that led off into some cow pasture. He drove along the bumpy mud road until he reached a gate that was locked. He pulled the truck as far off the road as possible without going into the nearby ditch and shut off the engine. The door squeaked when he opened it.

Cow dung clung to the air and burned his nostrils, making him sneeze. He wiped his nose and walked to the toolbox at the back of the truck, looking for something to use as a weapon. Aided by the dim light from the moon that smiled above, he spotted a hatchet at the bottom of the toolbox. He removed the leather cover and tested the blade. Nice and sharp.

Clutching the hatchet in his right hand and the address in his left, he set out to find 129 Piped Lane and the man responsible for wrecking his life, for pushing his wife into the raging rapids, for causing his daughter's death. *What if things go bad and I have to use this hatchet? What if I want to use it when I find Jake?* William shuddered. His sweaty palm made it hard to grip the hatchet. He had never considered killing someone before. He had been raised to think that killing was wrong, that murderers went to hell. *But the Bible does say that the wages of sin is death,* he thought, then stopped. *Does that mean I will die if I kill Jake?* He shook his head and trudged on. *I'll find Jake and Gaby Arthur, or whoever they are, and let fate sort out the rest.* Being good and trying to do the right thing didn't help his dad or his daughter. The time for trying to do the right thing was over. It was now time for action. Besides, he had absolutely nothing to lose.

William left the cow pastures behind and squeezed through the prickly wires of a barbed-wire fence. He found himself in someone's backyard. The house was at the front of the street, near the highway. He pressed his body flat against the house and slinked along to the front yard. Somewhere in the distant night a dog barked. He froze. He hadn't considered dogs. He peered around the house and looked at the street sign. If he remembered correctly, Piped Lane was the next one.

William scampered across the street and between two houses to the backyard. He made his way through another cow pasture, maneuvered through backyards and over fences and then, at long last, he stood staring across the street at 129 Piped Lane. There, in the driveway, sat the familiar white van—the same white Honda minivan that Jake Arthur drove. The house was a two-story dwelling. The front door faced the street. The main door looked like wood, but there was a glass outer door. That would be noisy. He'd have to get in through the back.

William looked up and down the poorly lit street. At first

he'd wondered about a family who had a street named after them. He now realized it was nothing more than a long shell driveway. Probably every neighbor on the street was related. The more reason to be careful. He clutched the hatchet and weighed his options. He could call the police, but they might not listen to him. They would immediately take him into custody. Besides, he'd come this far so he might as well see it through to the end.

He dashed across the street and threw his back against the wall of the Albert home. Everything was quiet. He crept along the side of the house and inched around the corner to the back. A short flight of steps protruded from the back of the house and led to a sliding glass door. He shook his head. *Isn't anything ever easy?* Maybe he could pry the door open without making much noise. Moving one step at a time, he made his way to the foot of the steps. He stared with mouth wide and tried to watch all of the windows at once as he planted his foot on the first step. He shifted his weight forward and lifted his rear leg. He eased onto the next step, and the next. When he reached the landing, he lay prone and scooted toward the sliding door. He lay breathless, listening. Not a peep from anywhere.

William raised up to his knees and scooted close to the door. He placed the blade of the hatchet between the door and the frame. He began to pry, but the door slid open easily. *Well, well, at least one thing is going right for me.* When the opening was big enough to fit his body, he glided through the hanging vertical shades and melded into the darkness of the room. All was quiet inside. He hoisted the hatchet and walked through the darkness, feeling his way with the tips of his shoes. The downstairs rooms were empty. Next, he moved upstairs. A soft light at the top of the stairway lit the way to a hallway that was lined with three doors. Had to be bedrooms.

William opened the first door he came to and, standing aside, peered into the darkness. He listened for the sound of breathing. No sounds, no movement. He could barely make out a shadow that represented the bed. There didn't appear to be anything on it. He moved to the next room and opened the door. Nothing. He opened the third door and still there were no sounds, nor was there any movement. A sweet smell cloaked the stuffy air. As he turned away, he saw a dark shadow on the light-colored carpeted floor inside the room.

Squatting low, William looked behind him. All was clear. He crept into the room and stopped when he was within touching distance of the object. He glanced at the bed. It was silhouetted against the moonlight and he could now make out a form on it. He moved closer, trying to detect the slightest hint of movement. Still nothing. Keeping both figures in front of him, he backed toward the doorway and felt for the light switch. Aiming the hatchet at the figures, he flicked the switch on. Light shot from the bulb and painted the room in brilliant color.

William dropped the hatchet and recoiled in horror when his eyes focused on the bodies. Gaby Arthur lay in bed. A crimson spot glared at William from her white nightgown and the blanket that partially covered her. Her eyes were closed. It looked like she was sleeping. Jake Arthur lay facedown in a heap on the floor. Blood stained the carpet around his body. A large steak knife was buried in the side of his neck.

CHAPTER TWENTY-NINE

12:10 A.M.
Saturday, November 19, 2005
Magnolia Parish Sheriff's Office Substation

I stared at my phone for a long moment. Finally, I sighed and called Debbie. "Guess what?"

"You're canceling on us."

"No. You know that child-killer who escaped?"

"Yeah."

"He might be here."

Debbie gasped. "What? Why? How do you know?"

"He claims somebody from here killed his baby, so the detective who worked the case thinks he's out to get them."

"What are you going to do?"

"I'll pass the information on to Dawn. She'll get a team together—"

"You're not going after him yourself?"

"I'd love nothing more than to go get this piece of shit myself, but I'm not breaking my promise to you again."

"You mean you're picking me over your job?" Debbie's voice was incredulous.

"Yes, I am."

There was a long pause. Finally, Debbie spoke again. "Brandon, go get that monster."

"What? Are you serious?" My heart rate increased ever so slightly.

"We can leave early tomorrow morning. I know how important this is to you. Besides, I don't want a baby-killer running around our parish and you're the best chance we have of catching him."

"Baby, I really appreciate this! I'll get home as soon as I can."

"Be careful."

I heard Dawn's sirens screaming five minutes before she pulled into the parking lot. She jumped out of her car and marched to where I leaned against the wall.

"What are we waiting on? Let's go get this asshole."

"I'm waiting on Buzz to get here with some backup. We don't want to go in unprepared and have this guy slip through our fingers."

Dawn nodded.

Shift Lieutenant Buzz Landry arrived within minutes of Dawn. He assigned four patrol cops to accompany us to 129 Piped Lane and they all arrived one by one. We were in the parking lot planning our approach to the house when the dispatcher called me over the police radio.

I smashed my transmitter. "Go ahead with your traffic, Headquarters."

"We just received a call about a suspicious subject walking through yards on Piped Lane."

I spun and ran to my unmarked car. Dawn was already there. "Let's go!" I called out to the patrolmen, who scrambled to their squad cars. "Run code!"

CHAPTER THIRTY

12:30 A.M.
Saturday, November 19, 2005
129 Piped Lane, Seasville, Louisiana

William stared wildly about the room. As he tried to think of what to do, tires screeched outside in the street. Car doors slammed. A siren screamed in the distance. *The cops!* He hit the stairs at a full sprint. Midway down the stairs, his foot slipped. He rolled end over end and crashed to the landing. As he tried to right himself, the front door burst open and flashlights stabbed at him through the darkness. More cars arrived outside and people were shouting orders.

"Stop and put your hands up!" an authoritative voice commanded from the open doorway. The light was blinding. William stared wide-eyed and began to back away.

"I said *stop*! Put your hands up before I shoot!"

William turned and made a frantic dash for the back door. He dove through the opening in the sliding glass door and ran down the steps. A shot rang out and William felt a whisper pass his right ear. Someone screamed, "Hold your fire, damn it!"

William ran across the backyard and crashed into a plastic above-ground swimming pool. The sides collapsed and he fell forward. The force of the gushing water shot him backward and he slid on his face. He jumped to his feet. Propelled by fear and the shouts of angry cops, he sprang forward. A cop slipped and fell in the wet grass behind him. He jumped over a fence and raced toward an open cow pasture. Feet drummed behind him. They drew nearer. His heart raced, lungs burned. Screaming legs strained to carry him away from the approaching footsteps. He stumbled and a huge weight landed like a meteorite on his back. He crashed to the ground with the full weight of his tackler sucking the air from his lungs. He skidded to a painful halt, his face grating against the rough ground.

William spat mud and grass from his mouth and blinked his smarting eyes. His arms were jerked roughly behind his back. Metal jaws clicked around his wrists.

"William Chandler, your days of killing and running are over."

The cop spun William to a seated position. He looked up at his captor. The man wore slacks and a dress shirt that was unbuttoned at the neck.

"I'm Detective Brandon Berger," the man said, leaning over to catch his breath. He looked over his shoulder when a female detective ran up. Her tight jeans hugged what the moonlight showed to be a shapely figure.

"They're dead," she said, out of breath. "Murdered. Both of them."

William shook his head. "I didn't do it! They were like that when I got here. I—"

"Not another word until I read you your rights," Detective Berger said. The female detective handed him a card, but he waved it off. "You have the right to remain silent, anything you say can and will be used against you in court . . ."

As Detective Berger spoke, William's head spun. *How can this be happening to me?* He searched his memory, trying desperately to figure out who could be framing him, who could have known about the Arthurs. His mouth dropped open. *What if Detective London is behind it all?*

Detective Berger interrupted William's thought process by tugging on his shoulder. "Get up," he said. "We're going to have a long talk."

William struggled to his feet. Two patrolmen walked up. At Detective Berger's direction, they took custody of William.

"Take him to the office and put him on ice," Berger said. "I'll be there as soon as I get things organized here."

The patrolmen ushered William to a marked cruiser that was parked in front of the Alberts' house. They locked him in the back seat. When the car was moving, he leaned over to relieve the biting pressure of the handcuffs on his wrists. His movement caught the eye of the patrolman who was riding shotgun. "You'd better sit still," the patrolman cautioned.

"Sir, I'm innocent. You have to believe me!"

The patrolman laughed. "Yeah, they all say that."

William lay silent in the back seat. When the car stopped in front of an official-looking building, he straightened and allowed himself to be helped from the squad car. The patrolmen escorted him through the front doors and down a long hallway to a small room. There was a plain desk and three chairs in the room. The walls were bare and off-white. The temperature was at least ten degrees south of the temperature in the rest of the building.

"Sit there and don't move," one of the patrolmen said. He pointed to a mirrored window on one side of the room. "We'll be watching from there."

William placed his head on the desk and closed his eyes. His thoughts drifted to a simpler time when his biggest worry was fighting the small-town traffic on his way home from work to see his wife and new baby.

Sometime in the early morning
William stirred. *Gracie's image began to fade. His father appeared and he was reaching for Gracie's hand. "No! No!"*

The sound of his own voice brought him fully awake. He

jerked his head up. He felt his face flush when he saw Detective Berger and the female detective standing over him.

"No, what?" the female wanted to know.

William shook his head. "Nothing."

The female bent over William and freed him from the handcuffs. William caught a whiff of a sweet fragrance and he closed his eyes. He hadn't smelled the scent of a woman for too long. When she straightened, the detective held out her hand.

"I'm Detective Dawn Luke," she said.

William took her soft hand in his and squeezed it gently. She nodded to Detective Berger. "You already met my partner . . . the hard way."

Detective Berger pulled a chair out and sat beside William. "You remember the rights I read to you earlier?"

William nodded.

"Keeping those rights in mind, are you willing to talk to me without a lawyer being present?"

"I don't need a lawyer. I did nothing wrong."

"Well, I have a detective who's en route from Cote Blanche Parish. He says you murdered your baby girl and some man who was camping in the woods."

"He's a liar."

"He also told me you were coming here to murder two more people. Gave me their names, address, everything." Detective Berger paused and then said in a solemn voice, "Seems he didn't lie about that."

"Look, I was set up. Someone pushed my wife into a raging river to distract me long enough for him to kill my daughter. At first we thought a bear killed her, but the doctor says she was dead before the bear attack. She was fine when I left her, so it has to be this same person, or people, who killed her."

"Why would someone want to do that?"

"Like I said, to distract me so they could kill my baby."

"No, I mean why would someone want to kill your baby? Why go through all that trouble just to kill your baby?"

"How should I know? I'm not a detective. That's your job, her job, Detective London's job. All I know is that I didn't kill my baby."

"What do you think should happen to the person who killed your baby?"

"They should get the death penalty."

Detective Berger glanced down at his notes. "What led you to our little town?"

William explained everything, from the break-in at the Ranger station to him using the police radio to check the license plate number. "From that point, I just followed the map and got here and found them dead. That's the truth."

Detective Berger leaned back and rubbed his chin. "Pretty resourceful of you. Ever been in the military, or a cop, or a security guard, anything like that?"

William shook his head.

"I hear you also disarmed two cops. Is that true?"

"I wouldn't call them cops, like what a person would think of as a cop. One was a kid and one was a grandpa."

Detective Berger nodded as he stared for a long moment into William's eyes. Finally, he spoke again. "So, are you pretty convinced that Jacob Albert and his wife are involved in the murder of your daughter?"

"They have to be involved. They're the only people we talked to out there—the only people we really saw, except for that army man, and he's dead."

"Is that why you sentenced them to death?"

William scowled. "What are you talking about?"

"Well, you said the people responsible for your daughter's murder should get the death penalty. My question to you is, is that why you killed Jacob Albert and his wife?"

William leaned forward and stared Detective Berger directly in his eyes. "I did not kill Jake and Gaby, or whoever they are, and I did not kill my daughter. The sooner someone starts believing me, the sooner they can get out there and find the real killer."

"Tell me, in detail, what you did from the moment you hit town to the moment I tackled you in the field."

William took a deep breath and began talking. He looked from Detective Berger to Detective Luke. They listened intently, but their faces did not reveal what they were thinking. When done, he said, "And I'd even take a lie detector test."

"Are you sure?" Detective Luke asked.

"Yes, I am."

She looked at Berger, who nodded and said, "Set it up."

Both detectives walked out of the room. They left the door slightly ajar and stationed a uniformed deputy just outside. Each time William glanced at the door, the deputy was staring right at him. He shuddered and tried to keep his eyes focused on the floor. He didn't look up again until nearly an hour later, when the door opened and a short, balding man walked in carrying a briefcase. The man placed the case on the table and flipped the snaps open. He removed a laptop computer from inside and placed it gently on the desk. He plugged a microphone into the computer, slid it across the desk until it was directly in front of William, and began stroking keys on the computer.

William felt the front of his chest thump with each beat of his heart. "What is that?" he asked, trying to keep the quiver from his voice.

"It's a CVSA—Computerized Voice Stress Analyzer. It'll let me know if you're telling the truth."

Finally, a chance to prove I'm innocent, William thought. He glanced at the mirrored glass. *I wonder who's on the other side of that mirror.* He suddenly shuddered. What if this was a trick? What if they would doctor the test to show that he was guilty? "I'm a bit nervous," he said. "Won't that have an effect on the results?"

"Not at all. I'll just ask a few questions and all you have to do is answer them. I won't hook any straps to you, no alligator clips, nothing like that. It's completely unobtrusive and pain-less. You won't feel a thing."

"How accurate are those things?"

"Over ninety-nine percent."

William scratched his head. "What about the other one percent?"

"Operator error." The man smiled. "Nothing to worry about . . . I'm the best operator in the country."

CHAPTER THIRTY-ONE

4:30 A.M.
Saturday, November 19, 2005
Magnolia Parish Sheriff's Office Substation
"You think he's telling the truth?"

I looked at Dawn. She stood beside me in the dim light that shone from the two-way mirror, her face nearly pressed up against the glass as she tried to read William Chandler's lips. I turned my attention back to William. He sat at ease in the chair across from Lieutenant Chuck Wayne, our Internal Affairs Officer and CVSA examiner.

"I want to believe him," I said, more to myself. I turned away from the window and walked to the kitchen. Dawn followed and we sat silently at the table, each with a steaming cup of Community coffee. Before I reached the bottom of my cup, my cell phone rang. I glanced at the display screen: some number I didn't recognize. "Hello, this is Brandon."

"Detective Berger?" the voice was frantic, but somehow familiar.

"Yes, ma'am, this is Berger."

"Oh, thank goodness! I don't know what to do. Tom . . . Tom's gonna kill Meagan! She's on her way here with Nikki. I'm afraid he's gonna find her and—"

"Slow down, ma'am, I can't understand what you're saying."

"I'm sorry, I'm just very nervous. I always knew there was something wrong with Tom and now he's killed someone and I think he's coming here and I'm worried about Meagan and Nikki."

"Okay, first, let me get your name."

"Bernadette . . . Bernadette Mayeaux. I spoke with you last year about my son-in-law, Tom Banks. He had taken Meagan and Nikki away and I hadn't heard from them—"

"Oh, yeah, now I remember. Okay, you said something about Tom killing someone?"

"Yes, sir. Tom came home tonight and told Meagan that he did something awful. She asked him over and over and he finally told her that he was involved in killing someone."

I waved Dawn up and motioned for her to follow me as I fast-stepped out the kitchen, down the hall, and outside to my unmarked. Dawn's eyes were curious, but she slipped into the passenger's seat without a word. "Do you know who he killed?"

"No. All she said was that he was involved in a murder."

My unmarked roared to life. I shoved the gearshift in drive and sped out the parking lot. "Where are you now?"

"I'm home."

"Address?"

"1720 West Holley."

"We're already on our way. When your daughter gets there, lock all the exterior doors and windows and then lock yourselves in the bathroom. I'll call when we're outside the door."

"What's going on?" Dawn asked when I slammed my cell phone shut.

"Remember that old lady last year whose daughter was missing and then showed up the day she called?" The flashing blue lights on my dash splashed off the windshield and painted Dawn's blue. I could see the blank look. "You know, the girl from that weird church."

Dawn's face lit up. "Yeah, now I remember."

"Her mom just called. Her daughter thinks her husband was

involved in a murder."

"The Alberts?"

"She doesn't know, but considering how this is the first murder we've had in many moons, it's worth looking into."

Dawn nodded. Neither of us spoke again until we reached Bernadette Mayeaux's house. It was separated from the highway by a long paved driveway. Floodlights were stationed at every corner and the manicured yard was lit up like daylight. There was a smattering of bushes around the house and several massive oaks stood guard in the front. Large sectional windows lined the front of the house. In one of the windows, I spotted a small toddler. Her right hand and face were plastered against the glass. Her dirty blonde hair dangled in front of her lonely eyes. In her other hand, she clutched a porcelain doll. The eyes on the doll were mere dots. Even from a distance they looked terror-stricken.

"I thought you told Bernadette to lock everyone in the bathroom," Dawn said when she noticed the little girl.

"Since when do women *ever* listen to anything I say?" I parked behind a silver Galant and stepped out with my hand on my pistol. "Keep a sharp eye out." My eyes pierced the shadows of the bushes as I dialed Bernadette Mayeaux's number on my cell. She answered in a trembling voice.

"Detective? Thank God it's you! I'm on my way to the front."

Dawn approached the front of the house and I waited until she was in the open doorway before I made my approach. Once inside, Bernadette introduced us to Meagan and Nikki. Meagan's face was streaked with tears and her bottom lip trembled as she spoke.

"I'll take Nikki to the playroom and leave y'all alone," Bernadette offered.

Meagan led us to a spacious living room and we took our seats around a solid oak coffee table with a glass center. "I'm so sorry," Meagan began, tears racing down her face. "I should've never gone along with it! I know I'm going to jail, but it has to stop! I can't take it anymore! It's driving me crazy! I just want to die!" Meagan buried her face in the plush arm of the sofa on which she sat. Her muffled moans grew in intensity.

Dawn moved beside Meagan and put her arm around her shoulder. "Take it easy. You're safe now. Just try to relax and tell us what's going on."

"We . . . we got a call from Father Isaac. He said Jacob called, something about a detective leaving a message saying that a William fellow was after them. Jacob said he was calling the cops . . . that he was getting out of it." Meagan rubbed her face with a stained sleeve. "Father Isaac told Tom to meet him at Jacob's house. I begged Tom not to go, because I knew . . . I knew . . ." Meagan fell into Dawn and shook uncontrollably. Dawn rocked her for several minutes. She finally lifted her head again, tears leaking past her mouth and down her chin, but she didn't seem to notice. "They killed them, both of them, to keep them quiet."

"Quiet about what?" Dawn asked in a soothing voice.

Meagan took a deep breath and began to rapidly tell her story. I listened with mouth wide and heart pounding. She was nearly through talking when I heard tires screech outside. I jerked my head around. Through the frosted glass, a large figure loomed. Before I could get to my feet, the door crashed open and headlights flooded the hallway, blinding me. Gunshots exploded. I heard a woman scream and turned to see Meagan clutching her stomach. Blood oozed between her fingers. Dawn dove into her and dragged her over the back of the sofa and onto the floor. I clutched at my belt, desperately trying to drag my pistol from my holster. Gunshots continued to explode. My nose burned and my throat tickled from the smell and taste of gunpowder. Screams and a baby crying pierced the night air.

My pistol jumped in my hand and it was only then that I re-alized I was pulling the trigger. I saw the large figure lurch in the hallway. His hand drooped and he slowly fell to his knees. As I rushed toward him, I saw a second shadow emerge from the gunsmoke.

CHAPTER THIRTY-TWO

5:45 A.M.

Saturday, November 19, 2005

Magnolia Parish Sheriff's Office Substation

"Did I pass?" William asked when the examiner closed his laptop.

The examiner's cold, dark eyes dug into William's. "You should know if you're lying or not."

"I know I'm telling the truth. I just want to know if your test—"

The door to the interview room burst open and an important-looking man in a uniform rushed inside the room, followed by two younger cops. "Lieutenant Wayne, we need you out at 1720 West Holley ASAP. There's been an officer-involved shooting."

"I'll be done in just a—"

"We need you to come now." The officer swallowed hard. "We have an officer down."

"Put him in a cell until I get back!" The examiner bolted from his chair and jogged out of the room.

One of the cops walked around the desk, grabbed William's arm, and jerked him to his feet. "Come on, you maggot!"

"Hey," William protested. "I didn't do anything wrong. I'm innocent."

The cop shoved William hard against the wall, knocking the wind from his lungs. "All I know is we ain't never had a cop shot until you came to town." The cop's sour, coffee-laden

242

breath gagged William. "If I find out you had something to do with it, I'm gonna gut you and throw you in the bayou alive so you can watch the alligators eat your insides."

The cop jerked William off the wall and shoved him down a long corridor and into a dank, dark cell that smelled of urine. The door clanked shut. He shuddered, felt his way in the darkness to a metal bunk, and sank to his back. He cupped his hands over his face and tried to squeeze back the tears of frustration. "What the hell did I do to deserve this *shit*?" he screamed out loud. He pounded the back of his head on the metal framework. "Why? Why?" His head began to swim and he felt dizzy. After several minutes, the spinning slowed to a stop. He lay absolutely still. The only parts of him that moved were his heart and his lips, as he mouthed a silent prayer for a quick and painless death.

William's eyes twitched. He stirred and the squeaking from the metal bed brought him fully awake. He didn't move. A familiar voice echoed down the corridor—that must be what had awakened him. It drew nearer and a key jingled in the lock. He rolled to his side and swung his feet to the floor. When the door opened, he squinted against the light and found himself staring up at Detective London and a uniformed cop.

London smiled. "It's been a long time."

William grunted. "Not long enough."

"Yeah, well, follow me anyway. We have some things to talk about."

William held out his wrists to accept the handcuffs, but the uniformed officer turned and walked away. London did the same. Confused, William followed them down the long hallway. London stopped near a door to the room that adjoined the interview room and motioned for William to enter. With a cautious hand, William opened the door and stepped inside. The only light in the room was from the two-way mirror. He glanced through it and saw Detective Dawn Luke sitting where he had sat several hours earlier. Her clothes were tattered, face smudged, cheeks ruby, eyes puffy. The lie detector man sat across the desk from her. He was recording what she was saying.

"What's going on?" William asked.

"Her partner was shot a few hours ago," London said in a quiet voice.

William's mouth dropped open. He felt his knees shake. "What do you mean?"

"They were involved in a shootout with the two men who killed the Alberts. Detective Brandon Berger shot one of them, but the other guy blasted him with a shotgun." London nodded his head in Dawn Luke's direction. "She returned fire and killed the man where he stood."

"Is . . . is Detective Berger okay?"

"He's in emergency surgery. Doesn't look good."

"Oh, my God!" William felt sick. "I . . . what . . . that's so terrible!"

London nodded. "Today was Berger's wedding anniversary. He wasn't even supposed to be at work."

Guilt slammed into William's chest like a freight train. He turned his back to the wall and sank to the ground. "This is all my fault! Had I not escaped he would be okay. I'm . . . it's . . . I did this!"

London squatted beside William. For the very first time William saw compassion in the man's eyes. "William, everything happens for a reason. I don't know why that good man is lying at death's door, but I do know this: You didn't kill your daughter."

William gasped. His jaw burned and his lips trembled as the flood began to well up deep inside his chest. "You mean you believe me?"

Detective London pursed his lips and nodded. William thought he saw a hint of wetness in London's eyes. London blinked and stood quickly. "Come with me."

William stood and followed Detective London. They walked down a long hallway, through a series of cubicles, down another hallway, and finally came upon a closed door. London stopped and turned to face William. "Before you go in there, I just want you to know that I was wrong . . . very wrong. I can never undo what I've done and I'll go to my grave regretting it." Detective London stepped aside and opened the door for William.

William hesitated, not knowing what to expect.

"Go on," London coaxed. "Go say hello to your daughter."

"*What?* Is this your idea of a sick joke?"

London shook his head, face wet with tears, and smiled. "It's no joke."

William rushed into the room. An elderly woman held a little girl in her lap. The girl wore a pink dress. A matching sash held her dirty-blonde hair in a sideways ponytail. *"Gracie?"*

The little girl jerked her head around and her mournful eyes seemed to brighten. She smiled wide and William noticed the makings of her two front teeth protruding from her gums. At that very moment, she looked so much like Claire that William allowed himself to believe. The elderly woman stood and placed the little girl on her feet. She looked up and said, "Gran, gran."

The woman pointed to William. "Go to your Daddy." She then hurried out of the room.

William dropped to his knees and held out his arms. The tears flowed freely down his face and splashed onto the front of his shirt. "Gracie? Come to Daddy!"

The little girl walked jerkily toward William. When she reached him, she stared up with mouth open. "Da-*dah*?"

William squeezed the little girl in his arms. He shook

uncontrollably as the torrent of emotion ripped from his body. "Thank you, God! Thank you, God!" he wailed, not caring who saw. He stayed there for what seemed like two lifetimes. When he relaxed somewhat and his convulsions subsided, he held the little girl at arm's length and stared into her eyes. Her expression had turned to one of concern.

"Cry?" she said in a sweet and innocent voice.

William smiled and nodded his head. "Yeah, Daddy's crying—tears of happiness!" He looked over his shoulder at Detective London. "How is this possible?"

Detective London walked around to sit where the elderly woman had sat earlier. "Ever heard of the pigeon-drop scheme?"

William shrugged. "The scam where you switch real money for fake money?"

"Something like that." Detective London leaned closer and continued eagerly. "Over the years, I've worked several cases involving pigeon drops. Even went to an investigative school that focused primarily on the subject, but I've never heard of anything like what happened to you. What they did to you was brilliant—and I'm ashamed to say they almost pulled it off."

"What on earth are you talking about?" William stared down at the little girl in his arms. "Are you saying this is not really Gracie?"

Detective London placed a reassuring hand on William's shoulder. "No, this is definitely your baby Grace. DNA evidence will prove that."

William shook his head. "But I saw Gracie's body. She was dead. She was—"

"It wasn't Grace. They switched the babies. They took Grace and left a dead baby in her place."

"Why would someone want to do something sick like that?"

"It all started here in Seasville. A preacher named Isaac Stewart had been telling his parishioners they couldn't go to the doctor, they had to believe in God to heal them. A couple by the name of Tom and Meagan Banks had a little girl named Nikki. She was about seven months old when she became ill and was running a high fever. They called Isaac and he came over to pray for the baby. They prayed for several days, but the baby got worse and finally died."

"What? You mean they wouldn't bring their little baby to the hospital?"

"Nope. And to think, maybe something as simple as aspirin could have saved the baby's life."

William rubbed his head. "But what does that have to do with us?"

"Well, when the baby passed away, Isaac told Tom the reason his baby had died was because Meagan's faith wasn't strong enough. They then cast demons out of Meagan, and Isaac said he could raise the baby from the dead—*if* their faith was strong enough."

"You've got to be shitting me?"

"Shit-*ting*!" Gracie exclaimed.

William gasped. "No, no, baby, don't say that!"

Detective London laughed. "No, I'm not *kidding* you. They began praying on the baby, but too many people in the church became aware of what was going on, so they left town. They took trusted friends Jacob and Gaby Albert—your Jake and Gaby Arthur—with them to the Skybald National Forest, where they figured they would have privacy. They prayed on the baby for two weeks before you showed up with Grace."

"It seems like we would've been able to smell something if there was a dead body around."

"They preserved the body by keeping it in a large ice chest. When you showed up with your little girl, Isaac told Tom and Meagan that God sent you. He devised a plan to kidnap Grace one night while you two were sleeping, but his plan was foiled when he thought Claire saw him by the river. He pushed her in and, well, you know what happened next."

"How did Jake and Gaby play into this?"

"When Gaby met you all, she went back and told the group about your baby. Isaac saw that as the perfect opportunity to bring Nikki back to life."

"And these two couples just went along with him?"

"Meagan and Tom were actually so grief-stricken that they were all for getting a baby to replace their little Nikki. In addition, Isaac convinced them they would all go to jail for allowing their baby to die unless they could return with a baby and convince everyone Nikki was alive and well. Now, Gaby and Jake, they knew nothing of the plan to kidnap your baby." Detective London frowned. "That is, until I called them and warned them you were coming. According to Meagan Banks, Jacob called and confronted Isaac. He threatened to call the cops and expose Isaac as a fraud." London shook his head. "Isaac didn't want to give up his multimillion-dollar business and his god-like status, and Tom didn't want to give up his baby girl and go to jail. You saw what they did to the Alberts."

William nodded and then suddenly remembered. "How did the poor army guy factor into all of this?"

"Wrong place at the wrong time. He walked up as Meagan was removing Grace's clothes and placing them on Nikki's corpse. When he demanded to know what was going on, Tom and Isaac attacked him. They dragged him off into the woods and stabbed him with your knife. They beat the dog with a pipe and stabbed it, too."

"How'd they get my knife? I swear I had it—"

"Claire picked it up after breakfast on the morning you all went to the beach. Tom watched you from the woods while Isaac rummaged through your things. He took the knife just to disarm you. He had no idea he would later use it to kill Jeremy

McAllister and that it would help to frame you for the murders."

"Did they use it to cut my brake lines?"

"Your brake lines weren't cut."

"But they had to have been—"

"Ice pick."

"What?"

"They punctured your lines with an ice pick." Detective London sighed. "I missed it when I checked your vehicle. Meagan said Isaac drained the fluid into a pan so there would be no evidence on the ground. Slick one, that guy."

William sat in silence for several minutes as he watched Gracie entertain herself with a string that was hanging from her dress. "Did Isaac and Tom shoot Detective Berger?"

Detective London's nod was solemn. "Tom did. Isaac accidentally shot Meagan and Detective Berger dropped him in the hallway." London shook his head. "Detective Luke said Tom came out of nowhere and mowed Berger down. Meagan died at the scene, but lucky for you, she gave a full confession before she passed." London stood. "I'll leave you alone with your daughter." He walked to the door and paused. "Oh, and I took the liberty of calling Claire. She left about two hours ago and should be here soon."

"I don't know how I feel about her right now."

"Well, I told her you were right and that you didn't do the awful things we accused you of doing."

William looked up at Detective London. "You shouldn't have had to tell her, she should've already known."

London nodded and William watched him walk away. He leaned against the wall and bounced Gracie on his knee. She giggled as her head bobbed from side to side. *I'll deal with the Claire situation later,* William thought. *Right now I have some catching up to do.*

ABOUT THE AUTHOR

BJ Bourg is a twenty-five-year veteran of law enforcement and has worked as a patrol cop, detective, police academy instructor, SWAT officer, sniper leader, and chief investigator for a district attorney's office. He is a former professional boxer and a lifelong martial artist. His stories and articles have appeared in dozens of venues, including *Woman's World, Boys' Life,* and *Tactical Response,* and he is the author of the police sniper novel *James 516,* and the YA novel, *The Seventh Taking.* He loves vacationing in the mountains and is especially drawn to hiking, climbing, photographing dangerous animals, and traversing wild rivers. Above all else, he is a father and husband, and the highlight of his life is spending time with his beautiful wife and wonderful kids.